DEAD OF WINTER

KERI BEEVIS

B

Boldwood

First published in Great Britain in 2025 by Boldwood Books Ltd.

Copyright © Keri Beevis, 2025

Cover Design by 12 Orchards Ltd

Cover Images: Shutterstock and Alamy

A CIP catalogue record for this book is available from the British Library.

Paperback ISBN 978-1-83533-601-4

Large Print ISBN 978-1-83533-600-7

Hardback ISBN 978-1-83533-599-4

Trade Paperback ISBN 978-1-80656-039-4

Ebook ISBN 978-1-83533-602-1

Kindle ISBN 978-1-83533-603-8

Audio CD ISBN 978-1-83533-594-9

MP3 CD ISBN 978-1-83533-595-6

Digital audio download ISBN 978-1-83533-597-0

This book is printed on certified sustainable paper. Boldwood Books is dedicated to putting sustainability at the heart of our business. For more information please visit https://www.boldwoodbooks.com/about-us/sustainability/

Boldwood Books Ltd, 23 Bowerdean Street, London, SW6 3TN

www.boldwoodbooks.com

To Cindi Peterson.
Authors write stories, but readers breathe the life into them.

PROLOGUE
EIGHTEEN MONTHS EARLIER

Norfolk, England

The first time I laid eyes on Midwinter Manor, I knew I wanted it to be my home.

Hidden away from the nearest village, within a tangle of brooding woodland and only accessible via a long dirt track lane, you could easily miss it. But venture closer, where the trees eventually part way and the lane widens, a gate set between two stone pillars will greet you, and through the wrought-iron bars you will have your first glimpse of the house.

It looks like something out of a dark fairy tale, with an almost unnatural stillness. Beautiful and imposing, but also timeworn and slightly intimidating; set over three storeys with wide watchful windows that catch the light in an unsettling way, and jutting crooked chimneys that crown its roofline.

Step inside and it will feel like you are crossing into another century. The cool air shifts around you, laced with the faint scent of old wood and candle wax. The entrance hall is

wide with a grand staircase, its banister touched by a genera-
tion of hands, and the rooms beyond are sprawling and
elegant, with floral cornices and fireplaces tall enough to
stand in.

To some, this house might feel daunting, but to me it is a
sanctuary.

It is a place filled with history. But also with secrets.

And after tonight, those include our own.

1

MONDAY 22 DECEMBER

Manchester

It was just before Christmas and the last place Lola Henderson had expected to find herself was on a train bound for the Cambridgeshire fens and the tiny city of Ely, with two days of meetings lined up.

The email from Rich Bradford, CEO of Safe Hands, a company that supplied and fitted hand sanitiser machines, had come as an annoyance given how close it was to the holidays.

Rich was one of her most demanding clients, so she supposed she shouldn't be surprised. It was irritating, though. He mostly sold to offices, many of whom would be winding down ahead of the festivities, so it was hardly a prime week for marketing activity, and their catch-up could easily wait until January. Instead, she would be spending her Christmas Eve working, then catching a late train home.

This time last year, she would have told him a flat no, but things had been different then; her mother had been sick and required round-the-clock care, and Lola had been very aware it was going to be their last Christmas together. Now it was just her and her kittens, and although she had been reluctant to leave them, there were no other plans on her calendar.

She had purposely turned down all invitations for the coming week, not yet ready to throw herself into celebrations. There had been plenty of offers, her friends aware that she had no other family, but this year she needed a quiet one.

It had been a sad and difficult year of firsts without her mum, and it was always a time they had celebrated together. All she wanted was to be alone and have some time to reflect on bittersweet memories.

On Christmas morning, she intended to head over to the remembrance gardens at Manchester Crematorium and place fresh flowers by her mum's plaque, then she would go home and enjoy some nice food, a few glasses of wine and a bit of a movie fest.

First, though, she had to deal with Ely.

Boarding the train at Manchester's Piccadilly Station, she had been lucky enough to find a double seat to herself, shoving her travel bag into the overhead rack. The only things she had kept out were her Kindle and a bottle of water she had bought in the station. The journey was going to take just under four hours and her plan was to read for the entire length of it. She already had the new Harper Reed book downloaded.

Well, that had been the plan, but her mind kept wandering, reminding her that Ely wasn't too far from the county of Norfolk, and Saham Toney, the village where her brother lived.

Thirty-five miles, in fact. She knew that because she had looked it up after trying to make contact with him.

Her mum had never hidden from Lola that she was adopted, but she also hadn't pushed her to find her biological family either. Perhaps out of loyalty to the woman who had raised her, Lola had never tried.

But then Kelly Henderson had died on a bright March afternoon, as the world around her was starting to wake up after a season of hibernation, and later, going through her personal belongings, Lola had come across a letter written in her mum's neat handwriting with her own name on it, urging her to reach out to her birth family and giving her details of her adoption to help her do so.

She had ignored it at first, but curiosity had eventually changed her mind.

That and the realisation that with her mum gone she had no family.

Her adoptive father had left when she was three and neither Lola nor her mum had seen or heard from him since, and her mum had never remarried. As for friends, Lola had plenty of those, but they didn't live in each other's pockets. Sometimes they went more than a couple of weeks without speaking. And there was no boyfriend on the scene. She hadn't dated in ages.

She never considered herself lonely, but now she realised she was completely alone in the world, and although she was pretty self-sufficient, the temptation of finding new family had grown in appeal. So it had come as a huge shock when she had learnt that both of her biological parents were dead. Her birth mother suffering a brain haemorrhage, while her father had been killed a couple of years later in a tragic accident.

It was the weirdest thing, grieving for something she had never even known, and she blamed herself for not trying to connect with them sooner.

Nigel and Annie Whitlock did have a son, though. Daniel.

And the adoption agency had tried to reach out to him, without success.

Through her own sleuthing, Lola had found out what she could about the Whitlocks, learning that her father's family was wealthy. In addition to family inheritance, Nigel had also traded very successfully on the stock market, and he and Annie had lived a blessed life in Oxfordshire.

Their son, Daniel, had been a talented chef working in London restaurants until a nasty skiing accident in his late twenties had resulted in a spinal cord injury that had taken the use of his legs, leaving him completely paralysed from the waist down. He had lived at home with his parents until their deaths, but now resided with his wife in Norfolk.

Lola had tried to stalk him online, finding him on Facebook. She wanted to know him, but couldn't really get a measure of the man. There were a couple of photos of him on mountain slopes, taken from a distance, and another one where he was in a Lamborghini with another man, both of them posing and grinning broadly at the camera, but they all had to be pre-accident. Other than a couple of nature shots, there was nothing more recent.

Should she leave him be? The fact he hadn't responded to the agency suggested he didn't want her to find him. But what if he hadn't received their message?

Since reading the letter her mum had left for her, Lola's curiosity had grown. Her birth parents might be dead, but Daniel, who was older than Lola by four years, would hopefully be able to give her answers as to why they had given her up for adoption. Plus, knowing they were blood related gave her hope that perhaps they might be able to build a relationship. Growing up as an only child, she had often wondered what it would be like to have a sibling. The idea of having a brother appealed.

It was over two weeks later when she had finally dared press send on the Facebook message she had typed, reworded and deleted a dozen times.

She couldn't even be sure she was contacting the right Daniel Whitlock, though the yellow Lamborghini he was in on the Facebook post had also appeared in a newspaper article about his father, parked outside the family home. It was a distinctive car so had to be the same one.

After another week of being ignored, she had bolstered the confidence to try again.

The reply she received had been crushing, and colder than expected.

Dear Miss Henderson,

Thank you for reaching out. I am indeed the right Daniel Whitlock. However, while I understand your curiosity, many years have passed and, to be bluntly honest, I have no interest in pursuing a relationship with you at this point in my life.

I wish you well for the future.

Daniel

Formal and tersely polite. His dismissiveness both surprising and shocking her.

Lola wasn't sure quite what she had been expecting and she was annoyed with herself for not being better prepared.

Was his rejection because he feared she might be after his money? She assumed he was the sole beneficiary of his family's inheritance.

She supposed she could see how it might seem. Wealthy man's long-lost sister suddenly appears.

She had never responded to his blunt message, but his words had played on her mind, and it had continued to eat away at her that without his help she would never know anything about her biological family.

She wondered, not for the first time, that if he knew she was near Norfolk he might relent and agree to just one meeting with her. Perhaps there was a nearby Costa where they could have a quick coffee together. It was worth asking, wasn't it?

After spending twenty minutes wording another message to him in her head, while trying to concentrate on her book, she set the Kindle to one side and pulled out her phone, opening Messenger.

Dear Daniel,

I know you don't wish for a relationship with me, but you are my only link to learning about our parents. I am working local to Norfolk over the next couple of days. Please will you consider meeting me for coffee? I promise if you allow me one hour of your time, I will respect your wishes and never contact you again.

Lola

She hesitated before hitting send, resolving that she had done all that she could. If he didn't reply or told her no again, she would have to leave her past behind her.

Determined that she wouldn't keep checking to see if he replied, she put her phone away and picked up her Kindle again, ignoring the thrum of activity around her as the train pulled into Stockport Railway Station, a few commuters disembarking, while several new passengers boarded.

The train was starting to pick up speed when she had the creeping feeling she was being watched.

Raising her gaze from her book, she locked eyes with the man sitting a couple of rows forward, his seat facing her.

Realising she had clocked him, he smiled hesitantly and Lola's eyes widened in recognition.

Quinn Mallory.

What the hell was he doing here?

2

After their last encounter, Lola had expected never to see Quinn again.

That day was still etched firmly in her mind, even though it was four years ago, and she remembered every word that had been spoken, how she had completely shut down – it was her way of dealing with the trauma, she guessed – and that one last look Quinn had given her – part anger, part frustration and way too much pity for her to be able to handle – before he closed the door of the flat they had shared, still haunted her.

Now he was here on the train heading to Ely. Perhaps he was getting off sooner, or maybe he was staying on all the way to Norwich. Either way, she didn't quite know how to react.

Apparently, he did – probably because he'd had the advantage of seeing her first – as he was getting up from his seat now and heading towards her, and Lola's heart started racing, threatening to beat out of her chest, her palms dampening, and her body overheating. All thoughts of Daniel Whitlock and the message she had sent him disappeared from her mind.

She didn't consider herself to be a nervous woman, and

usually she was responsive and quick to deal with unexpected challenges, but this was Quinn, who had seen her at her worst, at her weakest and most vulnerable. He was the one man she had ever truly loved, but she had driven him away.

'Lola. I didn't expect to see you here.'

You and me both, Quinn. You and me both.

She had often wondered how he would react if they bumped into one another again. Would he still be mad at her for how things had ended or would there be an awkwardness between them; a distance that made them strangers despite the intimacy they had once shared?

Somehow, the thought of that was worse than him being angry.

He didn't seem either. Surprised, certainly, but almost pleasantly so.

Four years. And he had barely changed.

He would be what, thirty-five now? Two years younger than her.

His straight hair, only a couple of shades away from black, held no sign of grey. It was a little longer than she remembered, almost touching the collar of his jacket, but then he had never been good at keeping up with the appointments to get it cut.

And he had a healthy tan. One which had brought out the smattering of freckles on his nose. Had he been abroad recently? Maybe on a holiday with his girlfriend – wife, even.

Lola resisted the temptation to look for a telltale ring, instead managing to keep her attention on his face.

The only sign things were different now was in his eyes. The spark of youth had died and his dark gaze holding hers seemed older, a little more jaded, reminding her he had seen things.

To anyone else, she doubted it would be noticeable, but she had known him in the before and the after, and she understood, because she had been through the same thing too.

'Where are you heading?' he asked her now.

'Ely,' she told him, finding her voice.

'Really? Me too.'

Well, that could be uncomfortable. Over three more hours stuck on a train together.

'I have to work,' she blurted.

'Three days before Christmas?' Quinn wrinkled his nose. 'That sucks.'

Lola managed a laugh, relieved it sounded light and natural instead of forced, like it felt. Every muscle in her body was tense. Not Quinn's fault. This was just so unexpected. 'Tell me about it,' she agreed. 'He's not the easiest client.'

'Are you still freelancing?'

She nodded. 'Six years now.'

'And you're still glad you did it?'

'I am.'

There were days when she was frustrated with her job, but for the most part she loved it, and working for herself gave her so much more freedom. When her mum had first fallen sick, she had been able to juggle her commitments, often working late into the evening so she was free for the many appointments.

'I'm proud of you, Lola. It was a big step to take.'

Quinn's eyes shone with genuine pride, and as she thanked him, an unexpected yearning stirred in the pit of her stomach for what they had once had, but lost.

He had always been supportive of her career, pushing her to believe she was good enough and deserved better.

When Lola had first met him, she had been working for a

marketing agency. While she had enjoyed her role, working with different companies, building websites for them and driving active sales through digital marketing, her bosses had been, in Quinn's words, 'piss-takers', expecting long hours for a below-average salary, while dangling promotions that never seemed to materialise.

It had been with his support and encouragement, pointing out that she already had the skillset, that she had branched out on her own. It had been scary at first, but now Lola knew it was the best decision she had ever made.

'Are you still in the police?' she asked now, both out of politeness, as, so far, he had been asking all the questions, but also with a healthy dose of curiosity.

Quinn nodded. 'I passed my sergeant's exam last year.'

'Really? That's brilliant.' Lola was genuinely pleased for him. 'So, what are you doing in Ely today? Are you there with work?'

'No. I'm getting a connecting train to Cambridge. Chloe and Darren live there now. They're away over Christmas, so I'm heading down to see them before they go.'

'Please say hi to Chloe from me. Are they going anywhere nice?'

Chloe was Quinn's younger sister and Lola had always been fond of her, though she personally thought she could do better for herself than Darren, who was a bit of a sexist pig. She knew Quinn wasn't a fan either.

She watched him hesitate now, his gaze quickly flicking to the empty seat beside her.

'Shall I grab my bag and come sit up here?' he suggested, instead of answering her question. 'It will be easier to talk.'

Alarm must have crossed Lola's face, because he backtracked quickly.

'Though you were reading. I don't want to disturb you.'

He wasn't. And yes, she had initially panicked when she had first recognised him, but this wasn't really that difficult, was it? They were being civil with each other. Friendly even. It was healthy putting the past behind them.

'No, I would like the company,' she said, offering him the brightest smile she could muster and shuffling across into the window seat to show she meant it.

Moments later, Quinn was pushing his duffel bag into the overhead rack beside her own luggage and dropping down into the seat beside her.

This close, the familiar scent of his aftershave wove its way into her senses and the warmth of his arm against hers stirred memories of a time that she often wished she could revisit.

Before things had turned bad. Before all of the pain.

He was the only man she had ever loved. And she realised now that, despite everything, she still loved him.

But the chance had passed. They had both moved on. No doubt Quinn was in a relationship with someone else. Over the course of the next couple of hours, she would likely find out, and the door to whatever it was she was feeling right now – she didn't want to be so bold as to call it hope – would firmly be shut.

That would be for the best.

Showing they could be on good terms was one thing, but too much had happened, and it had broken what they had once been. The unborn child they had lost sounding a death knell on their relationship.

It was too late to go back.

3

You have a sister.

I remember reading the words in the email from the adoption agency and completely stilling as I focused on the screen. My first thought was, this is unexpected, but then irritation stirred, quickly morphing into anger.

I knew all about her. She was the bastard child who had been given away, the dirty secret of her mother's illicit affair that had almost torn the family apart. But why the hell was she making contact now? The tears I wanted to cry at the news were out of frustration, not joy. After everything that had happened, after what we have done, what were the chances of her reaching out?

Lola Henderson needs to go away, and I hoped that by ignoring the adoption agency, she would take the hint, but instead she popped up on Facebook Messenger a week later, like some unhinged stalker. Bile had roiled in the pit of my stomach when the alert pinged, telling me she had sent a message.

I didn't respond at first, but she was persistent, and

although I didn't want to converse with her, I eventually realised that if I wanted her to leave us alone, I had no choice but to reply.

I told her politely to bugger off, hoping that would be the end of it. But no, she has just messaged again. Apparently, she is near Norfolk and she wants to meet up.

The very idea has me breaking out in a sweat.

Can't the stupid woman take a hint?

I'm tempted to ignore her again, but what if she has our address? I don't want her turning up here uninvited.

Unsure what to do, I spend some time googling her. I had briefly looked her up after the agency got in contact, so I know she lives in Manchester, but now I am more thorough in my search.

She has a website, Click and Bloom, offering a number of digital services from website building to online marketing, and according to her bio, she graduated from Lincoln University in 2010. That puts her – if my calculations are correct – at around thirty-seven years old. The age would be correct. And her job suggests she is techie. She will be able to find us if she wants to.

Her Instagram and Facebook accounts reveal that she has cats and a wide circle of friends, and that she likes music festivals, judging from the number of pictures in which she has been tagged. One close-up shot leaves me in no doubt that she's a Whitlock. The wide almond-shaped eyes, angular jawline and high cheekbones are a giveaway. Different hair colour, though. Hers is more of an ash-brown. It's the least remarkable thing about her.

There is only one other Henderson she is linked to and that is Kelly Henderson. A quick glance at her Facebook profile soon tells me Kelly is Lola's adoptive mother and, judging from a couple of sympathetic comments posted on her wall, she has recently passed away. This probably explains why Lola is suddenly so determined to reach out.

It worries me that, now she is nearby, she might try to show up on the doorstep, and as I close my iPad, I get the inkling of an idea, wondering if there is perhaps a way to satisfy her curiosity.

She has asked for one meeting, a chance to ask questions and give her closure.

Can I give her that?

If so, she will be out of our hair for good.

Not a coffee shop, though. I can explain it's not easy with accessibility issues, especially in bad weather. It's best if she comes to the house.

There are a lot of secrets here at Midwinter Manor. It is a big place, perhaps dauntingly so to those unfamiliar with it, with its maze of hallways, large rooms and dark corners.

People probably think we were mad to move to a house built in the late 1700s, so secluded from everywhere. But it's just how I like it. There is a stillness to the place, even as it creaks and echoes, and a grandeur too. Although we have modernised certain things, the history remains in the wide, open fireplaces, so cosy when lit in the winter, the delicately carved ceiling roses and the wood-panelled walls. If they could talk – and I often believe they do whisper to us – they would say they have seen things, but that the house has stood for centuries and we are safe here, hidden away from prying eyes.

Lola's visit will be brief. I will make sure of it.

But am I getting carried away, thinking this is a good idea, when, in truth, it is ruining my build-up to Christmas. It's a holiday I always embrace and several of the downstairs rooms are decked out with trees and garlands, while a sumptuous feast awaits us on Christmas Day.

I am a hypocrite, because I'm not particularly religious, but then I suppose that is for the best, given our sins.

Deciding to give Lola's visit some more thought, I sit back in my chair and try to roll the tension out of my shoulders, swapping my iPad for the cup of coffee sitting on the table. As I take a sip, realising I've left it too long and the water is now lukewarm, I am tempted to switch it for something stronger, to calm my nerves.

I have worked so hard for everything we have and I will do everything necessary to make sure we keep it.

4

Lola and Quinn hadn't planned for a baby. They had been dating for a little over a year and had moved in together just a month earlier. When Lola had first fallen pregnant, both of them had been in shock, though it had quickly turned to pleasant surprise, and as they became used to the idea, they found themselves looking forward to impending parenthood.

They could make it work. Lola's business was still in its infancy, but at least she had the flexibility of working from home, and Quinn did shifts, which meant he would be able to take over on his days off, so she could catch up on her accounts. Their parents, who were excited about a grandchild, had also offered to help.

At thirty-six weeks, they were fully prepared, the spare bedroom in their rented flat kitted out with a cot and everything they were going to need for their new son or daughter.

At thirty-seven weeks, Lola became aware that the baby had stopped kicking. Three days later, after an ultrasound had revealed the baby's heart was no longer beating, she had endured an induced labour, delivering their stillborn son.

Quinn had cried that day as he'd held the baby boy they had named Milo, but Lola – numb with shock – hadn't been able to shed a single tear, and as she went through the motions over the coming weeks – the sympathy visits, the funeral, and the follow-up hospital appointments – she had felt detached from her own body, like an interloper watching from afar and reacting on autopilot. She had been wracked with guilt at her reaction, knowing it wasn't normal for a grieving mother.

Counselling had been provided, but hadn't helped, and over the following months, she was aware that Quinn was growing more and more frustrated with her. He had tried his best to pick up the pieces of their life to move them forward, but despite wanting that too, Lola had felt frozen in time, and although she was aware she was doing it and wanted to stop, she had gradually closed him out.

Seven months after Milo's death, Quinn had moved out, realising they could no longer make their relationship work, and it was two weeks later, while dismantling the nursery – a room that had been left closed – determined to have a fresh start, that Lola had finally broken down. The well of despair deep inside of her emptying as she finally came to terms with what had happened.

Her mother hadn't been great during that time. Kelly Henderson was another one who wasn't good at expressing her emotions, and her stance was to blame Quinn for everything. It was easier that way.

For a while, Lola had been horribly alone, struggling to cope with everything that had happened, while trying to keep on top of her business. Eventually, the bills for the flat had become too much for her to deal with and she had been forced to move back home with her mother.

It had taken her a long time, but finally Lola had managed

to put the broken pieces back together as best as she could, and sitting here now with Quinn, it felt like the pair of them had finally come full circle.

She had never stopped loving him and suspected he would always be the one, but even after she had tried to fix herself, she couldn't bring herself to reach out.

After Quinn had left, he had severed contact. Or so she had believed.

It wasn't until her mother was on her deathbed that she had revealed he had stayed in touch, not wanting to contact Lola directly, aware it might upset her, but asking after her for at least a year following their break-up.

Kelly Henderson had never approved of their relationship and Lola had long suspected it was because her own husband had left her. Kelly was distrustful of men, expecting them all to be the same, and she had always been convinced Quinn would eventually let her daughter down.

Whether it was guilt, or perhaps worry that she might be punished in the afterlife, she had finally admitted the truth, and Lola had been torn between anger and frustration. It was too little, too late, but how could she stay mad at her mum when there was so little time left? As for Quinn, it felt too late. So much time had passed.

When she had first seen him on the train, she had been embarrassed and anxious, and the thought of being trapped with him for the next few hours had made her skin prickle. Now she understood that this forced proximity was a good thing. The pair of them were in an environment with no other distractions and finally they had no option but to talk. Something they should have perhaps done a long time ago. And as they did – the familiarity of him putting her at ease and making her realise just how much she had missed him – she began to wonder if this was fate.

Or perhaps divine intervention?

That was foolish Lola's pattern of thought.

Serious, logical Lola knew it was a ridiculous notion. That this was nothing more than coincidence, and despite the fact Quinn's ring finger was bare – she had finally given in to the temptation to look – it didn't mean there wasn't a girlfriend waiting for him back in Stockport.

Still, she had to know for sure.

'So, what are your plans for Christmas?' she finally dared to ask, hoping he didn't pick up in the slight tremor in her tone.

It bothered her that his answer mattered so much. She had never been a woman who had simpered after men, and in the before, hers and Quinn's relationship had been on a very even keel.

'I'm going over to Mum and Dad's. Kyle and Josie will be there, so it will just be the six of us.'

'Six?'

Kyle was Quinn's older brother, and Josie his wife. But who was the sixth?

Lola drew in a steadying breath, waiting for the answer.

'Elsie.' Quinn smiled. 'I forgot you haven't met her. Josie fell pregnant the autumn after...' He fell quiet, realising the implications of what he was saying.

That Kyle and Josie had been lucky.

Although her heart hitched, Lola reminded herself she was in a better place now.

Quinn didn't know that, though, and although her smile wavered, she reached for his hand, squeezing in reassurance, the sudden longing for what they had once had almost as strong as the love she had for the child they had lost.

When his warm fingers locked around hers, so comforting as they stirred memories warm and deep, she pushed herself to ask the question.

'So you're going alone?'

She tried to phrase it as casually as possible.

Whether Quinn knew what she was hinting towards or not, he didn't say. He nodded. 'Yeah, I am.' But then he angled his head, looking at her, dark eyes locking with hers, and adding, 'There's no one else, Lola.'

* * *

As the train rumbled into the station, it offered a view of the marina on the river, the low winter sun sparkling across the water, and Lola could see the cathedral in the distance.

She had never been to Ely before and knew only that it was one of the smallest cities in England. Now she could also see how pretty it was. Not that she was likely to have any time to explore.

'Have dinner with me tomorrow night?'

Quinn asked the question just after they disembarked the train. They were standing on the platform about to part ways, as a bitterly cold wind howled around them – Lola ready to head to her hotel, while Quinn would shortly be catching his connecting train to Cambridge.

When she stared at him, surprised he was asking, a rush of words tumbled out as he tried to persuade her.

'We haven't seen each other in four years. I know we've just been sat on the train together, but there's still more to say. I'm not ready to say goodbye again. Not yet.'

Neither was Lola, but she had to be pragmatic.

'I thought you were travelling back up north in the morning?' she reminded him. 'I'm stuck here until Christmas Eve.'

'I can change my train, get a room in Ely for the night.'

He looked hopeful and Lola considered her schedule. Was there a way she could make this work?

She would be in a meeting with Rich Bradford for most of tomorrow, then her plan had been to chill in her hotel, maybe order room service. That was unless she heard from Daniel Whitlock. She wouldn't have time to see him on the Wednesday, as she had more meetings scheduled with Rich that morning and a late-afternoon train booked to take her back to Manchester. Daniel probably had plans anyway, what with it being Christmas. Did he have a family? she wondered. She knew he was married, but did he have kids?

Could he have kids?

He was paraplegic and she didn't know how that might affect things for him.

Anyway, he might even be away. Which would explain why she hadn't heard back from him.

She had checked her phone as the train had pulled into the station, her heart sinking when she saw her message hadn't even been read, and she was already resigning herself to the fact she was unlikely to hear back from him.

That did mean she was potentially free for dinner with Quinn. And he was right. There was still more to say.

'Can I say a tentative yes?' she asked, wishing she could give him a firm one. 'I don't want to commit in case I hear from my brother.'

'Of course,' Quinn said, understanding.

Lola had told him about Daniel during their train journey. Quinn had known since early on in their relationship that

Kelly Henderson had been Lola's adoptive mother, and he understood how important this was to her.

'How about we keep in touch and you let me know what your plans are tomorrow?' he suggested. 'You still have the same number, right?'

'Yes, and you?'

He nodded and leant forward to give her a brief hug and an affectionate peck on the cheek. The touch and the scent of him was so familiar, so inviting, and for a moment Lola just wanted to hold on.

But then they were parting company and he was giving her a crooked smile.

'Stay safe, Lola.'

It was a phrase he had often used when they were together. Any occasion really when he wasn't going to be around should she need him.

She had always found it amusing – a little old-fashioned, even – sometimes reminding him she could take care of herself, but more often or not, doing as she did now: smirking at him and giving a salute, before she turned and walked away.

She was about to spend two days in an office with a man who set her teeth on edge, even though he paid well. Quinn had nothing to worry about.

5

TUESDAY 23 DECEMBER

The message from Daniel Whitlock came after a long morning of frustrating meetings with Rich Bradford, who wanted to slash his digital marketing budget for the following year, despite Lola showing him proof that her growth plan for the company was working better than anticipated. He expected the same results, just for half the price, and she couldn't seem to get it through to him that she wouldn't be able to deliver.

By the time they broke for lunch, she had a headache from repeatedly banging her head against the wall and her mood had soured. The only thing keeping her going was knowing that in a few hours she would be seeing Quinn again.

She had agreed to his dinner suggestion when he'd messaged her that morning, wanting to know if he should skip his train.

At that point, her message to Daniel had remained unread and she had given up hope that she was going to hear from him.

Now, seeing his invite, offering for her to come to his house and saying he would give her an hour of his time, she debated what to do.

Quinn had changed his plans to accommodate her and Lola was really looking forward to seeing him again, but she also wanted to meet Daniel. She had pleaded for this one chance and he had relented, but she was certain if she messed him around, she wouldn't get another.

Was it possible she could do both? Go to Saham Toney, then have dinner with Quinn?

The timings would be tight. Probably too tight.

She couldn't leave until her afternoon meeting with Rich had wrapped up and Saham Toney was about an hour away. She would have to get there and back, and that wasn't even factoring in the time she would want to spend with her brother. It just wasn't doable.

Deciding Quinn deserved an actual conversation rather than a message, she decided to call him.

'Hey,' he greeted her. 'Is everything okay?'

'Will you really hate me if I have to cancel on you tonight?'

If he was annoyed or disappointed, he hid it well. 'Have you heard from Daniel?' he asked, understanding before she had even explained.

'Yes, he's offered to meet me after work. I'm so sorry, Quinn. I've really messed you around.'

'He's your brother. Forget about me; we can have dinner another time. This is more important. I'm still in Cambridge and haven't sorted a hotel room yet, so I'll just hang here for another night. I can always make sure I catch the same train back as you tomorrow, and we can catch up some more.'

Even though he was making this easy, she still felt guilty. 'Yes, I'd like that. I was looking forward to tonight, but I don't think I can get to Saham Toney and back in time.'

'Saham Toney,' Quinn repeated. 'You're going to your brother's house?'

Now she heard the frown in his voice.

'Yes, I'm hoping to hire a car as it will cost a small fortune to go by taxi, and it looks like the bus only goes to the nearest village.'

'Can't he come and meet you halfway?'

'He's in a wheelchair. I don't want to make it difficult for him when he's doing this for me.'

'I get that,' Quinn said patiently, 'but it's a long way to go, Lola, especially if there's snow.'

'Snow?'

'Haven't you seen the weather? There's a blizzard forecast for later on tonight.'

She hadn't, though it didn't surprise her. It was bitterly cold.

'It's not that far,' she reasoned. 'I've looked on Google Maps. I reckon it's about an hour's drive. I can hopefully be there and back before it hits.'

'Norfolk isn't like it is up north,' Quinn argued. 'It's all single carriageway and a lot of it is on B roads.'

She supposed he would know. Unlike Lola who had grown up in Cheshire, Quinn's family had lived all over as his dad had been stationed in the RAF. They had frequently moved between bases.

'I'll be okay,' she insisted, determined not to miss the opportunity to meet her birth brother. 'I'll drive carefully.'

Quinn was silent for a moment. 'Let me come with you,' he suggested.

He would do that for her after all this time?

Lola indulged herself for a moment, liking the idea of having him by her side as she made the journey to see Daniel.

Although she was pushing them down, nerves jittered in her belly at the prospect of meeting a brother she hadn't realised existed.

It wasn't a good idea, though. Firstly, she hadn't mentioned bringing anyone with her. And this wasn't a coffee shop or cafe. Daniel had invited her to his house and his wife, possibly family, might be present, so it felt wrong to invade their space with someone else when they had so hesitantly welcomed her alone.

Besides, Quinn was a distraction, and she needed her focus on this meeting.

'No, I have to do this alone,' she told him, 'but thank you for offering. It means a lot.'

It really did, and it was a stark reminder of what she had lost when their relationship had ended. He was a good man and he had always put her first, even when she hadn't deserved it. Was there a way they could find a path back to one another? Right now, it seemed possible, but so much had happened between them. It was going to take more than one encounter on a train for them to rebuild what they had lost.

Quinn accepted her decision to travel in the worsening weather and to do so alone, but then she guessed he didn't really have a choice.

'Do me a favour,' he asked before they ended the call, 'let me know you get there safely, okay?'

'If it makes you feel better,' Lola joked, keeping her tone light.

'It will,' he insisted, and his words stayed with her as she replied to Daniel, accepting his invitation.

His reply came back promptly, agreeing to the time she had asked to meet and giving her his address – the name of his house, Midwinter Manor, sounded imposing. There were no pleasantries, but then she supposed he didn't know her.

Yet.

After going online and booking a rental car, arranging to have it delivered that afternoon, she stopped for a sandwich, then headed back up the road to the Safe Hands office for round two of meetings.

She was almost there when a spit of something wet landed on her cheek.

Sleet, she realised, though not snow. Not yet.

Hopefully it would hold off long enough for her to get to Norfolk and back.

She had come so far and she wasn't going to miss the opportunity to meet her birth brother and seek some answers for the sake of thirty-six miles and possibly a bit of snow.

Plus she had the return journey with Quinn to look forward to.

It was all going to work out.

6

'I can't believe you're letting her come here. Are you both stupid?'

Jimmy's laugh was harsh, his tone insulting, and Rose was tempted to snap at him. Instead, she bit down on her temper, knowing sweetness was usually the way to go when she wanted something from her older brother. He might be five years her senior, but often she felt like she was the responsible one of the two.

He could be argumentative just for the sake of it, especially when he had sobered up after sleeping off one of his drinking sessions and was nursing a mammoth hangover. It wouldn't last long, though, and she noticed he was already eyeing up the vodka bottle that sat on the kitchen counter.

'It's only going to be a brief visit,' she pointed out. 'She messaged Daniel saying she's working locally and asked to meet him. What were we supposed to say? She's his sister.'

'Nothing! You were supposed to say nothing.' Jimmy's eyes, which had once been a mirror of her own, were now puffy and bloodshot; the blue of his irises bright with anger against the redness around them. 'Ignore her and she'll go away. It's too dangerous.'

'It will be fine,' she assured him, keeping her tone smooth and thinking to herself that the only danger came from Jimmy and his big, clumsy mouth. Especially once he started drinking. 'We couldn't risk her showing up uninvited.'

She didn't want Jimmy here when Lola Henderson came to the house and hoped she would be able to persuade him to go out to the pub.

Honestly, if she could find a way to get him to move out, then she would. It was Daniel's fault he was here. Her husband was too soft on Jimmy. And now it was too risky to force him to go; the terrible thing they had done binding them closer together.

'What if she figures it out, if she realises what you did?'

What you did.

Rose's temper spiked at his phrasing. Not what we *all* did. Jimmy was taking himself firmly out of the equation.

Typical of her brother. Run at the first sign of trouble.

They had let him live here. Putting a roof over his head and meals on the table. They had provided for him when he'd hit rock bottom and had nothing, and this was his way of saying thank you.

'She's not going to find out,' she insisted, keeping her smile pleasant, even though she was gritting her teeth. 'She's going to come to the house, we'll try to answer her questions, then she will leave. She's given her word that she will back off. After today, we never have to see her again.'

'You hope,' Jimmy goaded. 'When she sees the size of this place, she'll want to stay. Get her feet under the table and make sure she's in the will.' He shook his head in disgust. 'Why the hell did you invite her here to the house? You could have gone somewhere else to meet her.'

'Because it's safer. For all of us.'

Rose glanced out of the window at the sleet that had started to fall again. She had seen on the news the predictions for a white Christmas, and she knew that snow was forecast for tonight.

With any luck, Lola Henderson would realise how bad the roads were and she would turn back.

Then they wouldn't have to go through this charade at all.

7

Lola needed to be in Saham Toney no later than 7 p.m. and, aware she had to allow extra travelling time for the poor weather conditions, she decided that she needed to leave the Safe Hands office when they closed at 5 p.m. It would give her half an hour to nip back to the hotel and quickly freshen up before hitting the road.

Unfortunately, it seemed Rich Bradford had other ideas.

'I thought we could order in some food and talk things through some more,' he complained when she tried to draw their meeting to a close. 'I have a couple of marketing ideas I still want to discuss with you.'

'We can go over them tomorrow,' Lola said, keeping her tone amenable as she buttoned her coat. It was one she didn't wear often, tending to reserve it for client meetings, when she made more of an effort with her appearance, and the soft caramel shade complemented the understated black jeans and jumper underneath it. Right now, she was glad she had brought it with her; the calf-length woollen coat would keep her warm against the elements.

'I don't understand why we can't just carry on tonight,' he argued. 'You're only going to be sitting around in a hotel room.'

She bristled at his words. Even if she was intending to do that, it was her free time, and she pointed this out now, reminding him that she had already accommodated his request for meetings so close to Christmas. 'Besides,' she added, 'I won't be at the hotel. I have plans.'

'Really?' He sounded intrigued. 'What plans?'

None of your business, she wanted to say, but he was a client and she wouldn't be rude, even if he was.

'I'm seeing family,' she told him, deciding to keep it simple. Rich had no business knowing about Daniel or why she was meeting him.

'I didn't know you had anyone in Ely.'

As it wasn't a question, she didn't attempt to explain that she was actually going to Norfolk.

'I'll see you in the morning,' she said instead, eager to be on her way.

He nodded brusquely before managing the hint of a smile. 'Don't stay out too late. I want to get an early start tomorrow. I was thinking we could meet here at 8 a.m.'

'Fine.' She would give him that one concession. Besides, an earlier start meant she might be able to get away sooner. 'I'll see you in the morning.'

It surprised her that Rich wanted to stay late at the office. She didn't know much about his personal life, but a photo sat on his desk of a smiling woman holding a toddler, suggesting that he had a family waiting for him at home.

No, this was all about work and trying to get extra for free. Plus, the man appeared to enjoy making life difficult for people. He didn't have a huge workforce, hence why he outsourced his marketing, and Lola felt sorry for his employees. There wasn't much Christmas spirit about the place, with just a tiny tinsel tree on the front reception desk.

She pushed the main door open, stepping outside into the dark night, the bitterly cold temperature stealing her breath. Although she could hear the faint hum of traffic on the city roads, there was no one else in the car park, and she hurried over to the Peugeot she had rented. It sat beneath the one security light at the far end of the car park, its bonnet glowing where sleet had melted. For now, the dark sky was clear and full of stars, and there was a stillness to the air, as if in anticipation of the blizzard Quinn had mentioned. Lola hoped to be back in Ely before it hit.

Letting herself into the car, she locked the doors, cranked up the heating and quickly familiarised herself with the dashboard and indicators before heading off.

Arguing with Rich had eaten into her precious half an hour, so she only had time for a quick freshen up when she arrived at the hotel, switching her black jumper for an olive-coloured blouse, the long, wide sleeves and elegant neckline smartening up her appearance. Given his reluctance, it would probably be the one and only time she would get to meet Daniel and while he might not care or even notice, she wanted to make a good impression.

Ignoring the jittery nerves in her stomach, she touched up her make-up and ran a comb through her hair, spritzed on perfume, then wrapped up warm again in her thick coat and scarf. Thinking practically, she grabbed one of the bottles of water from the minibar, then her phone and charger.

As she went to slip the phone in her coat pocket, she spotted she had a WhatsApp message from Quinn, wishing her a safe journey.

She replied, thanking him and letting him know she would

be leaving shortly, promising – because it would put his mind at rest – that she would let him know once she had arrived safely at Daniel's house.

It was weird, she surmised, seeing Quinn's name popping up on her phone screen again. Though, in a good way. And she was already thinking ahead to their train ride home tomorrow. He seemed keen to spend time with her and she wondered if this was the start of rebuilding a friendship with him. Possibly more.

Although she had always been a firm believer in never looking back, their relationship breakdown had been borne of a tragedy and neither one's fault. They had been different people then.

He remained on her mind as she drove out of Ely, her only company coming from the satnav, and the radio, which she had on low, the steady stream of festive songs providing a comforting background noise, while at the same time evoking memories.

Lola had spent every Christmas with her mum, at the home where she had grown up. There would always be a beautifully decorated tree and her mum's Christmas dinner, then bubble and squeak leftovers and cold meats, pickles and salads the following day. They played boardgames, watched festive movies, and Kelly had made sure there were always gifts under the tree. Last year, the roles had reversed, as Lola had tried to make things special for her mum, and it had been bittersweet, both of them realising it was the end of a tradition.

Perhaps it was good that she was here and focused on meeting Daniel. At least it was a distraction.

As another flurry of sleet started, and the radio station cut to the news and local weather, warning again of the approaching blizzard, she was glad of the warmth inside the car.

Her belly was rumbling with hunger pains, but there had been no time to grab food, and if she was completely honest, she wasn't sure she would be able to eat anything anyway.

The nerves that were present in her tight shoulders and jittery stomach were only natural, she supposed. This was hardly an everyday event.

When she left Daniel's, she would find a McDonald's.

Quinn was right about her route being mostly B roads, but apart from getting stuck behind a lorry for one stretch, the traffic wasn't too bad.

As she spotted signs for Saham Toney, the sleet became heavier, turning into snow. The wind had picked up speed and thick white flakes were hitting the windscreen from all directions, reducing her visibility, even as the wipers tried to bat them away.

Lola was glad for the directions from the satnav, even though it skirted her around the edge of the main village, where several of the houses were decked out with fairy lights and Christmas trees twinkled in the glowing light of windows, before heading back out into the countryside.

Pockets of fir trees were sprouting up now on the sides of the road, caught in the glare of the headlights, and replacing the hedgerows and open fields that had been her view for much of the journey. As her path ahead twisted then narrowed, the trees became more closely intertwined, thickening into longer stretches of woodland.

The satnav was assuring her she was only one minute from her destination, but it looked more like she was in a remote Christmas card scene, and she hadn't seen any houses for at least the last couple of miles.

Lola was a city girl, used to the bright lights and bustle of central Manchester, and this was a world away from what she was accustomed to. A world away from Ely, too, and it was hard to believe the city she had left behind was less than forty miles away.

The road twisted again, this time the bend sharper than she was anticipating, and as the tyres skidded on ice, she almost lost control of the car.

Almost.

As she righted the vehicle, drew in a deep breath to steady her nerves, she thanked God she had been driving so slowly.

Was she mad coming here in these conditions?

Quinn had thought so.

Perhaps she should have taken him up on his offer when he'd suggested coming with her.

No, they had only just reconnected. It wouldn't have been right.

Besides, she was almost at her brother's. She wouldn't try to outstay her welcome and hopefully the snow would stop before she made the journey back.

'You have reached your destination,' the satnav announced, directing her off the road and onto a lane that appeared to snake through the trees.

No. This had to be wrong. It was just woodland.

Slowing the Peugeot to a halt, Lola pulled her phone out of her bag on the seat beside her. She had no mobile number for Daniel and her only form of contact was Messenger, but she could try to call him through that. She would explain she was lost and hopefully he could guide her to the house. It had to be close.

Her hopes of reaching him were dashed, her heart sinking, when she realised she had no signal.

Was it the weather affecting things or was she in a mobile dead zone?

Now what was she going to do?

As fresh tension knotted her neck and shoulders, she reversed back onto the road, holding her phone up, desperately hoping for a couple of bars, but there was nothing.

Think, Lola.

If she backtracked to the village, would she get a signal?

Realising it was the only choice she had, she started to turn the car around in the lane. As she did so, her headlights swept over what appeared to be lettering.

Was that a signpost?

It was almost hidden from view behind a tangle of overgrowth, but she could see the beginning of a word. Mid.

Daniel's home, Midwinter Manor?

But there was no house in sight, and this location certainly didn't resemble the address she had earlier googled.

Although she was reluctant to leave the warmth of the car, she needed to know what the rest of the sign said. Keeping the engine running and the lights on so she could see, she reluctantly pushed open the driver's door.

An icy breeze carrying a flurry of snow almost took her breath away as she stepped from the car and she wasted no time going over to the sign, unnerved by how isolated her location was.

As her fingers pulled at the weeds covering it, the rest of the wording was revealed, and the shiver running down the length of her spine as she saw it was indeed Midwinter Manor, had little to do with the cold.

So the satnav was right. She really was supposed to follow the track into the woods.

What the hell was she doing here?

It was two days before Christmas and she was in the middle of nowhere in a snowstorm. She couldn't see any house.

Spooked, Lola was ready to turn around. Drive back to Ely before the weather worsened and to the safety of her hotel room.

That was when rational Lola, the version of herself that didn't easily give in to paranoia or fear stepped up. The darkness wasn't helping and it was making her overreact.

The sign said Midwinter Manor, so she had to be in the right place.

So what if she couldn't see a house? Some of the trees ahead were thick pines and obscured her view. She had no idea what might lie beyond them, but having travelled here to meet her birth brother, that's what she was going to do.

Back inside the car, she steadied her breathing, ignored her accelerated heart rate and released the handbrake.

She had come this far. There was no turning back now.

8

Quinn glanced out of the window in his sister's kitchen, where he stood at the counter peeling potatoes, noting the worsening weather and hoping the snowstorm hadn't yet reached Norfolk. The swirling flakes might look pretty from behind a pane of glass, but it meant the roads would be treacherous.

Although she had a driving licence, the Lola he remembered preferred to use public transport, saying she found it more convenient to hop on a bus or train. She had never taken their car out much and whenever they had gone anywhere together, Quinn had usually been the one to drive.

Her lack of experience in this weather bothered him more than it should, as did the fact she was going to a remote part of Norfolk on unfamiliar roads, to meet a brother she hadn't realised existed. It had been difficult to step back and remind himself that it wasn't his place to look out for her any more.

He had offered to go with her and she had turned him down. Although he had wanted to, he hadn't pushed it. Instead, he had asked her to send him a quick WhatsApp message, so he would at least know she had arrived in Saham Toney safely.

Not that he should have requested that, either, but he needed some peace of mind.

It had knocked him for six when he had seen her on the train yesterday and for a few moments he had barely been able to gather his thoughts.

By the time he had, she had noticed him staring at her, and there had been no time to consider how to approach her. He had acted on instinct, determined to push aside the awkwardness and shock of seeing her after four long years.

He still felt guilty that he had given up on their relationship, though, in truth, he had been left with little choice after she had completely shut down on him and closed him out.

Not that he could blame her for that. It had been her way of coping after the trauma they had been through. Quinn had struggled, but he knew for Lola it had been worse, both mentally and physically.

Even then, he hadn't moved on. Keeping tabs on her via her mother.

Kelly had repeatedly made it clear that there was no going back and eventually he had ceased contact. For his own sanity, he knew he needed to move on. Still, he had thought about Lola often since they had parted, hoping she had found her own peace and been able to rebuild her life.

It had been a relief to see her looking so healthy, and to learn of her success with her business. And once she was over her initial shock at seeing him, it had surprised him how easily they had fallen back into a familiar pattern with each other.

Lola Henderson had always been the one for him. And, if he was honest, she still was.

He remembered back to the very first time he had seen her.

His brother, Kyle, had hired the firm Lola had been working for at the time to help with the marketing for his fledgling furniture business and she had been the digital marketeer assigned to his account.

Quinn had stopped by the office early that spring to meet his brother for lunch and instead had come face to face with Lola. She had been focused on her computer screen at the time and had spared him no more than a polite smile and a brief hello when Kyle had introduced them. She had ignored all of Quinn's attempts to flirt with her while he waited for his brother, so instead he had watched her tapping away at her keyboard, her ash-brown hair pulled back in a messy ponytail, and a pair of sexy dark-rimmed glasses perched on her nose, her brow furrowing and the tip of her tongue running along the corner of her top lip whenever she frowned at the screen.

She seemed a little more serious than the women he usually went for, but, regardless, he had been smitten straight away, and he had peppered Kyle with questions about her during their lunch.

It had taken a few more visits to the office, but eventually he had managed to talk her into having dinner with him.

That night, she sadly hadn't worn the glasses, but he had seen her eyes were an earthy shade of olive green. And he was wrong about her being serious. She had a wickedly dry sense of humour. He had also learnt towards the end of the evening that she almost hadn't showed up for their date, having him pegged as a shallow serial flirt.

They had both misjudged each other.

What started off as tentative quickly grew in intensity, and by the time summer ended they were already spending all of their free time together. The following year, they rented a flat, and shortly afterwards, Lola had fallen pregnant.

Unplanned, but not unwelcome once they had adjusted to the idea. Things seemed so perfect, Quinn had felt like he was living in a Richard Curtis film. That was until their lives had derailed.

There had been no happy ending for them.

Yesterday had been unexpected, but the way they had slid straight back into their old familiar roles after years apart had ignited a flame. Was it possible they could reconcile?

Quinn was currently single, having ended his last relationship a couple of months before Christmas, and Lola hadn't mentioned seeing anyone.

Perhaps he was foolish to hope, but he couldn't help it.

Just as he couldn't help worrying about her journey to Norfolk in the bad weather.

He glanced at his phone now. Lola had messaged just over an hour ago to say she was leaving Ely. She would be in touch again soon.

'I think it's starting to settle.'

Chloe, who had been putting Quinn's nieces, eight-year-old Lois and six-year-old Mia, to bed, came back into the kitchen, moving to stand beside him as she peered out of the window. She handed him a glass of red wine. Feeling useless, wishing he could be there with Lola, but knowing he wasn't needed, he took a sip, hoping it might help him to relax and shake off the feeling of unease that was kneading at his gut.

'Has Lola messaged yet?' Chloe asked, as if reading his thoughts.

He shook his head and managed a smile for his sister. 'No, but she's probably taking it slow in these conditions.'

Chloe took the peeled potatoes and put them into a pan to boil.

'She will be,' she assured him. 'Lola's no fool.'

Her certainty reassured him a little. And Quinn told himself he was just on edge because they had only just reconnected. He took another sip of the wine and ordered himself to relax. He needed to pull himself together and get some perspective on the situation.

Everything was going to be okay. He had to believe that.

9

When the trees parted and the lane widened and Midwinter Manor came into sight, Lola was left in no doubt that she was at the right place.

After Daniel had given her his address, she had looked up the property online, but the photos she had seen didn't do it justice, or prepare her for quite how big or imposing it was, standing on an incline and hidden away in the middle of the woods.

Two huge cone-shaped pillars flanked the edge of the driveway and the wrought-iron gate that stood between them was wide open. Beyond the entrance was the house: a three-storey grey stone building that looked to be several hundred years old. The building seemed to be in good repair, but its sheer size was a little intimidating, as was the large gargoyle carving in the wall above the wooden front door; some kind of mythical creature with its face twisted into a grotesque scream.

Tall chimneys jutted out of the snow-covered roof, smoke billowing from one of them, and pointed arch windows stared at her. A couple of them on the ground floor were lit, but those on the levels above were dark and foreboding, and as she drove through the open gate, her headlights chasing shadows as her tyres cut tracks through the dusting of snow on the ground, she couldn't help but feel like the house was watching her approach.

Perhaps it was the wintery weather, the remote location, or simply the reason why she was here, but something about this place unsettled her, and the butterflies that had been fluttering away in her belly were now raging a storm.

There were no other vehicles on the large driveway, so she parked the rental car close to the house.

Before she had even killed the engine, the front door opened. Her arrival had been watched.

Not by Daniel. It was a woman who waited in the doorway, her hands clasped and a half smile on her face. By her side sat a black Labrador and, as Lola climbed out of the car, the dog ran towards her, tail wagging.

'Monty!' the woman shouted after him, trying to get him back inside.

He was an older dog, Lola realised, watching as he limped towards her, the grey and white fur around his mouth a telltale sign of his age. He met her halfway, friendly brown eyes looking up at her, and despite the falling snow, she paused briefly to make a fuss of the animal.

'I'm sorry about him,' the woman said, sounding a little exasperated.

'It's fine. I like dogs,' Lola assured her, straightening, as Monty glued himself against her.

'Come on,' the woman beckoned them both. 'We're letting the cold in.'

She ushered them inside a large porch with a high ceiling and a black and white checked floor, closing the heavy door against the worsening weather as Lola brushed icy flakes off her coat.

'The weather is terrible,' she continued without introducing herself. She seemed certain of who Lola was, though, so perhaps she had googled her. 'We half thought you might cancel.'

She had a soft Scottish lilt, and was a similar age to Lola. And although casually dressed, her grey wool trousers were fashionably high-waisted and wide-legged, and the string of pearl beads against her black top appeared expensive and chic. Her dark hair was clipped back, her skin smooth and pale, and perfectly made up, and the only colour in her outfit was from the blood-red slash of lipstick painted on her mouth.

Standing next to her, dressed in jeans and tired from her drive, Lola felt woefully inadequate.

'The roads weren't too bad,' she downplayed. Truthfully, she wasn't looking forward to the drive back. The snow had already started to settle, and although it was only a dusting at the moment, if it kept falling, that could change.

'I'm Rose. Daniel's wife.' At last, the woman was introducing herself, holding out a manicured hand that sparkled with a large diamond ring. It cut against Lola's fingers as she politely shook it.

'Lola. Thank you both for inviting me here. I promise I won't take up too much of Daniel's time.'

So this was her sister-in-law. Another relative, though not by blood. It was a strange feeling, meeting family for the first time.

She wondered where her brother was, peering past Rose into the daunting house. It felt odd that he had been the one messaging with her, but he wasn't here at the door to greet her.

Though she supposed that might be because he was in a wheelchair. It was perhaps easier to send his wife to the door.

'Let me hang your coat up for you,' Rose offered, taking it from Lola and putting it on a peg next to a Burberry jacket and a fur-lined animal-print trench coat. 'This way,' she gestured, leading Lola through into a large hallway.

A huge Christmas tree dressed in reds and golds twinkled at the bottom of a wide staircase, its banister wrapped in a holly garland, and the tiled floor looked polished to within an inch of its life. On the wall beyond the tree, Lola spotted ornate carved wooden doors.

'It's a lift,' Rose said, seeing her looking. 'Came with the house. Daniel didn't want some plastic monstrosity installed to take him upstairs.' She turned up her nose, as if the idea of a disabled lift disgusted her. 'So we looked for a property that already had one.'

Unsure how to react, Lola simply nodded.

Rose had assumed she knew about Daniel's accident. Did she guess Lola had been googling her brother?

'Let me go and tell him you're here. Come on, Monty.'

There it was again. That half-smile, as if she was too wary to let her lips fully curve.

Lola watched the dog get up and plod after Rose, as she disappeared through an archway, and she drew in a breath to try and calm the flutter of nerves in her stomach.

This was an unusual visit, she supposed. It wasn't every day that unknown family came crawling out of the woodwork.

Taking the opportunity while she was alone to message Quinn and let him know she had arrived safely, she pulled her phone from her bag, dismayed when she saw that she still had no signal. It must be the remote location of the house. When Rose returned, she would ask if she could hop on to the Wi-Fi.

For now, she waited, putting her phone away, aware how cold it was without her coat. Although it was warmer inside the house than out, it was a big place to heat, and she only had on a blouse. Her own fault for not picking something warmer.

As she rubbed at her arms, she took in more of the room she was in. It was elegantly but very traditionally decorated, its dark linenfold panelling and huge chandelier hanging from the high ceiling giving off an air of formality, and the few pieces of furniture – the grandfather clock, a console table and a rustic monk's bench – were antique in style. To both sides of the cavernous hallway, dimly lit corridors led off, and given the size of the house from outside, she suspected they led to a rabbit warren of rooms. It felt more like a museum than a home; the kind of place you visited where everything was cordoned off by rope barriers, and it was a world away from what she was used to.

Now Rose had gone, the lingering of her perfume was fading and Lola noticed a slightly musty odour clinging in the air, and the faint whiff of cigarette smoke. It only added to the unsettling atmosphere.

Minutes passed, the silence broken only by the ticking of the grandfather clock, and Lola was wondering how long they were going to leave her waiting in this draughty entrance hall, when the clip of footsteps signalled Rose's return.

'Sorry for keeping you,' she apologised. Monty again trailed behind her. 'If you want to come this way, Daniel will see you now.'

It all sounded very formal and again Lola considered his disability. She assumed he used a wheelchair and could move around, but did she have that wrong?

'Um, could I just ask a quick favour? I don't suppose I could use your Wi-Fi? I'm supposed to message a friend and I have no signal.'

'You won't have,' Rose agreed. 'We're in a dead zone here and have to use Wi-Fi calling. I keep meaning to get a landline phone connected, so we're not cut off when the signal drops out. Come and meet Daniel and then I'll get you the code.'

Fresh nerves jittered in Lola's stomach. It was like being at an interview or waiting to see a doctor.

Drawing in a steadying breath, she smoothed a hand over her hair, wishing there was a mirror in the hallway so she could quickly check over her appearance.

It mattered, she realised, his first impression of her.

Which was ridiculous. She wasn't trying to be someone else.

Keeping that thought in mind, she followed after Rose.

10

Lola followed Rose and Monty into another longer hallway. This one was much narrower than the first, but with the same dark panelling on the walls, giving it an oppressive feeling. Most of the doors were closed, and those that were open led into dark rooms where it was impossible to make out their function. At the end of the hall was a large living room, much cosier than the rest of the house, and dominated by a huge lit fireplace that was warming the space.

She didn't take in any other details of the room, her sole focus on the man in the wheelchair who sat in front of the fire, watching as it crackled and blazed with dancing orange flames.

Had he heard them enter the room? He made no attempt to turn around and Lola stood awkwardly just inside the doorway, next to Rose, unsure whether to approach.

She was about to speak his name, when Rose called to him. 'Daniel. She's here.'

Taking that as her cue, Lola stepped towards him, relieved when he finally turned his chair.

She recognised him instantly from the Lamborghini photo,

but he was no longer clean-shaven, instead sporting a full beard. It was a couple of shades lighter than his dark hair.

Scowling eyes looked her up and down. 'Miss Henderson.'

'Lola, please. Thank you for meeting with me, Daniel.'

He seemed to bristle a little at her use of his first name, but gestured to a nearby sofa. 'Take a seat.'

It sounded more like an order than an offer.

'I'll go make some drinks,' Rose told them, hastily leaving the room.

Alone with her brother and the dog, who slumped to the floor beside the sofa, Lola lowered herself onto the leather seat, unsure where to begin. She had wanted this meeting and had a list of questions for Daniel, but she hadn't expected such a formal greeting. He had been terse in their messages, but she had convinced herself that things would be different once they were face to face. Instead, he was staring at her like she was a stranger. Which, she supposed, she still was. They might be brother and sister, but they had never met before.

'What is it you want to know?' he asked abruptly, catching her off guard.

Lola scrambled her frazzled brain, determined to focus. She had come here for answers and she wasn't going to let him guilt her into leaving before she had got them. She had already accepted that there would be no relationship, but he owed her the courtesy of this one meeting.

'What were our parents like?' she asked, holding eye contact, despite his permanent scowl. It was a broad question. One that required more than a one-sentence answer. Now she was getting the measure of this man, she was determined to hold her own and not let him off the hook.

'They were just regular people. My dad, Nigel, was a

banker. Quiet, hard-working, though he had a temper when pushed.'

Lola smarted at his use of the word 'my'. Had he said it on purpose to try to exclude her?

'What about *our* mother, Annie?' she asked, refusing to acknowledge the slight.

'She was a receptionist in a hotel when they met.'

'Was this in Oxford?'

Daniel nodded. 'Yes. She didn't stay there long, though. I was born not long after they married and then she stayed at home looking after me.'

'What was she like?'

He shrugged. 'Not as serious as Dad. She was the fun one, I guess.'

She continued with her questions, trying to break down that barrier. Asking more personal ones about Nigel and Annie, trying to get him to react and engage. But there was no connection. He didn't want to talk about them, at least not with her. If anything, he seemed bored of their conversation, bored of her, and he wasn't even trying to hide it.

'Do you have any photos of them?' she asked. If he wouldn't give her any information, perhaps he would let her see pictures. She hadn't been able to find anything online.

Daniel didn't get a chance to answer, as Rose timed that moment, arriving with a tray laden with tea things. It all looked very formal as she set the tray down on a coffee table. There were cups with saucers, a teapot, milk jug, and even sugar cubes in a little dish.

Was this something they only brought out for guests or did they live like this all the time?

'How do you take your tea, Lola?' Rose asked, and although

she was friendlier than her husband, there was still a stiffness about her.

'Just a little milk, please.'

She watched Rose pour the drink, noticing that her hands were shaking slightly.

Was she nervous having Lola in her home? It made no sense why she would be.

Lola thanked her as she took the cup, turning her attention back to Daniel.

'Photos of our parents,' she pushed. 'Do you have any?'

'Of course.' His tone was sharp.

'Am I able to see them, please?' Lola was annoyed that he was making her ask.

Seeming determined to be the peacemaker, Rose gave what appeared to be a warning look to her husband to play nice. 'I'll go get some,' she offered. 'You two drink your tea.'

As Rose left the room, Lola realised she had forgotten to remind her about the Wi-Fi password. She asked Daniel for it now.

'I promised I would check in with a friend,' she explained, hoping he would sense her urgency and not think she was being rude for asking.

'I don't have it on me,' he said dismissively. 'Rose will have to get it when she returns.'

Lola must have looked frustrated, because he gestured to his legs and shrugged, before adding, 'I rely on her to do a lot for me these days.'

It was frustrating, but she would have to wait. Would Quinn be keeping an eye on the time? She knew the bad weather had bothered him and he was worried about her making it safely to Saham Toney. He was still at his sister's, though, so perhaps he was being distracted by his nieces and hadn't given it much thought. She would message as soon as she was able.

'How did you end up in the chair?' Lola asked, deciding to try a different approach with Daniel, even though voicing the question aloud made her a little uncomfortable. So far, her questions had been all about their parents. Perhaps if she asked about him personally, he might engage more.

'A skiing accident.'

'Were you very old?' Lola already knew he had been twenty-nine, having read about it online, but he didn't need to know that.

He fell silent, seeming reflective, and she waited, hoping she hadn't conjured up bad memories for him.

'No,' he said quietly. 'I wasn't. It happened a couple of months before my thirtieth birthday. I didn't believe the doctors when they told me I would never walk again. But I guess I didn't know shit, because here I am.'

The harshness of that last sentence seemed at odds with the man she had been talking with and Lola was unsure how to react.

'I'm sorry,' she said. What else could she possibly say?

Daniel's lips curved into a smirk as he studied her, and for a moment it seemed he was noticing her properly for the first time.

'People say that to me a lot, you know. *I'm sorry*. It's a bit of an empty phrase, don't you think? You're sorry for what, I want to ask them. That it happened? That it was me and not them? I don't need anyone's sympathy, Lola. It was a long time ago and, look, I have this fancy chair on wheels to ride around in. I have everything I need here, and I get by just fine.'

Was he trying to embarrass her? Although her cheeks heated, it was more with anger. Why was he being such an arsehole? Okay, she might have pushed to meet him, but that was because he was her brother and the only one who could give her information about her family. He still could have said no.

'Good for you,' she managed, biting down on her annoyance, though she couldn't stop her sarcasm slipping through.

She sipped at her tea as a silence descended upon them, forcing herself to swallow the too-hot liquid over the growing ball of frustration that had built in her throat, while Daniel stared at the tea tray.

He had yet to touch the drink that Rose had poured for him.

Why had Lola kidded herself this would be different once they had met? She had believed she would somehow win him over, but now she understood the truth, that Daniel had never been up for this. She should have left well alone.

If she hadn't messaged him again, she would be back in Ely having dinner with Quinn. Instead, she faced a horrible drive back on the icy roads.

'What's your story, Lola?'

The question came out of left field, completely catching her off guard.

They had reached a stalemate. Daniel making it obvious she wasn't welcome and Lola, seeing no way forward, was beginning to wonder if she should cut her losses and leave. But now he had broken it, and he was showing an interest in her.

It took her a moment to try to gather herself to respond, unable to decide if he was genuinely interested in her answer.

'What do you want to know?' she asked cautiously.

'You're in marketing, right? Have your own business.'

'Yes,' she confirmed. 'That's right.' She was surprised he had looked her up.

'Are you married? Engaged? A boyfriend?'

He steepled his hands, forefingers pressing into his chin as he waited and she thought of Quinn. Of what they had once had and lost.

'Right now, I'm single.'

'No children then?'

Her breath caught. 'No children,' she managed.

Her voice sounded strained to her own ears and she hoped he hadn't picked up on the emotions clogging her throat as she spoke the words.

'Well, that's good, I guess. We don't want any little nieces or nephews popping up out of the woodwork trying to lay a claim to Uncle Daniel's estate.'

It took a second to register his words, and the heat behind them.

There it was, the accusation laid bare. He thought she was after his money.

Lola wanted to defend herself, but shock and fresh anger choked her. How dare he suggest she was only here for his money?

Rose chose that moment to return to the room and if she picked up on the tension, she didn't say. She held something in her hand and as she neared, Lola saw it was a couple of photographs.

'This is your mother, Annie, and your father, Nigel,' she said, taking a seat beside Lola, and handing her the first photograph. 'It was taken on their wedding day.'

Lola studied the picture. The tall, stern-faced man standing next to his smiling bride. Her mother, Annie, wore a long-sleeved puffy gown, her light-brown hair falling in ringlets around a heart-shaped face.

So these were the people who had created her, but then abandoned her.

She would be a liar if she claimed not to be upset by their actions, but, equally, it saddened her she would never get the chance to meet them and learn their history. That was why she had come here today, for answers. It had nothing to do with money.

Rose pushed the other photo into her hand. 'This was your mum with Daniel when he was younger.'

Much younger.

Annie and her brother as a child were on a beach, and seeing Daniel's toothy grin, it was hard to reconcile him with the man sitting next to her.

'Do you know why they gave me up?' she asked Daniel, readying herself for another harsh answer, but needing to know the truth. It made no sense to her why they would have one child, who it appeared they loved, yet when another baby came along, they weren't interested.

He shrugged, and for a moment she didn't think he was going to answer. 'I didn't know about you until a few years back. I was still very young when you were born and I didn't realise Mum was pregnant. They never discussed it in front of me. All I remember was they were fighting a lot and then Mum went away for a while. I didn't realise until much later that there had been complications with the pregnancy and they'd had to keep her in for observation.'

The look he gave her suggested he held her responsible for those complications, and it was a reminder of the wall he had erected between them.

As far as he was concerned, she wasn't his family and without her birth parents here to ask, she was never going to know the full truth about what had happened.

She went to hand the photos back to Rose.

'You can keep these,' the other woman told her, insisting. 'We have copies.'

At least she would be leaving with something, Lola supposed, even though the people in the photographs were strangers, despite their blood bond. 'Thank you.'

She slipped the photos in her bag, finished the rest of her tea, and started to get up. She had been here for just under the hour she had asked for, but there was no point in outstaying her welcome. Besides, she was eager to get back before the snow worsened.

'You're going?'

Was Lola mistaken or did Rose sound relieved?

Still, the woman had been much friendlier to her than Daniel had, even if there was something a little off about her.

'Yes, I have to drive back to Cambridgeshire. Thank you for your hospitality, though, and for the photos.'

She glanced at her brother, tempted to leave without saying goodbye to him. But she was better than that. She wouldn't stoop to his level.

'I appreciate you talking to me. I won't bother you again.'

He nodded, his expression blank.

Rude bastard.

Daniel made no attempt to leave his position in front of the fireplace and as Lola followed Rose back through to the main hallway, Monty again following, then through to the entrance porch, the heaviness of nerves started to lift.

She should never have come here. She knew that now. But it was over and she wouldn't have to see Daniel again. It was disappointing not to learn more about her birth family, but it was time to close the door on this history.

Rose was already taking Lola's coat and scarf from the peg,

hovering over her as she put them on and reached in her pocket for the car fob.

'Safe travels,' she said, opening the door, and Lola wasn't sure if there was a hint of relief in her tone.

As she thanked Rose again and said goodbye to her and the dog, Lola went to step outside, the scene before her taking her by surprise. It had stopped snowing, but everywhere was white; the light dusting that had been on the ground had been replaced with a much heavier coating, that looked several inches deep.

'Oh,' Rose gasped beside her.

Oh, indeed. How had so much snow fallen so quickly?

Quinn had warned Lola not to come. Now she was going to have to drive back in this.

Staying wasn't an option. She had another meeting with Rich Bradford lined up for the morning and a train back to Manchester booked for the afternoon.

Besides, the thought of stepping back into Midwinter Manor held zero appeal.

'Are you going to be okay to drive in this?' Rose asked.

Lola nodded. 'I'll be okay. Thank you, again.'

She trudged her way towards the hire car, glad she had her boots on, then spent a few minutes brushing fresh snow from the windows and roof. By the time she pulled the driver's door open, her hands were freezing and the front of her coat damp.

Inside the car, she tried the engine, her breath catching when at first it didn't start. But then it spluttered to life and she tried to roll the tension out of her shoulders.

It would be okay. She just had to get back on the main road.

She cranked up the heating, waiting for it to clear the windscreen, turning on the headlights and then the wipers as a fresh flurry of snow started to fall. As they batted back and forth across the windscreen clearing the white flakes, she glanced in the wing mirror.

Rose hadn't gone back inside. Instead, she stood watching from the open door, Monty still beside her. Gingerly, Lola eased the car forward, aware from the way it started slipping around on the snow that there was little traction.

Getting back to Ely was not going to be an easy task.

She took it slowly and had almost made it down to the gate, when she broke the number one rule of driving in icy weather, touching the brake as she turned the steering wheel. As she lost control, the Peugeot skidding to the left, she continued to pump the brake uselessly. Unable to break the swerve, the front of the car slammed into the left post, jolting her sharply against the seatbelt, the sound of metal hitting metal making her wince. The engine stalled, then something under the bonnet hissed and smoke rose into the air, only just visible through the swirling snow.

Even though she knew she was wasting her time, Lola tried the ignition, her heart sinking when it coughed and spluttered, then cut out again. She was still sitting there trying to get the car to start when, a minute later, there was a knock on the driver's side window, and she glanced back to see Rose.

The woman had gone back inside to grab the fur-lined coat and was hugging it around her as she urged Lola to open the door.

'Are you okay?'

'I am, but I'm not so sure about the car. I hope I haven't damaged the gate post.' She could already imagine Daniel's irritation. 'Obviously I will pay if I have.'

'It's fine,' Rose said, waving away the offer. 'But the car definitely won't start?'

Remembering the reception she had received in the Whitlock home from Daniel, Lola tried the ignition again, but this time there was nothing.

She shook her head. 'It's dead.'

Rose was silent for a moment. 'Come on, you'd better come back inside the house,' she said eventually. Although there was a hint of stiffness in her tone, the smile she offered appeared genuine.

Reluctantly, Lola got out of the car, mad at herself for crashing into the post and already thinking ahead to how this affected everything.

Would she be able to get anyone out to fix the car tonight?

The snow seemed to be getting heavier, and the wind was picking up too, the icy flakes swirling around her face, batting in her eyes and stealing her breath.

'We should head indoors,' Rose urged. 'It's getting worse.'

Knowing she didn't have a choice, Lola followed after her, ignoring the jitter of unease as she glanced towards the house.

Like it or not, for now she was trapped here.

11

NINE YEARS EARLIER

Oxford

Rose Campbell almost hadn't gone to the interview the day she met Daniel Whitlock.

She had moved into private care work a couple of years earlier and was enjoying the benefits of a better wage, as well as getting to pick and choose what jobs she took on, and caring for the paraplegic adult son of Nigel and Annie Whitlock didn't particularly appeal.

When the agency she was registered with had first contacted her about the job early in the spring, she had initially said no. She already had enough clients and didn't need the extra hours.

But then the agency had mentioned how much the Whitlocks were willing to pay, and Rose had decided there and then to push her concerns to one side.

The morning of the interview, it had seemed that the world was conspiring against her leaving the house. First, her mother had called in a state, as she'd had a bad fall. Despite Jimmy being just round the corner, she had contacted Rose, who lived over 400 miles away. Typical of her selfish mother, and after going through the motions of calming Agnes down, it had been left to Rose to track down Jimmy and get him to take responsibility for the situation.

Finally off the phone and knowing she was going to be late, she had choked on a mouthful of cold coffee, spilling it down her clean white blouse.

After a change of clothes, she had got into her car, only to have the engine splutter and die.

Everything was working against her and she decided it was a sign that she wasn't supposed to meet the Whitlocks. It was only the temptation of the money that kept her focused and calling for a taxi.

The ride had been expensive, the Whitlocks living twenty minutes outside of Oxford, but as she caught her first glimpse of Hartleigh House, where the family lived, her annoyance slipped away, her mouth dropping open at the size of the place.

No wonder they were willing to pay well.

The grandeur of the building had her smoothing out the creases in the replacement blouse and running an anxious hand over her hair. She wished she had a mirror on her, so she could double-check her appearance. This was a different world to what she was used to and it suddenly seemed important that she make the best impression possible.

As it turned out, she need not have worried. Annie Whitlock was down to earth and welcoming, brushing away Rose's apologies that she was late and sympathising over her mother's fall, her brow creasing in concern.

'I hope she's okay. You must be worried.'

'It was a bit of a scare,' Rose had agreed, playing the role of the doting daughter.

Nigel hadn't been home that day, having been called away to an important meeting, but Rose did get to meet Daniel and they clicked instantly.

His story was a tragic one and she couldn't begin to imagine his internal anguish at losing his freedom and, in turn, everything he held precious. Not only had he been a keen sportsman, regularly enjoying golf, rugby and cricket, as well as skiing, which, of course, had taken the use of his legs, but he had also travelled extensively. Something that he could still do, though it now came with its limitations.

Before, he told her, he had enjoyed camping on safari in Tanzania, rock climbing in Spain and kayaking on the Amazon River. Now, if he travelled, every tiny detail needed to be planned and assessed. Adventure holidays were no longer an option and had to be traded for more traditional hotel packages that catered to his needs.

He was a paraplegic man who had been forced to swallow his pride and accept help for some of his most basic needs, but still he remained positive, explaining to her as he stroked the black Labrador puppy by his side, that he hadn't given up hope of walking again. Willing to try anything and with money no object, he had looked overseas for pioneering treatment and was currently in contact with a team of doctors in the US who were working on a cure for spinal cord injuries.

Later, when the two of them were alone again, Annie told Rose that her son believed the doctors would soon be able to fix him. He was grasping at straws, though, and refusing to accept that a cure was unlikely to happen for decades – certainly not in his lifetime – if at all. The research was still in its infancy and there were a lot of obstacles to overcome.

For now, Daniel needed help and company, and that was where Rose came in.

Annie had initially wanted to employ someone on a permanent basis, but Daniel was against the idea, and Rose tended to agree that he didn't require full-time care either. He was fiercely trying to protect what little independence he had and she understood that.

She was glad Annie had put her son's wishes first too, in part because she would have had to turn the job down if it was full time, but after meeting with the pair of them, she agreed to their twenty hours a week request.

At first, caring for Daniel Whitlock was the same as looking after any of her other patients. It was just a job that came with better pay, a nicer setting, and someone she genuinely liked looking after.

She got along well with Annie, appreciating that the woman didn't try to interfere with her job, and although she was less fond of Nigel, who was a little sharper around the edges, he was seldom at home whenever she was there.

That was better for Daniel too, who she sensed had a difficult relationship with his father, the pair of them scarcely seeing eye to eye, and Annie was often left to play peacemaker between the two of them.

The first year with the Whitlocks flew by and by the time spring came around again, Rose had dropped her other clients, increasing her hours to look after Daniel. He hadn't necessarily required the extra time, but equally, he hadn't complained.

As their friendship steadily deepened, priorities shifted.

Despite her job role, Rose had never seen herself ending up with someone who had a disability, but her needs adjusted. When Daniel proposed, she didn't hesitate to accept. Yes, the lure of great wealth was a factor, but Daniel was an attractive man and he was kind too. It was no hardship being with him, or helping him to look after his dog, Monty, and she would never want for anything. She would be a good wife to him.

Annie had been delighted. Nigel more reserved. He was suspicious of her motives. Rose understood she was marrying into money and she was determined to prove him wrong. So, it stung when Nigel told them they needed to have a prenup in place, making her feel as if her motives for marriage were devious.

She told Daniel she would sign it to keep the peace, but he was insistent they didn't need one. Following an explosive argument, though, he and his father didn't speak for several days, while Rose and Annie walked on eggshells around them, and knowing something had to give, Rose had talked Daniel into letting his father draw up the paperwork. It was just a document, she told him. And it would never be needed, as they would be together always.

The wedding ceremony was low-key, neither Daniel nor Rose wishing to draw attention to themselves, but while Annie smiled and wiped tears of joy from her eyes, Nigel was cordial, but stony-faced. Even with the prenup, Rose sensed he didn't like her joining the family.

Once married, she gave up her flat, moving in with the Whitlocks. She had hoped to persuade Daniel to move out so they could have their own place, but he was insistent they stay with his parents for the time being, arguing that there was plenty of space.

Rose wasn't looking forward to sharing a home with her father-in-law, but reminded herself she was built of stern stuff and would not cower to him.

It helped that she continued to care for Daniel after the

wedding, and Rose knew that Nigel was quietly impressed she hadn't been quick to throw her job in.

She would win him over eventually, she figured.

And if she didn't? Well, the man was in his seventies, much older than Annie, and he didn't lead the healthiest of lifestyles. It was only a matter of time before he met his maker.

12

PRESENT DAY

Jimmy had only been in the Black Horse pub a handful of times, so he was surprised that the bartender recognised him.

Maybe it was because the man knew he lived at Midwinter Manor. The place was far bigger than any other property in the surrounding area, and they liked to keep to themselves a lot of the time. People were probably curious about the elusive Whitlocks.

Usually, Jimmy preferred to drink alone, but Rose had given him thirty quid, offering to treat him to a few beers, and he wasn't stupid enough to turn her down, even though he knew full well why she wanted him out of the way.

It was because of her. Lola Henderson. Daniel's sister.

For some inexplicable reason, they had invited her to the house and Jimmy hadn't held back in telling them what a stupid idea it was. No wonder they wanted him gone.

Jimmy often rued the day he had moved in with his sister and her husband, just as he bitterly regretted going along with such a dangerous plan.

Rose had dangled the carrot, though, and he had been too

weak-willed, too greedy, to walk away. The irony was that he'd liked Daniel when he moved in, and they got along well.

But that had been before. Now, all thoughts of his brother-in-law left a nasty taste in his mouth, and he avoided being anywhere near him.

The size and grandeur of Midwinter Manor had at first enthralled him. It was like something out of a fairy tale, and when he had shown up to visit his sister in the summer of 2023, he had been green with envy.

How quickly things had changed.

He had nothing left to his name, though, the alcoholism that had consumed him, destroying his marriage and getting him sacked from his caretaker job, stealing his home and emptying his bank account. He had been grateful when Rose took him in.

Despite there being five years between them, they had enjoyed a close relationship when they were younger, though they had grown apart in more recent years, especially after Rose had moved to London to train to become a nurse. She had wanted to get away from the quiet Scottish village where they had grown up, claiming life there was too boring, but Jimmy had been happy to stay. At least before his fortunes had changed.

Here in Norfolk, he hoped he might have a fresh start. What had started as a visit turned into something longer, even though none of them ever had a conversation about whether this was a permanent move. Jimmy surmised that Rose and Daniel had plenty of money, and it wasn't as if they didn't have the space to put him up.

He even made an effort to cut back on the booze, and for a while he had felt truly content.

But then his sister had asked him to do something for her,

and, scared that he might lose everything if he refused, he had agreed. It was the biggest regret of his life.

Of course, she had allowed him to stay. She couldn't risk him shooting his mouth off. Neither of them could.

It was why they mostly left him to his own devices, letting him drink himself stupid – because there was no way he could stay sober after what he had done.

And for his part, Jimmy kept quiet.

This was his life now. He hadn't chosen it, but he would have to live with the role he had chosen.

As he finished his third beer, he dreaded the thought of returning to the house.

The bartender was clearing tables and as Jimmy waited for him to return, ready to order another drink and debating whether to move on to something strong, he glanced around the room. It was much emptier than when he had first arrived. Emptier, in fact, than when he had ever been here before. A young couple sat at a corner table and three older men were at the other end of the bar, but other than that, it was Jimmy and the bartender.

'Where is everyone?'

He was still sober enough to notice he was slurring his words.

The young bartender glanced up, tray of empty glasses in his hand. 'It's the weather. Everyone wants to get home before it worsens.'

'The bookies will pay out big time on Christmas Day if it doesn't clear,' one of the men at the end of the bar muttered.

It had been snowing on and off during the mile and a half walk to the pub, but Jimmy hadn't taken a whole lot of notice, but now he moved to the window, blinking in disbelief as he took in the wild scene outside the pub. The benches and tables in the beer garden were covered in snow and white flakes were furiously batting the windows.

It took his alcohol-soaked brain a few seconds longer to register that he too had to walk home in this.

Fuck!

He didn't suppose he would be able to get a taxi. Besides, it was only just after 8 p.m. and Daniel's sister would probably still be at the house. Rose would be annoyed if Jimmy made an early return.

Returning to his bar stool, he decided he would have a double whisky and wait a little bit longer, before he attempted to trudge back to the house. The longer he stayed away, the better for everyone.

13

'Could you let me have the code for your Wi-Fi, please? I'll see if I can get someone out to look at the car.'

Lola had waited until their damp coats were discarded in the foyer before she asked the question. She was hurrying to keep up with Rose, who was leading the way down another hallway towards the opposite end of the house from where Lola had met with Daniel.

For a moment, the other woman didn't appear to have heard her, but then, as they stepped through into a ginormous kitchen, she turned to face her.

'It's on my phone. I'll go get it. Stay here.'

She almost barked the last words as an order before disappearing out of the kitchen, leaving Lola wondering what the rush was for.

As when she had first arrived, she was left to wait and as she glanced around the room, she realised she felt just as uncomfortable as the first time Rose had abandoned her.

At least Monty was here, she realised, spotting the black Labrador lying in a tatty-looking dog bed on the far side of the room. Noticing he had company, his tail started thumping and he rose unsteadily on tired old legs to bring her a soft ball.

As Lola scratched behind his ears, grateful for the company, she took in the circular room.

It was beautifully designed and, unlike the rest of the house, it looked fresh and modern, with navy-coloured units and a glossy white worktop. A large Aga cooker heated the room, and all of the appliances – the microwave and air fryer, the coffee machine and toaster – were shiny, new and expensive brand-name labels. The American fridge-freezer looked top of the range, while a large central island held a vase filled with a decorative winter floral display.

Everything was spotlessly clean and there was no clutter, but as with the rest of the house, something about it made Lola uneasy.

Perhaps it simply was the isolated location on a bitterly cold winter's night, or maybe it wasn't the house at all. She couldn't quite put her finger on what was troubling her.

She couldn't even blame the feeling on Daniel and his treatment of her, as the creeping up her spine sensation had been there from the moment she had stepped inside.

Was this why Rose was acting so edgy? Was she fearful of telling Daniel what Lola had done to the front post?

Wishing like hell she wasn't stuck here, she went over her mental checklist.

Once she had access to the Wi-Fi, she would contact the rental company. If they couldn't get help to her tonight, she would leave the car behind for now and get a taxi back to Ely and the comfort of her hotel room. It would be costly, but worth it, and at least she wouldn't piss Rich Bradford off. He was such an awkward client and she had no idea how he would react if she wasn't there for their meeting tomorrow. Not well, she suspected.

Although this wasn't technically her fault, she knew from history he didn't accept excuses. He had even been a little tetchy with her when she had to take some personal time to be with her mum.

The last thing she needed was to lose his account.

Once she had sorted the car, she would message Quinn, too. Let him know what had happened so he didn't worry as he hadn't heard from her.

Having a plan of action settled her and she was relieved to hear approaching footsteps, wanting to get things moving.

Rose returned to the room a little more relaxed than she had left it, though tension lines still creased her forehead. She wore a brittle smile and had a bottle of red wine in her hand.

Was it really so stressful having Lola there? It wasn't as if she had a choice, or even wanted to be here.

Rose held up the bottle. 'Wine?' she offered, the smile almost cracking.

'Wi-Fi?' Lola reminded, trying her best to keep her tone patient. 'I don't want to waste any more of your evening than necessary.'

'Yes, I have it.' Rose set the bottle down and reached into the pocket of her trousers for her phone.

Lola pulled her own phone out and clicked into the Wi-Fi settings, the knot in her stomach loosening a little as Rose read out the code and the signal bars appeared on the screen.

Within seconds, she was getting email and WhatsApp notifications. A lot of it junk, but the message that popped up from Quinn quickened her heartbeat. Three simple words. Are you okay? Telling her that he was worrying about her.

'Which breakdown service are you with?' Rose asked.

'I'm not.'

'Oh.'

There was no point. Lola had a car, but living centrally, she seldom used it.

'There's a garage in the village,' Rose said, not hiding her disappointment. 'Though I doubt they will still be open.'

Lola shook her head. 'It doesn't matter. I need to report it to the rental company. They will be able to advise what to do next.'

And then she would reply to Quinn. Put his mind at rest.

She opened up the hire car agreement and found the out-of-hours emergency contact number. As she waited for the call to connect, she watched Rose drink the glass of wine she had poured.

Noticing, Rose held the bottle out. 'Did you want some?' she offered again.

'No, thank you.' A glass would relax her, but Lola was starving hungry and it would go straight to her head. Besides, if there was any chance she would still be driving back to Ely tonight, she wanted her full faculties about her.

Frustratingly, the rental company number cut to an answerphone. With no other choice, Lola left a message, citing her name and booking number and explaining what had happened. She was just about to give the address of the manor when the lights in the kitchen flickered ominously.

Rose paused pouring and the pair of them exchanged a glance.

Moments later, the room went dark.

14

Quinn cleared away the dinner things and cleaned the kitchen, while Chloe put the kids to bed, and his brother-in-law, Darren, who had arrived home as dinner was being put on the table, now sat on his arse playing video games.

For the hundredth time, Quinn wondered what the hell his sister actually saw in her husband. Darren never lifted a finger around the house to help and he seldom spent time with Lois and Mia, preferring the company of his online mates as they blew up buildings and raced cars on the TV screen.

Even now, a pile of unwrapped Christmas presents was hidden away in the understairs cupboard that his brother-in-law could start wrapping. Chloe had dropped a hint to Darren before going upstairs to tuck the kids in, but he had barely acknowledged her and hadn't made any attempt to get up.

Quinn wanted to say something, but Chloe had already made him promise not to have a go at Darren, who never reacted well when Quinn called him out for his lazy behaviour.

'It's Christmas, and you're only here for a couple of days,' she had reminded him. 'I don't want to be caught in the middle of you two fighting.'

Instead, he finished washing up, biting his tongue as he heard Darren talk into his headset to one of his online mates, 'Cover me. I'm going up the back stairs.'

Screw Darren. Once he had finished tidying up, he would help Chloe wrap the gifts.

As he wiped down the countertop, his mobile vibrated in his back pocket and dumping the cloth in the sink, he dried his hands on his jeans and snatched out the handset.

Was it Lola? He still hadn't heard from her.

While it was probable she had just forgotten, perhaps over whelmed in the excitement of the moment of meeting her brother for the first time, he wanted to know she was safe.

His heart sank, realising the message was from one of his mates in a WhatsApp group about their Christmas Eve drinks tomorrow night, reminding them of the time and venue.

Quinn was planning to go for a couple of pints, though it of course depended on the weather and if the trains would be running.

Right now, the snow was still falling heavily and he couldn't see it clearing by the morning.

Chloe, Darren and the kids were meant to be leaving in the morning, heading to Wales, where they were supposed to spend Christmas with Darren's parents, but Chloe had told Quinn they wouldn't go unless the weather improved, in which case he was fine to stay with them over the next few days.

That was all good and well for him, but what about Lola?

He knew the invitation would extend to her too, but was it weird? They had only just reconnected and he had no idea if it was as friends or if there was a chance of rekindling their relationship. He didn't want to scare her off by moving too fast.

And right now she wasn't even here. What if the weather was too bad for her to travel back to Ely?

'Have you heard from her?'

Chloe's voice interrupted his thoughts and as Quinn looked up, she nodded at the phone still in his hand.

He shook his head. 'Nothing yet.'

'Lola's not stupid, Quinn. If the roads are really bad, she's probably stopped somewhere. Have you messaged her?'

'I did a short while ago, just to check she's okay. She's read it but hasn't replied. I don't want to hassle her.'

No, spooking her was the last thing he wanted to do. He wasn't her boyfriend. Not any more.

He kept his tone light, changing the subject as he slipped the phone back into his pocket. 'Do you want a hand wrapping up the kids' stuff?'

'That would be great, if you don't mind.' Chloe sounded relieved to share the job.

Quinn knew she was on a deadline and needed everything done by the morning, just in case the weather had improved enough for them to leave.

As she went to fetch everything, he stopped by Darren's chair, signalling to his brother-in-law to pause the game.

'What's up?' Darren's tone was impatient.

'You want to help us with Lois's and Mia's presents?'

Darren glanced at the living room door, where he could see Chloe's backside sticking out of the hallway cupboard. 'Uh, no, it's good. You guys go ahead.'

As he turned back to his game, Quinn bit down on his irritation, reminding himself of his promise to his sister not to antagonise Darren. He didn't want to add to her stress.

Chloe returned to the room with bags full of gifts and rolls of wrapping paper under her arm and put everything down on the floor. As Quinn made a start, she disappeared through to the kitchen, reappearing moments later with a bottle of Baileys and two glasses.

He hesitated, thinking about Lola.

If anything had happened and she needed him, he had already had a glass of wine. Perhaps he should knock the alcohol on the head.

No. He was being irrational and panicking because he didn't want to lose the tenuous reconnection they had made yesterday.

He reminded himself that she had turned down his offer to go with her to Saham Toney, and that she was a grown woman who didn't need him hovering over her.

He wanted her back, but it had to be on her terms. She would contact him when she was ready.

Accepting the glass from his sister, he watched as she filled it.

Sitting down beside him, ignoring Darren, who was still absorbed in his game, she poured her own glass, then held it up to Quinn.

'Cheers,' she said, as they clinked glasses.

'Cheers,' he replied, one more brief thought of Lola before he took a sip of the drink.

It was all okay. She was going to be fine.

15

FIVE YEARS EARLIER

Oxford

Annie Whitlock passed away in hospital in February 2020, five days after suffering a brain haemorrhage, and it soon became clear that she had been the lynchpin holding the family together over the past four years.

As Rose, Daniel and Nigel came to terms with their loss, the big house in Oxford, which Rose had once thought of as the perfect home, started to feel more like a prison.

Nigel, who had always ruled over the family, a mighty presence in all of their lives, seemed to deflate after Annie's death. Although Rose never saw him shed a tear and he refused to speak of his grief, at least not in front of her and Daniel, she knew losing his wife had affected him deeply, and he spent much of his time alone, only joining them for meals, where conversation was muted.

Meanwhile, Daniel, who was far more open, had struggled with his father's reaction and the restrictions keeping him in the house. He had already lost so much, he complained to Rose, and now the pandemic was impeding him further.

Rose had never heard him sound so aggrieved and at first it had been a shock. But while he was becoming more frustrated with her, he no longer sparred with Nigel. It seemed that without Annie there to referee them, neither man had the inclination or the heart for a fight. Their relationship, which had once been passionate and fiery, was now almost non-existent.

For her part, Rose missed Annie too.

She had been hesitant when Daniel had first told her he wanted them to remain living with his parents, but in the time before and after they were married, Annie had never been intrusive and she had always been kind.

Rose's relationship with her own mother had made her wary of maternal figures and she had often wondered why Agnes Campbell had wanted to have children. Rose and Jimmy's dad had worked on the rigs and was away more than he was home. When he had been there, they had functioned as a normal family. It was while he was gone that things were bad.

Agnes veered between strictness and neglect, and when she was in a particularly bad mood, her punishments became more creative. Both Rose and Jimmy had learned to fear the kitchen cupboard from a young age. It was a small, dark, dank space where Agnes kept her brooms, mops and cleaning products, and Rose had spent many a long night locked in there, hungry and scared, simply because she had spoken out of turn or managed to get dirt on her clothes.

She had longed for the times when her dad was home, but then one day he had stopped coming back. It wasn't until later that Rose and Jimmy had learnt he had left their mother for another woman, and the hurt, knowing he had abandoned them too, was at times too much to bear.

The punishments had stopped for Jimmy not long after he became a teenager and Rose had become her mother's sole target. Sometimes she resented her brother for turning a blind eye and not trying to protect her. They had always been so close growing up, seeking solace with one another to cope with their mother's cruelty, and it was difficult not to feel betrayed.

It was a wonder that Rose had managed to mature into a normal functioning adult, but here she was, and she had even taken the high road, doing things for Agnes as her health had started to fail.

The scars were still there, which perhaps was why she had initially kept Annie Whitlock at an emotional distance. But, over the past four years, she had learnt to trust, and the pair of them had grown close. When Annie passed, Rose had felt her loss almost as acutely as her husband and father-in-law did, but as Daniel and Nigel were becoming more fractured, Rose found herself having to pick up the pieces.

By the following summer, she was struggling to hold everything together. Nigel had recovered his bluster, but this time it was with a nasty streak, and he spent much of his time complaining and belittling Rose, trying his best to get a reaction out of her.

It was almost as if he had become a child, and, try as she might, nothing she did seemed to please him. She was cooking and cleaning and doing her best to run the household efficiently, but he continually berated her, picking holes in every little thing, until she was mentally and physically exhausted.

And it galled her that, like Jimmy years earlier, Daniel no longer had her back.

He seemed happy to leave Rose to run their day-to-day

lives but turned conveniently deaf whenever his father started playing up, instead disappearing out into the garden with Monty, and she suspected he just wanted an easy life.

At least his mood had improved a little, but she now understood how reliant he had been on his mother. Somewhere over the last year, Rose had stepped into Annie's role and when she realised just how much he was taking her for granted, she knew it was the beginning of a downhill spiral.

Despite his spinal injury, the pair of them had found ways to be intimate. Their sex life wasn't conventional, but they had adapted and made things work. In recent months, though, sex had become non-existent, and Rose was beginning to feel more like Daniel's mother than his wife.

Frustration grew as her needs weren't being met and despite her best attempts to seduce her husband, he ignored every one of her advances. It seemed the man had simply lost interest in her.

As the darkness of winter approached, Rose was growing increasingly bitter with her situation. She had not anticipated any of this when she had married into the Whitlock family, and while she had vowed to continue looking after her husband in appreciation of the lifestyle he had given her, she expected more from their life.

Nigel was infuriating her and growing even more difficult to deal with, and things weren't improving with Daniel.

But then Nigel had fallen down the stairs of the Oxfordshire home, succumbing to a nasty head injury and it was just the two of them.

Perhaps she should have been ashamed to say her first reaction was relief, but was this a turning point for her and Daniel?

There had been a police investigation, much to Daniel's

chagrin. It had been a senseless accident, he had snarled, clashing with the police. Did they really believe that he and his wife had anything to do with it? He was a paraplegic, he had raged. Did they think he had pushed his father with his wheelchair?

It was Rose's suggestion that they move to Norfolk.

There were too many bad memories in Oxford and she was aware of the whispers, people speculating that Nigel's fall had not been an accident. That someone had pushed him.

The police had never believed that, but some of the locals and the internet sleuths did. People who knew nothing of the circumstances and were far too ready to draw their own conclusions.

At first, Daniel had been hesitant. This was his family home, and his mother was buried close by. But eventually Rose persuaded him a move would be good for them both.

What she didn't tell him was that she had already found the perfect place.

She had seen Midwinter Manor mentioned in an online article listing the most desirable properties for sale in the UK and had immediately fallen in love with the huge gothic-style house. Built in the 1700s, it was so grandiose, with its huge arch windows, the chimneys jutting up out of the roof, and the decorative, slightly sinister gargoyles on the brickwork, and she had immediately thought of Manderley in the du Maurier book, *Rebecca*. It was exactly how she pictured it. The only thing that was different was the location. Rather than on the Cornish coast, where the crashing waves hit the rocks below, the manor was in a fairy tale setting, tucked away in the middle of the woods in Norfolk.

They would be the lord and lady of the manor.

The remote location and the size of the property had

initially put Daniel off. They should look for somewhere smaller and more practical, he insisted. But Rose wasn't about to give up her dream that easily, and perhaps it was her enthusiasm, or that he simply grew tired of her pestering him, but eventually he agreed to go and look at the house.

'See, I told you. It's too isolated,' he had grumbled as they drove through the village and followed the track into the woods. 'This is the back end of nowhere.'

But then he had laid eyes on the manor and, as Rose hoped, he fell in love with it too, suddenly looking for solutions, instead of placing obstacles in the way. The fact they discovered it had a lift between the ground and first floor was also a game-changer, and it didn't take much more persuasion for Daniel to agree.

The lead-up to the move had been fraught with problems, buyers pulling out of their Oxford home and then issues with the conveyancer which dragged the process out, but fate was meant to be – Midwinter Manor seeming as if it was waiting for them – and eventually, in the spring of 2023, just over three years after Annie's death, they packed up everything they owned and, along with Monty, made the move to Norfolk.

The place was far too big for just the two of them and the dog, but Rose was in her element as she decided which parts of the house to update and what should be restored. As spring blossomed into a warm summer, Daniel was drawn to the extensive gardens. The outdoors had always appealed to him and while he might not be able to explore as he had once done, at least he was able to enjoy beautiful views.

And then Jimmy came to visit.

Initially, it was meant to be for a few days, but Rose knew her brother had recently lost his job working as a caretaker for a property maintenance firm, and she soon found out he had been served an eviction notice on his house, after failing to pay the rent.

They never discussed how long he would stay, but the house was more than big enough and Daniel didn't seem to mind.

Jimmy being at Midwinter Manor had its pluses. He made an effort to cut back on his drinking and had developed quite a skillset in his caretaker role, able to help with the many jobs that needed doing around the old house.

And it didn't leave Rose so tied to the place. She was able to keep up with her hair and nail appointments, and her shopping trips, without feeling guilty, knowing Jimmy would be there if Daniel needed him.

Here, tucked away from the rest of the world, and with so much space, they weren't rubbing each other up the wrong way, and the three of them settled into a routine.

Everything seemed so blissfully perfect. What could possibly go wrong?

16

Stay calm and consider all options.

Lola breathed deeply, focusing on her plan as she waited for Rose to reappear.

For a moment after the lights had gone off, the kitchen plunged into darkness, neither woman had spoken, and the only noise had come from the wind, which had picked up and was howling outside, rattling against the windows.

Rose had reacted first. 'Crap,' she had muttered, not sounding at all happy.

Lola had been in the middle of leaving the manor address on the rental company answerphone when the light went out and she pulled the phone from her ear. Unsure if the call was still connected, she tapped the screen, her heart sinking when she saw it wasn't.

In the faint glow of the device, she glanced in Rose's direction, saw the woman staring back at her.

Rose shook her head. 'Power's out. That's not going to work.'

As the phone screen darkened, plunging them back into

blackness, the implications of her words resounded and Lola stood numbly for a moment, even as she heard the sound of a drawer open and the clatter of its contents being moved around.

When light returned, it was blinding and white, and it took her a second to realise Rose was shining a torch in her face. As she put her hand up to shield her eyes, the woman dropped the beam, pointing it towards the door.

'I don't suppose you have a backup generator?' Lola knew larger houses sometimes had them. The isolated location of the property certainly warranted one.

'No,' Rose answered sharply. 'I did suggest we get one after the last power cut, but—' She paused abruptly, seeming distracted for a moment, muttering to herself under her breath. 'Daniel didn't think we should bother,' she said eventually, as though remembering she had been in the middle of a sentence. She gave Lola a tight smile.

'Maybe it will be temporary,' Lola said, trying her best to be optimistic, but Rose's words dashed her spirits.

'I wouldn't count on it. The last time this happened, we were without electricity for three days,' Rose continued. 'And the weather wasn't as bad as this.'

Okay, that wasn't good.

'I don't suppose you would consider giving me a lift to the nearest town?'

Lola hated asking, realising what an imposition it was, especially with the weather so bad. Rose and Daniel wanted her gone, though, so they might oblige.

'I would, but I've been drinking.' A tight smile briefly touched Rose's lips. 'I'm sorry, but you're stuck here.'

As her words sunk in, Lola understood how dire her situation was.

Tomorrow was Christmas Eve and she was stranded. Unless the power came back on, there was no way for her to call for help. The thought of being trapped in this big, unfriendly house, which had been overwhelming even when the lights were on, tightened the ball of anxiety in her stomach.

She could try to walk to the village, get help that way, but the temperatures were freezing outside, the blizzard showing no signs of slowing. Even if she managed to find her way there and didn't get lost, there was no guarantee that the power would be on or that she would be able to find anyone to help her.

No, she couldn't leave by foot.

'I guess I'll have to make up a bed for you,' Rose said, and although she probably didn't mean to, she sounded so inconvenienced, Lola was tempted to apologise.

She didn't. Instead, she pointed out a little snappily, 'I don't want this any more than you do.'

Whether it was her tone, Rose seemed to catch herself, finding her manners. 'I'm sorry. That was rude of me.' She sighed, shaking her head, moving around the kitchen now, the beam of the torch sweeping across the room, exposing dark corners and shadowy countertops, as she opened and closed cupboards, pulling various items out.

'Is there anything I can do to help?' Lola asked, feeling useless just standing by watching.

Rose dumped everything down on the counter and Lola could now see she had candles and packets of tealights. She pulled open a drawer, taking out a box of matches that she threw at Lola. As Lola caught the box, Rose nodded to the candles. 'Yes, you can light these,' she said, before adding, 'Please,' almost as an afterthought.

She focused the torch while Lola lit a candle that was already in a jar.

'You'll find holders and jars for any that don't have them in the cupboard under the sink,' she instructed. 'I need to go and check on Daniel.'

'Wait,' Lola called after the woman's retreating back, but Rose either didn't hear her or chose to ignore her, disappearing out of the kitchen, and with the absence of torchlight, Lola was left with the one flickering candle, its flame making shadows dance up the walls.

She glanced over at Monty, who grinned at her, his tongue hanging out of his mouth.

'At least you seem glad to have me here,' she told him and his tail thumped against the stone floor in response.

Using the matches Rose had left, Lola lit the rest of the candles and tealights.

Now, as she waited for the woman to return, she tried to work out a plan of action.

She couldn't go anywhere, so there was no point in wasting energy on trying to do so or getting frustrated at her situation.

Quinn knew where she had gone, but he was the only one, and she hadn't contacted him as she had promised to let him know she had arrived safely. Would he be concerned that he hadn't heard from her?

They were supposed to be catching the train back together tomorrow. That was if the trains were actually operating. Right now, it seemed doubtful.

And Rich Bradford. He would be expecting her at their meeting bright and early in the morning.

Would either man raise the alarm when she didn't show up as planned?

Being stuck at Midwinter Manor, and with no change of

clothes, was not an ideal situation, but she was going to have to make the best of it. Rose had said she would sort a bed. Hopefully there would be an offer of food too. Lola was starving.

Rose had said that the previous power cut had lasted days, but hopefully she would be able to walk to the village for help tomorrow. If Lola could get back to Ely, she would happily pay extra to stay in the hotel over Christmas until the weather improved.

She wondered how Daniel was reacting to the news she was still here. Rose had been gone a while.

Outside, the wind roared, lashing thick white flakes of snow against the old leaded windowpanes. It was definitely getting worse instead of better.

As the seconds ticked by, she wondered if Rose had forgotten about her. Lola couldn't be certain how long she had been waiting, but it felt as though several minutes had passed. Rose had said she was going to check on Daniel, but it shouldn't take her all this time.

Unless something had happened.

Deciding to check on them, Lola started to reach in her pocket for her phone before changing her mind. She didn't want to use the torch and drain her battery. Instead she picked up one of the candle jars and headed towards the kitchen door, Monty climbing from his bed to follow her. The flame flickered ominously as she stepped out into the dark hallway and, fearful it might go out, she slowed her pace, cupping her hand around the top of the jar.

Away from the kitchen and the warmth of the Aga, the house was much colder, and it was a reminder that with the power out, none of the radiators would be working.

The blouse she wore offered little protection and as she

followed the passageway back to the main hallway, she couldn't help shivering.

Perhaps Rose would lend her a jumper or cardigan. She would ask.

Lola assumed both Rose and Daniel were in the living room and that was the way she headed, candlelight guiding her through the darkness, not liking the creaking sounds the house made as it was battered by the storm. As she reached the living room, she paused abruptly, hearing voices through the crack in the door, which hadn't been shut properly.

'You know we can't do that,' Rose hissed. 'She'll freeze.'

Had Daniel just proposed they kick her out of the house? He surely wouldn't do that.

'We should have known better than to invite her here,' Lola heard him grumble in response. 'Now we're stuck with her.'

He sounded so bitter and, despite how coolly he had already treated her, it was a fresh sting, knowing he had never wanted her here.

She was about to push the door open, wanting to at least try to make him feel guilty for wasting her time, for making her drive out here in the bad weather for nothing, but Rose's next words had her hesitating.

'Look, it's just for one night, then she'll be gone and you won't ever have to see her again.'

'You're playing with fire, Rose,' Daniel warned. 'This could end very badly.'

'Don't be so dramatic, darling. It won't.'

'For her sake, you'd better be right. Because if she finds out what I did... what *we* did, she'll wish she'd never come here.'

Daniel spoke softly and, had the door been closed, Lola might have missed what he had said. Instead, she heard every word, fear chilling her spine at the quiet threat in them.

As she stepped back, she willed Monty to stay quiet and not reveal her presence. She needed to get back to the kitchen. They mustn't realise she had overheard their conversation.

Perhaps whatever they had been discussing wasn't as bad as she thought, but in this isolated setting, trapped in the dark house with people she didn't really know, her imagination was running riot.

Again, the temptation to leave, to take her chances with the elements and try to make it into Saham Toney seemed a better option. She wasn't a fool, though. Although she was confident she could make her way back to the village, there was no guarantee she would be able to find anyone to help her. She knew nothing about the place or how big it was so had no idea if there would be any petrol stations, pubs or convenience stores open. And she didn't fancy the idea of knocking on random doors.

No, she was better off here, and she tried to reassure herself that the current weather outside was far more threatening than anything at Midwinter Manor.

She was starting to make her way back along the dark hallway, trying to tread softly so her boots didn't clatter against the hard floor, when the living room door pushed fully open, the beam of Rose's torch finding her.

'Lola?'

Blinded by the sharp light, Lola couldn't see Rose's expression, but she heard the surprise in her tone, and the uncertainty too.

'There you are. I was just coming to find you,' she said hastily, hoping her voice carried no trace of the lie. 'I wasn't sure if everything was okay.'

'It's fine. Come on.'

Rose shone the flashlight ahead, pushing past her and

seeming on a mission as she led the way back to the kitchen. Did she suspect that Lola had overheard the conversation with her husband? If so, she didn't say.

'We have some paraffin lamps in the storeroom. Help me with those and then we'll light the dining room fire. We need to get some warmth in the rooms.'

'Okay,' Lola agreed as she followed after Rose. She was relieved to be doing something instead of standing around uselessly.

'Once we're sorted downstairs, I'll make up one of the guest rooms,' Rose continued, sounding focused. 'Hopefully the storm will have passed by the morning.'

Lola hoped so too. She didn't want to spend a moment longer in this house than necessary.

17

It had been a stupid idea to walk home from the pub after a skinful.

Jimmy realised that about a third of the way into his journey. The effects of the alcohol, which had at first numbed the cold, were now intensifying it.

He had already slipped over a couple of times, the first time landing on his bum, which was now soaking wet, the second, falling face first into the snow. And the biting wind didn't help, nor the flakes that kept getting into his eyes, impeding his vision and making it difficult to see where he was going.

They had all tried to stop him leaving, the bartender and the other drinkers, telling him it wasn't safe and he was best to wait until the weather calmed down. Jimmy, in his usual wisdom, hadn't listened.

It was only a fifteen-minute walk, he had told them, laughing that they were overreacting. He would be home in no time.

Now he was bitterly regretting it, the journey taking twice as long.

When the torch he carried finally picked out the sign for Midwinter Manor, he was ready to cry.

Just a few more minutes and he would be back in the warmth of the house and able to shed his wet clothes. He would have a bath, he decided, already dreaming of sinking into the hot, soapy water. The cold night air was starting to sober him and he could feel every one of his aching muscles. Maybe he would have a measure or two of whisky as well to help numb the pain again.

As he approached the gates, it took him a moment to realise the house was in darkness. Possibly it was because the curtains were drawn in the rooms that were lit, but he had left the porch light on.

Belatedly, he remembered the pub had briefly lost power. It had happened as he was finishing his last pint, plunging the bar into darkness before the backup generator had kicked in. Was Midwinter affected too? He hadn't even considered it might be.

Stupid, Jimmy. He should have stayed put.

The last time the house had lost power it had taken days to fix. At least it had been late summer. The absence of electricity had been an inconvenience, but easier to cope with thanks to the longer, lighter evenings. Things would be a lot different this time, especially with it being Christmas.

Trudging forward, he almost missed the black Peugeot parked on the side of the drive.

Who did that belong to? Daniel's sister?

Jimmy had assumed she would be long gone by now.

Unless she had broken down.

The car had hit the post, he realised, shining his torch

across the bonnet. Had she lost control in the snow? If so, he assumed she hadn't left.

This could be interesting. Rose would be upset that he had returned, but what choice did he have? It wasn't his fault if Lola was still here.

He had warned them they were being foolish, inviting her to the house. There were too many secrets at Midwinter Manor.

More than a little curious to meet Daniel's sister, Jimmy stumbled forwards towards the house.

18

The bedroom Rose had put Lola in was on the top floor, which seemed to be the creepiest part of the house, but perhaps that was because Lola had only seen it in the glow of the paraffin lantern Rose had left her with, with shadows dancing up high walls and dark corners hidden.

And it didn't help that she was up on the second floor, accessed by a steep, narrow staircase and along a dark corridor. Had this room once belonged to a housekeeper perhaps? There was a musty odour as if it hadn't been aired in a while, and as well as the icy temperature, it felt a little damp.

The room had a fireplace, but Lola had soon learnt it wasn't a functioning one. Instead, it contained a small electric stove, which was of no use to her whatsoever.

'We haven't blocked it up, as we were planning on restoring it at some point,' Rose had helpfully added, as the wind whistled down the chimney, bringing in a cool draught.

Lola wasn't sure what was worse: the freezing cold or the eerie sound.

Surely there was another room, but she didn't like to ask. Rose already seemed put out by her extended visit.

The room was dominated by a four-poster bed that looked like it should be in a museum, with heavy velvet curtains and ornately carved head and footboards, that Rose told her had been one of several relics that had come with the house.

At least she had clean sheets. And the mattress was comfortable when she sat on it. Still, she didn't think she would be getting much sleep tonight.

She had helped Rose make up the bed. The two of them worked mostly in silence, and although Rose was perfectly polite as she had fetched extra blankets, then showed Lola where the nearest bathroom was, providing her with fresh towels, toothpaste and a toothbrush, as well as a cardigan to help ward off the chill, Lola couldn't stop the conversation she had overheard playing on a loop in her head.

This could end very badly.

She'll wish she had never come here.

Nothing made sense about this family. Daniel and Rose weren't that old, yet they lived in this huge house, far too big for two people, and miles from anywhere.

As for the secrets, what exactly were they scared of her finding out?

Was this to do with inheritance? Nigel and Annie Whitlock had left Daniel their fortune. Was he scared Lola might try to take some of it?

Perhaps she needed to make it crystal clear that she wasn't interested.

That may be foolish on her part. They had been her parents too, and she had no idea if legally she was entitled to anything. Perhaps not, as there had probably been a will, but it didn't matter anyway. In fact, it was irrelevant. It had never been about the money for her. She led a comfortable enough life. No, she wasn't rich, but she worked hard and had been shrewd over the years. She had some savings.

Daniel could keep his inheritance. He seemed to be the perfect example that money didn't equal happiness. Had he always been like this, so ill-mannered and grumpy, or was it her presence here causing him to be this way?

Rose had left her to get settled, going downstairs to put together a late supper. She told Lola to join them when she was ready.

Although the thought of spending time with these people was unappealing, Lola was ravenous.

One meal, one night. She could do this.

There was very little she could do in terms of settling in, as she had nothing to unpack, but she used the bathroom further along the dark corridor to freshen up.

It was almost as big as her flat, and as she washed her hands and dabbed cold water on her tired eyes, she was struck by the similarity of this room with the infamous bathroom in the film *The Shining*. The colour was different, black and white instead of green – at least it was in the light of the paraffin lamp – but there were twin sinks along the side wall, both with arch mirrors above them, while the bathtub was set back into a tiled alcove with what looked like a gold rim and a white curtain drawn across it.

Lola shuddered, remembering what Jack Nicholson's character had found behind that curtain and decided she would be locking the bedroom door tonight. She had already noticed there was a key in the lock of her bedroom door, and given the size of the house and the conversation she had overheard, bolting herself inside was probably a wise idea. She would feel safer knowing that one space was hers and that no one could get in unless she let them.

There was no point locking it now, as she would take her bag downstairs with her, liking the idea of having her phone close, even if she couldn't use it right now.

As she picked it up from the dresser, she noticed the charge had dropped to 30 per cent. Her charger was still in the rental car, but it would be of no use to her unless the power came back on.

She glanced out of the window at the white scene below. Big, fat snowflakes were swirling in front of her and had this been her cosy hotel room in Ely or back home in Manchester, snug in her flat, she might have enjoyed the view. Instead, now, it was a stark reminder that she was trapped here and that the worse the weather became, the harder it would be for her to leave.

The Peugeot was parked at an awkward angle where she had left it after hitting the gate post. It was still visible, though a thick layer of snow now covered the roof and bonnet. If the blizzard continued, getting into the village tomorrow and then back to Ely was going to be a gruelling task. Something she didn't even want to contemplate right now.

Supposing she should head downstairs and join Rose and Daniel, Lola stepped away from the window and was about to turn away, when a flicker of movement caught her attention down by the car.

At first, she believed it to be an animal, but then she saw the beam of light. A torch. And whoever it was moved into her line of vision.

Male, she thought, though she could have been mistaken. On foot and dressed in a dark coat and woolly hat.

Was he coming to the house?

Possibly another stranded motorist or a friend of the family. Maybe someone with a vehicle or network coverage, who could help her get back to Ely.

All at once curious, apprehensive and a little bit hopeful, she picked up the lantern and headed back out into the corridor, making her way over to the narrow staircase, keen to find out who this stranger was.

The steps creaked as she descended to the first-floor landing, and for a moment she found herself disorientated, trying to recall which way she had to go. The wider passageway stretched in both directions, all of the doors closed, and the shadowy darkness didn't help, as there was nothing to help her get her bearings.

Taking a chance, she headed left, realising when the corridor turned to reach one last room and a dead end that she had chosen wrong.

As she turned to go back on herself, a groaning noise came from behind her, and she froze.

It's just the wind.

To reassure herself, Lola glanced over her shoulder.

No one was behind her, and stepping over to the nearest window, which gave her a view of the front of the property, she could see the blizzard was raging a storm outside.

Annoyed she was allowing this old house to spook her, she started to walk away.

Click, click, click.

Her head shot around, recognising the sound of a doorknob twisting, and she expected to see the door opening, but there was no movement.

She held her breath, the paraffin lamp shaking slightly as her trembling hand tightly clenched the handle.

Although the door remained closed, the muffled sound of a cough came from within.

Someone was definitely in the room.

It had to be Rose. This was probably her and Daniel's bedroom. She obviously hadn't gone downstairs yet.

Not wanting to get caught outside the door and for Rose to think she was snooping, Lola quickly made her way back along the corridor, passing the steps that she had come down a few moments earlier and finding her way to the wide landing at the top of the grand central staircase. Further back on the landing was the lift and it briefly struck Lola as odd, as she headed down the stairs, that Daniel would pick a bedroom so far away from the lift.

Downstairs, she headed straight for the kitchen, knowing it was warm from the Aga. She would wait in there. Perhaps when Rose came downstairs, Lola could help her with this supper that she was putting together. Anything to stop feeling like a spare part.

As she neared the room, the heat reached out to welcome her, while the warm glow of the flickering candles made it seem cosy. Entering the room, she was surprised to see Rose, along with another man.

So it hadn't been Rose that Lola had heard upstairs.

Had Daniel ridden up in the lift? He had a motorised wheelchair, so it was possible. Though, with the power out, would it work?

Lola supposed it depended on whether there was a battery backup.

Rose and the newcomer were talking quietly by the window, but as they heard her footsteps, both abruptly stopped their conversation. As the man looked at her, Lola realised he was the same figure she had seen approaching the house.

The hat and coat had been discarded, his greying hair dishevelled and his face ruddy, but it had to be him.

After all, who else could it be?

He had a smile on his face now, though it didn't quite reach his eyes. They seemed to be assessing her, and Lola suspected he already knew who she was.

'You must be Daniel's sister,' he announced, confirming her suspicions, the smile growing wider as he stepped towards her. It looked fake. He had a Scottish accent, like Rose, and Lola guessed this was her brother before he introduced himself. 'It's good to meet you,' he said, though Lola wasn't sure his words were sincere.

'Lola, nice to meet you too,' she told him, shaking his ice-cold hand, and pulling away when he gripped hers a little longer than she was comfortable with.

This close she could smell alcohol on his breath.

'Jimmy?' Rose was watching them carefully. 'Go upstairs and change out of your damp clothes. I'm putting some supper together.'

He glanced at his sister, a hint of irritation on his face, and she gave him a pointed look. 'Okay, I'm going,' he muttered, raising the torch he held and pointing it towards the doorway. He nodded to Lola as he went. 'I look forward to catching up with you later.'

She noticed there was a slight slur to his voice.

Was he drunk?

And if he had clothes here, did he live with Rose and Daniel at Midwinter Manor?

Had Rose said he did?

Lola couldn't remember, but she had mistakenly assumed he had his own place, perhaps in the village or nearby.

'Please ignore my brother,' Rose said once she knew Jimmy was out of earshot. 'He's been in the pub and tends to spout a load of nonsense when he's had a few drinks.'

That would explain why he had arrived at the manor on foot.

Was the pub far away? She was surprised Rose hadn't mentioned it.

Lola toyed briefly with asking where it was, but then dismissed the idea. Rose had gone to the trouble of making up a bed for her. She needed to accept the fact she was staying here tonight.

It was just one night.

'Can I help with anything?' she asked, watching Rose taking armfuls of jars and packets out of the fridge.

'No need. Everything's in hand. The table's set in the dining room and the fire is lit. Daniel's already in there. It's nice and cosy.'

'He's downstairs?' Lola asked, remembering the noises she had heard behind the door on the first floor.

Rose looked at her quizzically. 'Of course. You seem surprised by that.'

She was about to tell Rose what she had heard, ask her if there was someone else in the house, because if it wasn't Rose, Daniel or Jimmy, then who the hell was it?

Something had her hesitating, though. Perhaps it was the way Rose was staring at her, head cocked slightly on one side, seeming wary of what she might say.

Instead, Lola shrugged, making an effort to keep her tone casual when she spoke. 'I thought I heard something when I was coming downstairs, but it was probably just the wind.'

Rose's blood-red lips tightened. 'Yes, I'm sure that's what it was.'

19

She is not what I imagined.

As the four of us sit around the dining room table, tucking into our supper in the light of the candles on the table and the flickering flames of the log fire, I surreptitiously study her, this long-lost sister.

We might be related, but I don't know her at all and she is a stranger in our home.

I had read up about her after she made contact, wanting to get a measure of who we were dealing with, but I guess online articles and photos can be deceptive and they don't really prepare you for how someone will be in real life.

Physically, she is less petite than I expected. Taller and prettier too, though in a plain way. She relies on what God has given her, rather than enhancing her looks with make-up, jewellery and clothes. And her accent surprised me, even though I knew she was from Manchester.

She is polite, too, but I think part of that is down to nerves.

Despite those nerves, I suspect she has a backbone of steel. I see moments of it in the quick flash of her smile and when something is said that she doesn't agree with. She takes care with her words and doesn't challenge as such, but she isn't afraid to make it clear if she has a different viewpoint.

Things were a little uncomfortable at first, as we all gathered around the table. She doesn't want to be here, not after how she was treated earlier, and she definitely isn't wanted here. We have too many secrets and we can't risk her uncovering them.

Still, I grudgingly find myself liking her. There is something about her that draws you in, and I have to remember softening my approach is dangerous. We cannot drop our guard, not until she leaves.

Jimmy needs to get the memo on that.

The cold walk back from the pub had sobered him, but now he is on the wine, knocking back generous glasses, and the bottle of red on the table is already empty.

Sober Jimmy knows the risks we have taken allowing her to come here, and the consequences we would face if anyone ever learns what the three of us did. But drunk Jimmy doesn't give a flying fuck and he likes to dance with the Devil.

He knows damn well what is at stake here, and he is aware of just how bad things will be for him if he reveals what we have done. How bad things will be for all of us.

Still, the more he drinks, the less he cares.

The man is a liability and we should never have agreed to him staying here without cleaning up his act.

Though, truth be told, he would be dangerous anywhere he went. I guess at least here we can keep an eye on him. Make sure he doesn't shoot off his big mouth.

I watch him carefully, trying to catch his eye and giving him warning looks whenever his glazed gaze briefly looks my way, though I'm not sure how much he sees in this muted light.

He needs the reminders that we are playing a high-stakes game, but it doesn't seem to be sinking in and when he utters the name 'Brett', I flinch, certain this is going to be our downfall.

She can't find out about Brett.

Conversation is about Christmas, which should be a safe subject, but Jimmy, in his infinite wisdom, manages to go back two years, reminiscing about one particular Christmas.

'That was when Brett showed up,' he tells Lola, who I can see is scrambling to recall any previous mention of his name.

'Brett?' she asks, puzzled.

'Just an old friend,' I quickly smooth over. 'He spent Christmas with us before heading on his way.'

I shoot Jimmy another warning look.

Do not mention Brett again.

We just have to get through this supper. Everyone will go to bed and then we are safe until morning. Hopefully the snow will have started to thaw and Lola can find her way back to the place she has come from.

Until then, we just need to keep up the pretence we're a nice, normal family.

20

TWO YEARS EARLIER

Norfolk

When Rose had first met Daniel, he'd had a wide circle of friends, though she soon learnt only a few of them lived locally. Although he kept in frequent contact with everyone, very few of them visited, and their engagement was through social media, text messages and phone calls instead.

He was so gregarious and full of life, at first she had been surprised, but then she supposed there were limitations as to the activities he could participate in. Many of his friends were sports enthusiasts – skiing, cycling, rugby and paddleboarding. Sometimes invitations were extended for him to come along and watch or to meet for lunch afterwards, but he turned most of those down.

Rose understood it had to be difficult for him.

After they were married, the contact with his friends became even more sporadic, and by the time they moved to Norfolk, taking up residence in Midwinter Manor, he was barely in touch with them at all.

So when Brett Corrigan reached out over social media, it had been unexpected.

'We were at university together,' Daniel explained to Rose later that evening. 'I haven't seen him since I've been in the chair.'

'Does he know?' she had asked, aware Daniel's social media feed contained only older photos from the time when he had been able-bodied.

'I'll tell him,' he said, brushing off the question. 'There's plenty of time to catch up.'

That was when he explained that Brett wanted to visit them.

'He's been living in New Zealand. But he's home now.'

As Rose learnt about Brett, the more hesitant she became.

Brett was estranged from his family after falling out with them years earlier, and according to Daniel he was between jobs. That was why he was back here, hoping to put down roots and planning to talk to the banks about a possible loan for a business venture he had in mind.

From the way her husband described him, the man sounded like a smooth talker with expensive tastes, and a cynical part of Rose couldn't help but worry whether the only reason he was back in touch with Daniel was because he was hoping for a handout.

Although she couldn't stop Brett visiting, she decided she would keep a close eye on him.

By the time he showed up, a week before Christmas, she had psyched herself up for the worst and was dreading his visit, ready to hate him, but the man who climbed out of the 2013 plate Range Rover was not at all what she expected.

For starters, he was far more down to earth than she was

expecting and, although he was charming, there was nothing smooth or sleazy about him at all.

He seemed delighted to see Daniel and completely unfazed to find him in the wheelchair. As Rose had suspected, Daniel hadn't told Brett about his accident, but other than asking a few straightforward questions, Brett seemed to shrug it off.

He had shown up with gifts. Apparently, Daniel had told him about Rose and Jimmy, though evidently not Jimmy's alcohol problem, and Rose had prickled watching her brother accept an expensive bottle of Scotch. Her own gift was a lilac silk scarf, while Daniel received a personalised poker chip set and there was a new squeaky toy for Monty.

'Good job I didn't get you new ski goggles,' Brett had commented drily, as Daniel opened his gift, and Rose had caught her breath, unsure how he would react.

To her relief, he laughed.

They all liked Brett, Jimmy included, so when Daniel suggested he stay until the New Year, everyone agreed it was a good idea.

When Rose looked back now, she could clearly see that had been the beginning, the spark that had ignited the flame and sent them on a downward spiral.

If Brett had never shown up on their doorstep that Christmas, if he had just stayed away, then things might not have escalated. But, instead, emotions had simmered, frustrations boiling over, and what happened in the months that followed could never be taken back.

The frightening thing was, Rose knew she would do it all again in a heartbeat.

21

PRESENT DAY

Rose's supper was an elaborate affair considering it was gone 9 p.m. and something she had supposedly thrown together. The four of them sat around the large mahogany table next to a roaring fire. Monty had positioned himself on the floor between Lola and Daniel and kept glancing up hopefully every so often in case snacks were passed his way.

The food was set out in dishes surrounding two lit candelabras and consisted of cheeses and pickles, smoked salmon, giant prawns that had been marinated in a garlic sauce and cuts of ham. There were also bowls of homemade potato salad and coleslaw and chunks of crusty bread with plenty of sauces for dipping.

It reminded Lola of the buffets her mum had often prepared on Christmas Day night if they had guests.

Normally, she loved this kind of picky food, but tonight she was struggling to eat. It wasn't that she didn't have an appetite – she was ravenous – it was just being here in this house, sharing a meal with people she didn't know. It was unnerving, especially given the noises she had heard upstairs and the conversation she had overheard earlier.

Perhaps she was overreacting. This whole situation was stressful and the Whitlocks didn't want her in their home any more than she wanted to be here. Maybe what she had overheard wasn't as sinister as her mind was imagining.

As for the noises upstairs, had it been the wind?

Deep down, she didn't believe it was, but she had to keep trying to convince her brain, otherwise she wouldn't sleep tonight.

Daniel hadn't been impressed when he had found out she was still here, but to her relief he had thawed a little during the meal, joining in on the bland conversation.

Finding him watching her now, Lola offered him the hint of a smile, hating the kick of disappointment in her gut when he didn't return it.

'Whereabouts is it you have been working?' he asked, in a sudden change of subject that caught her off guard. 'Earlier you said you had to drive back to Cambridgeshire.'

She had told him that, though she had never mentioned which part.

'Ely. I've had meetings with a client.'

'Which firm?'

Was it her imagination or was there a hint of suspicion in his tone? Did he think she was making it up? That there had been no work meeting and she had especially driven all the way down here from Manchester just to see him?

'Safe Hands,' she told him, annoyed that he was doubting her. 'They make sanitiser machines.'

'Sounds riveting,' Jimmy joked, necking the rest of his glass of wine and immediately reaching for another bottle.

Lola didn't miss the warning look Rose gave her brother,

that he chose to ignore. She didn't seem happy with the amount he was drinking.

Did he have an alcohol problem?

Lola picked up her own glass and took a sip, hoping that the wine might ease some of her tension. Her intention was only to have the one drink, though, as she was keen to keep her wits about her.

'So you do their marketing for them?' Daniel pushed, keen to stay on this new topic.

'Yes. Their CEO wanted a meeting to discuss our 2026 approach.'

'This close to Christmas?' He sounded surprised. Incredulous even.

'What can I say? He's a demanding client,' Lola told him, keeping her tone firm.

'So it's a case of he says jump and you say how high.'

'Not exactly.' She refused to let him press her buttons. 'He is one of my biggest accounts, so I try my best to keep him happy. My schedule was free, so it wasn't an issue to head down to see him.'

'No plans for Christmas then?'

The temptation to down the rest of her wine, as Jimmy had done, was overwhelming, but she wouldn't give in. Still, familiar tension crept back into her shoulders.

She gave him a tight smile. 'I'm meant to catch the train back from Ely tomorrow, if they're running, but no, I don't have any plans.'

Daniel nodded, studying her. 'I suppose without a husband or family waiting back home for you, there's no one for you to celebrate with.'

His words stung and Lola flinched, but it was Rose who gasped, seeming appalled at what her husband had said.

'Daniel, stop being so personal,' she chided.

'I don't see what the problem is,' he challenged. 'We're family. Lola came here to ask me questions, so what is the harm in me doing the same?'

It was not the same, but Lola sensed he wanted a reaction, that he was hoping she would bite. Tempting as it was to give him what he wanted, she didn't care for him to know that the family she had lost – the adoptive mother and stillborn son that she grieved – were her Achilles' heel. She suspected that if Daniel knew her vulnerability he would use it against her, which was why she took a measured breath before responding.

'Sure. Ask me anything,' she challenged. 'But I expect the same courtesy.'

'Very well.' She could tell that her response had amused him. 'Don't you ever get lonely being all by yourself?' he asked, jumping straight in.

'I'm not alone. I have plenty of friends and a good social life. And I recently adopted two cats. They're still kittens,' she told him, thinking of Casper and Tilly, and how less empty her flat was since they had moved in with her. She had left a key with her neighbour, who was popping in to feed them, and hoped they weren't missing her too much.

'Cats are vicious little bastards,' Jimmy piped up from across the table. 'One nearly took my eye out once.'

Yes. He was definitely slurring his words.

'Because you were tormenting it,' Rose pointed out. 'It was our neighbour's cat,' she explained to Lola. 'Poor creature wanted to be left alone to sleep, but my brother here thought it would be fun to keep picking him up and holding him in the air.'

Lola knew she shouldn't judge, as she had only met Jimmy a short while ago, and she knew very little about him, but

Rose's words didn't surprise her. Although Jimmy didn't strike her as cruel, there was something in his demeanour, perhaps a carelessness, that suggested he was a little self-absorbed and didn't have much empathy for others. Physically, he shared Rose's sharp features and blue eyes, but while Rose had a quiet elegance about her, Jimmy seemed to be more of a buffoon.

She didn't react to his comment about cats, instead turning the tables back on her brother.

'How about you, Daniel? Don't you ever get lonely living out here in the middle of nowhere?'

'I'm not alone, am I?' he told her mildly, indicating to Rose and Jimmy.

'No, but you are limited with that chair. You can't just nip out to the shops or to see people. You're completely dependent on your wife and brother-in-law to get anywhere. That must be quite emasculating.'

Had she pushed things too far?

Normally, Lola would never speak so cruelly, but she wanted to make it clear to Daniel that she would give as good as she got. If he pushed, she would shove right back.

He regarded her for a moment as he considered her words, the shadows of dancing flames flickering across his face, his lips carving into a snide smile, before he looked to Rose.

'So she has some spark, this little sister of mine. Thank God for that.'

'Daniel,' Rose urged again. She seemed uncomfortable with the conversation.

'At least I can believe now that you're a Whitlock,' he said, ignoring his wife as he addressed Lola.

'Well, half a Whitlock,' Jimmy sniggered.

'What?' Lola thought she had misheard him. 'What do you mean by half?'

Even as she asked the question, she saw the panic on Rose and Daniel's faces and understood that Jimmy had slipped up.

'He doesn't mean anything,' Daniel said angrily. 'Ignore my idiot brother-in-law. That's his poor attempt at humour.'

Lola looked at the faces around the table. Rose was glaring at Jimmy, who was shrugging his shoulders and mouthing 'sorry' to her, while Daniel was stony-faced.

The comment 'half a Whitlock' could only mean one thing. She and Daniel only shared one parent.

'Explain the joke, please,' Lola asked, keeping her tone diplomatic, even though deep down she was fuming. She had come here in the bad weather to get answers about her family and they had lied to her. But for what reason?

'There is no joke.' Rose was flustered. 'Jimmy says things to get a reaction when he is drunk. He meant no harm.'

'So you just made it up?' Lola glared across the table at Jimmy.

Even though his eyes were glazed, his gaze flicked from side to side as he answered. A sure sign he was lying. 'Yes, I'm sorry.'

'And Annie and Nigel are definitely my parents?' she demanded of Daniel.

'Of course.' Daniel sounded belligerent. 'Why would I have told you otherwise?'

Lola had no idea why he would do such a thing, but she didn't believe he was being honest with her. And Jimmy's admission – because she was certain his remark hadn't been a joke – would make more sense in terms of why she had been given up for adoption.

When she had first learnt that that she had a brother, Lola had struggled to reconcile why her parents would have given her up. It had never been easy, knowing she had been unwanted, but finding out her parents had been married with an older brother when they fell pregnant with her had stung. Why had they not wanted Lola – or whatever they had named her. Had they even named her? – when she was born? Had they been set on having only one child or was it some old-fashioned sexist reason that she was a girl and they only wanted boys? Or had they simply looked at her and decided she didn't fit into their family?

The questions had plagued her, but if her mother – she was going to assume Annie was her birth mother – had been having an affair, it would explain that perhaps Nigel hadn't wanted to keep her.

But why would Daniel and Rose not be upfront about it?

It made no sense and Lola couldn't understand what they would have to gain.

Part of her was tempted to continue to push the point, but they were boldly lying to her face and Lola was unable to prove otherwise.

She couldn't shake the conversation she had overheard. Was this the secret they wanted to keep from her?

This could end very badly.

If she finds out, she'll wish she had never come here.

Daniel's words still disturbed her and it was for that reason she decided to drop the subject – for now.

'Just forget it. Like you say, it was a poor joke.'

Let him think she believed him, then once she was back home, she would try to do more digging.

After a few more moments of awkwardness, the subject changed to safer topics, though Jimmy's words continued to play on Lola's mind as, appetite gone, she discreetly fed bits of the food left on her plate to Monty. The subject was still on Rose's and Daniel's minds too, she guessed, from the furtive looks they continued to exchange, while Jimmy remained conspicuously quiet throughout the rest of the meal.

After they had eaten, Daniel and Jimmy headed through to the living room, while Lola helped Rose clear the table and load the dishwasher. Then, when they were finished, Rose invited her to join them for a nightcap.

'Do you mind if I don't?' Lola asked, feigning a yawn. 'It's been a crazy day and I'm exhausted.'

'No, not at all.' Rose seemed glad with her decision. 'Is there anything you need?'

The things Lola needed were not to be found in this house, but she smiled graciously, said no and thanked Rose for letting her stay. But the relief at being away from the Whitlocks was weighed down by her sense of foreboding as she ascended the stairs, her lantern cutting a pathway through the darkness. It was deathly silent as she crossed the first-floor landing, the wind outside having stilled, and her nerves jangled waiting for any sound to come from the room at the end of the corridor.

There was nothing, except the sound of her own footsteps, and she wasted no time climbing the narrow staircase up to the second floor. This house might be grand, but there was something unnerving about it, and she had felt it before the blackout.

It was bitterly cold in the bedroom, the temperature having dipped considerably since she was last upstairs, and part of her regretted her decision to come to bed early. She wouldn't go back down and join the Whitlocks, though. They made her too uncomfortable.

Briefly, she used the creepy *Shining* bathroom, peeing and brushing her teeth, then hurried back to the bedroom, closing the door and reaching for the key, her fingers instead finding the lock empty.

As her heart thumped, she shone the lantern on the door. What the hell had happened to the key? It had definitely been there earlier. She knew she hadn't imagined it.

The brave part of her wanted to go downstairs and challenge Daniel, Rose and Jimmy. Demand to know who had taken it. She already knew, though, that she would be wasting her time. Her accusation would be denied, and, realistically, it couldn't have been her brother. The lift didn't serve this floor. Given that Daniel had been the hostile one up to now, it made her wary of Rose and Jimmy. It had to have been one of them who had taken the key. But why?

Lola was certain now that she wouldn't get any sleep, but she might as well get under the covers. Leaving the lantern burning and deciding to stay dressed, she kicked off her boots, then threw the extra blankets on the bed and huddled under the heavy feather duvet, trying to get warm.

She was too cold, though, and the tension in her body wasn't helping. As she lay in bed shivering, wishing to hell she had heeded Quinn's advice and not come to Norfolk – at least not alone – she heard the distinct creak of a floorboard out on the landing.

For a moment, she froze, catching her breath, every part of her stiffening, except her heart, which was pumping overtime.

Someone was outside her room.

Was it Jimmy or Rose?

As she eased out a long, trembling breath, she forced herself to push back the duvet, snatching up the lantern and briskly crossing the room, determined to catch the culprit.

Twisting the knob, she pulled the door open, blinking into the empty shadows.

No one was there.

She raised the lantern and cast its light in both directions, but the corridor was empty.

Her fraught mind replayed the sound she had heard. Had she imagined it? Or was it simply the groans and creaks of an old building?

If only she could leave, but the blizzard had trapped her here. She had no choice but to wait things out till morning.

As she stepped back into the room and closed the door, she shone the lantern around, looking for anything she might be able to use to protect herself. Other than the furniture and the heavy drape curtains, there was very little else. Only a few decorative pieces that looked like antiques. One of them was a tall candlestick and after setting down the lantern next to her useless phone, she tested its weight.

It was a lot heavier than she expected and could definitely do some damage if needed.

After moving it to the table beside the bed, she climbed back under the covers, telling herself she was overreacting. She didn't need a weapon and wouldn't be forced to defend herself. She was simply getting spooked by an old house and the hostile welcome she had received from her brother.

It was all going to be okay and in the morning she would get to the village, sort the car and find a way to contact Quinn. This time tomorrow, they would be laughing about what had happened.

But as she continued to shiver under the duvet, wide awake and listening for any tiny sound in the silence, she suspected it was going to be the longest night of her life.

22

Quinn had never even considered becoming a dad before Lola had fallen pregnant.

It wasn't that he never wanted kids. It was just that he hadn't ever thought about parenthood in depth. He liked children fine, and adored his nieces, but he and Lola had only recently moved in together. It was far too early to go down that path and he had assumed they would get married first and concentrate on their careers for a bit before having that discussion.

But then she had become pregnant, something that had shocked both of them, and after coming to terms with the news, they had decided they wanted to keep it and he had fallen in love with the idea of having a baby with her.

No, it wasn't what they had planned for their immediate future, but priorities shifted.

Nights out with friends turned into evenings in their flat, as they saved and prepared for their impending arrival.

While Lola shopped for baby clothes and nappies, Quinn, along with his best mate, Dino, had decorated the spare room a neutral sunny yellow and beige with a safari theme.

Names were picked – Milo for a boy, Ella for a girl. And the soft toy elephant they had bought, that they hoped would become a childhood favourite, sat in the cream cot awaiting his owner's arrival.

A week later, everything had changed, Lola freaking out because she couldn't feel the baby kicking. The three days that followed were the worst of Quinn's life, as they learnt that placental problems had led to insufficient oxygen and nutrient delivery. Their baby boy dying in Lola's womb.

Quinn didn't consider himself to be an overly emotional man, and he had dealt with loss before, but this grief was on a different scale, and holding the body of his perfectly formed tiny son, knowing that Milo would never get to feel his touch or hear his voice, was devastating.

It was worse for Lola, who had been forced to give birth, and she blamed herself for not keeping their son safe and alive, despite everyone telling her otherwise.

Back home in their flat, the door to the baby's room stayed shut, neither of them able to face going inside, but as Quinn openly mourned, Lola refused to acknowledge what had happened.

It was shock that had made her close down, that was what the counsellors told him, and he knew it was true, having seen a similar reaction in some of the crime victims he dealt with.

Trying to look after Lola while coping with his own emotions almost broke him too. Still, he hadn't given up on her. At least not until he realised that he had to let her go if he wanted to help her.

It was one of the hardest things he'd ever done.

Although he had tried his best to move forward, he still

carried the grief of his loss with him, along with guilt that he had let Lola down by leaving, even though deep down he knew she had never given him a choice.

They had been so tight together, such a good fit, but in the presence of tragedy, they had slowly unravelled.

He still loved her and after they had reconnected on the train yesterday, he was confident the feeling was mutual. Time apart had allowed them to deal with their loss and both of them were aware they were being offered a second chance. That was why it was bothering the hell out of him that Lola hadn't made contact.

It hadn't been some simple bumping into an ex and exchanging pleasantries. It was more than that and he knew she realised the significance too.

Was it the weather? Had her car come off the road somewhere?

What if she was lying in a ditch, unconscious – or worse?

He had promised himself he would relax and have a drink with Chloe while they wrapped presents, but now he was regretting it, the alcohol making him paranoid and now, fearing for Lola's safety.

He couldn't lose her again, not when he was on the cusp of getting her back, and he had given into the urge to try to contact her again, not liking that his phone calls went straight to voicemail. He had called the hotel where he knew she was staying. Although he understood they couldn't confirm if she was there, he left a message with the reception team asking them to pass it along.

Chloe knew he was on edge and she was doing her best to calm his fears, but Quinn knew the only thing stopping him from borrowing his sister's car was the alcohol in his bloodstream.

His job as a detective required a certain amount of intuition and he didn't like any of this situation. But it was Lola he was worrying about. Was it possible that their personal connection was clouding his normally reliable judgement?

He kept checking both his phone and the local news, relieved when it eventually stopped snowing, and he decided that if he hadn't heard from her in the morning, he would head out to find her.

23

'You're both overreacting.'

Jimmy had known he was going to pay for opening his big mouth at dinner. It had been a complete shitshow, Rose had angrily told him, her tone furious, but her voice low, just in case Lola made a surprise reappearance.

She wouldn't, Jimmy assured them. She had already gone to bed.

It had been a silly mistake. He had slipped up, but no harm was done. Lola was none the wiser as to who Brett Corrigan was and they had managed to convince her that both Nigel and Annie Whitlock were her biological parents. Her real father's name hadn't even entered the conversation.

'We're not overreacting,' Rose snapped. 'You knew how much was riding on tonight. Why the fuck do you think I wanted you out of the way? Because you're a bloody liability, Jimmy.'

'Well, I didn't know she was going to crash her car and have to stay over,' Jimmy bit back. 'It was a stupid idea inviting her here in the first place. I told you so.'

'It wouldn't have been if you hadn't opened your big mouth!'

Rose lit a cigarette, holding it between shaking fingers as she inhaled deeply.

It was a habit that Daniel disapproved of, especially indoors, but his sister had never been one to take orders.

Ironic that she had trained as a nurse and knew all of the associated health risks that came with smoking, Jimmy thought, conveniently ignoring the fact that he had been drinking like a fish long before he was sacked from his job.

They both had their addictions.

He snatched up the open bottle of brandy, pouring himself a double measure and downing it quickly. The liquid heated his belly, having barely touched the sides of his throat as it went down.

'I don't need to listen to this,' he snarled, thumping his glass down. 'I'm off to bed.'

He received no objections and didn't miss the shared look of relief at his departure. Out of the way was safer for everyone.

Things had changed since he had first come to Norfolk. Back then, he had felt welcomed. Daniel had never spoken unkindly to him, but everything was different now and he knew he only had himself to blame. He should never have agreed to their plan, not realising the huge repercussions it would have on his life.

Why had he been so weak-willed, instead of saying no?

He should have known things could never go back and realised how the dynamics in the house would change.

Now they hated him.

The witch and the manipulator. That was how he often thought of the pair of them these days.

They let him stay here in the house, knowing it was the safest place for him to be. Here they could keep an eye on him, and they allowed him to drink himself silly because they didn't trust him. Keep Jimmy the fool content and stop him from shooting his big mouth off about the terrible secret they all shared.

Not that he would ever confess to their sin. He wasn't an idiot.

In his more sober moments, Jimmy was fully aware of what was at stake. Often the horror of what they had done that summer's evening eighteen months ago woke him up in the middle of the night in a cold sweat.

It was why he kept a bottle of whisky in his bedside cabinet. Drinking himself into oblivion was the only way he could escape his nightmares.

24
_____

For what felt like hours, Lola had lain awake. The ominous silence of both the house and the weather outside hindered her efforts to fall asleep, as she listened for any tiny sound that might suggest her visitor had returned.

She had thought sleep would be impossible and had resigned herself to the fact she would lie in this cold bed fully alert until morning – which perhaps would be a good thing, given that someone had taken the door key – but exhaustion had finally won, her eyes drifting shut.

It wasn't a noise that disturbed her slumber or the icy temperature of the house, but instead a light tickling caress against her skin. She didn't suddenly start awake, instead slowly growing aware of the sensation as she gradually drifted towards consciousness.

In the dream she was having, the hand cupping her chin and the thumb gently stroking her cheek belonged to Quinn, but as her surroundings became familiar, and she recalled the disastrous visit to Norfolk to meet her brother and all that had followed, the last pull awake was as sharp as a slap across the face.

She was still in his house, still in the four-poster bed on the second floor, and it was still dark outside. The only thing that was different was she was no longer alone. Someone was leaning over her.

Not Quinn. And not Rose, Jimmy or Daniel.

In the flickering light of the paraffin lamp was an older woman, her soft, cold finger stilling against Lola's cheek as she stirred, her long hair falling in a tangled curtain around her shoulders, close enough for Lola to breathe in its rancid scent.

Lola's immediate reaction was to scream, jerking away from the woman's touch as she did so and scooting back across the mattress.

Instantly, the woman's demeanour changed and she became wild-eyed, for a moment looking as if she was going to attack, but as Lola half scrambled, half fell out of the bed, trying to put more distance between them, the woman turned and fled from the room.

What the hell?

Lola's heart was thumping in her ears, her adrenaline so spiked she barely noticed the cold, and as she clumsily reached for the paraffin lamp, she accidentally knocked it to the floor.

For one terrified second, she thought it was going to ignite, but as the spilled oil covered the wick, the flame died, plunging the room into darkness.

No!

The curtains were still open. She had never drawn them, wanting that tenuous connection to the rest of the world, and as her eyes gradually adjusted to the sliver of moon, she could see the blizzard had passed and the clear sky was illuminated with a glassy light from the snow, appearing brighter towards the horizon.

Snatching up her phone from the bedside table, trembling fingers activating the torch, she followed after the woman. Whoever she was, she had a head start, but Lola was determined to find out what the hell was going on.

What had just happened was not okay.

A quick check of the corridor and the bathroom showed her they were both empty. There was one other door, but when she tried to open it, she found it was locked.

Had it been a ghost?

The thought was only fleeting. She knew what she had seen was real.

But who was she? Rose hadn't mentioned anyone else living in the house and she hadn't been with them at dinner.

Leaving the locked door, Lola headed down the staircase to the first-floor landing.

Too many doors to check on this level.

Were Rose and Daniel still up? They would know who this woman was, so Lola resolved to go downstairs and find them.

As she was about to descend the main staircase, a muted, almost childish giggle came from behind her, and she swung around, the beam of her phone torch darting from one side of the landing to the other, as she looked for where the noise had come from.

No one was there.

But then she realised she hadn't considered the lift. Was someone inside the carriage?

Tentatively, she stepped towards the door, nerves creeping in and weakening the edges of her anger. She was summoning up the courage to pull open the door when another voice spoke, and she almost jumped out of her skin.

'It doesn't work, you know. Not just because of the power cut. It hasn't done in ages.'

Her head shot around, the light landing on Jimmy. He stood across the landing, hair dishevelled and wearing checked pyjamas. The lower buttons of the shirt were straining over his stomach.

His appearance had caught her off guard and she hadn't registered his words properly, too focused on everything else that had just happened.

'There was a woman in my room,' she told him, watching as he frowned.

'A woman?' he repeated.

At first, Lola thought he didn't believe her, but then she realised that because of the alcohol he had consumed, he was struggling to focus on her words. He seemed even more pissed than he had been at dinner.

'She was an older lady,' she pushed, hoping to stir something in his drunken brain. 'Maybe in her seventies or eighties, and she was wearing a white nightdress.'

The giggle came again from the lift shaft and this time both their heads shot towards the door. The sound seemed to sober Jimmy slightly, as a look of panic crossed his face.

'Who is she?' Lola demanded.

'You should go back to bed,' he slurred, waving his hand dismissively. 'I'll deal with this.'

Honestly, Lola wasn't sure he was in a fit state to deal with anything. Besides, after being so rudely awaken, she deserved to know who the woman was.

'I'm up now, so I'd like to stay,' she said firmly.

Jimmy didn't even try to argue, shrugging his shoulders as if he couldn't be bothered with any of this. As he took a stumbling step towards the lift, the concertina door was pulled open from inside, and Lola could see the woman who had been in her room, a childish look on her face as she stared at them through the bars of the outer gate.

'Come on, Mum,' Jimmy sighed, pulling the gate open and reaching his hand out, huffing when the woman refused to take it. Instead, she stepped back to the rear of the carriage, pressing at the buttons on the side panel, like they were playing some kind of game. 'Let's take you back to your room.'

Rose hadn't mentioned anything about their mother living with them. Not that it was any of Lola's business, but it seemed odd that she hadn't joined them downstairs for supper.

Perhaps it was because she didn't seem well. Lola wasn't a medical professional, but she suspected the woman had some form of dementia. It would explain the odd behaviour, though not so much her appearance. Her white nightdress was torn in places and covered in stains, her hair in desperate need of a brush, and her poor bare feet – which must be so cold – were filthy.

Did they not look after her properly? Given how impeccable Rose was with her own appearance, Lola would have thought her mother's care would have been a top priority.

Looking at the poor neglected woman before her, a rush of sympathy surged, along with guilt at how she had reacted when she had found her in her room. Okay, it was understandable she had been a little freaked waking up to find someone looking over her, but the woman had meant no harm.

'She likes to play with the buttons,' Jimmy said, exasperated, as his mother drew her focus away from the control panel to stare curiously at Lola. 'Come on, Mum. Now, before Rose realises you're out of your room. You don't want her to get mad at you.'

Angry? Why would Rose get mad? This was her mother.

Lola remembered when Kelly had become ill. Her mum had been so sick with the chemo and then, towards the very end, she had needed help with the most basic functions, even breathing. She had wanted to remain in her own home and, although she had a palliative care team coming in, Lola had been with her, taking time away from work to do whatever was needed, right up until the very end. And yes, at times she had been frustrated, angry even – though only ever at the cruel disease – and she had been terribly sad, but she had buried all of those negative feelings, determined to put a brave face on and keep those last awful days as stress-free as possible.

'What is your mum's name?' she asked, sensing Jimmy needed help. He could barely keep himself standing upright and wasn't in a fit state to help anyone.

'What?' He heavily blinked at her, as if he had forgotten she was even there, but as his eyes zoned out, then seemed to refocus, he answered her question. 'Agnes.'

Agnes. Lola nodded.

Stepping forward, she offered her hand to the woman, careful to keep her movements slow and steady, not wanting to spook her. 'Agnes, it's nice to meet you. I'm Lola.'

At first she thought Agnes was going to ignore her, but then she started to move towards her.

Unfortunately, Jimmy chose that moment to almost dive at his mother, grabbing her in an awkward hug. 'I've got it. Come on, Mum. Back to your room.'

As he manhandled Agnes, who was getting more distressed by the moment as he half dragged her across the landing, Lola hurried after them, appalled at what he was doing.

'Jimmy?'

The voice that came from behind them sounded shocked and annoyed.

They all paused and Lola turned, locking eyes with Rose.

'What's going on?'

Rose's gaze flickered to Jimmy, before landing back on Lola, both her tone and her glare accusing, and Lola's hackles rose. While she was appreciative of the Whitlocks for letting her stay, she was not going to be spoken to as if she had done something wrong.

'I woke up to find your mother standing by the bed,' she answered, keeping her tone cool.

Rose was silent for a moment as she processed Lola's words.

'How did she get out of her room?' she snapped, not sounding at all happy.

This time, her focus was on Jimmy, who still had hold of Agnes. He pouted at his sister, a little sulkily, but guilt was all over his face, and his glazed look had gone, Rose's sudden appearance seeming to sober him up.

'I nipped in to check on her when I came up to change. I thought I'd locked the door behind me. I swear.'

They locked Agnes in her bedroom?

Lola tried to reserve judgement. She knew very little about dementia – assuming it was that. Perhaps it was for their mother's own safety.

Still, briefly, the mention of locked doors reminded her of the missing key to her own room and she wondered again if it had been Jimmy or Rose who had taken it and with what intention.

'I'll take her back,' Jimmy told his sister. 'No harm done.'

Was Agnes's room at the end of the corridor, where Lola had heard noises coming from before going down to supper?

She remembered how she thought the doorknob had turned. Had that been Agnes trying to get out?

Rose huffed out a breath and for a moment it looked like she was going to respond, but then she shook her head in either disappointment or annoyance – perhaps both – and took charge of the situation.

'No,' she shook her head. 'I'll do it.'

She spoke quietly but firmly to Jimmy, taking her agitated mother by the arm, and gave him a warning look to back off. Then, barely sparing Lola a glance, she walked Agnes across the landing and out of sight, leaving Jimmy and Lola standing awkwardly at the top of the stairs.

'Bloody cold up here,' Jimmy said, the first one to break the silence. He rubbed at his arms as though noticing the low temperature for the first time.

'It is,' Lola agreed. She was not looking forward to returning to her freezing room, though making painful small talk with Jimmy was just as uncomfortable.

'I'm going to head down for another nightcap and warm myself up. The fire is still lit in the living room. Want to come?'

'What time is it?'

Jimmy glanced at his watch. 'Just after 1 a.m.'

So, late then, but there were several hours to kill. Lola didn't want any more alcohol, but the thought of the fire still crackling away downstairs was tempting, and she was really thirsty. 'I could use a glass of water,' she said, following after him.

It was as they were almost to the foot of the stairs that Jimmy's earlier words came back to her.

When he had found her standing by the lift, he had said, *It doesn't work, you know. Hasn't done in ages.*

At the time, Lola hadn't paid much attention. She had been

so preoccupied, wanting to know who was inside the carriage. But now she thought of her brother.

Rose had told her that she and Daniel had purposely picked a house with a lift already installed. So if Jimmy was correct and it hadn't worked in a long time, how did Daniel manage to get up and down the stairs?

25

Lola played for time before going through to the living room, making a fuss of Monty, who was back in his bed in the corner of the room, then drinking two glasses of tap water whilst enjoying the warmth from the Aga and looking at the view out of the window.

The tealights that had bathed the room in a warm low glow had now burnt out and perhaps because of the darkness inside, the snow gleamed bright; it was crisp and untouched, and the scene looked perfect and peaceful.

Growing up, Lola had always hoped for a white Christmas. Sometimes snow fell a few days after, and on one occasion it had made an appearance a month early, but never on the actual day itself. How ironic that today was Christmas Eve and she finally had her wish, but the weather was trapping her somewhere she had no desire to be.

It's just until daylight, she reminded herself, still trying to put a positive spin on her situation. She would hopefully be home in time for Christmas Day or at the very least back in her hotel room in Ely.

Away from Daniel and Rose and their secrets.

She would be a liar if she said she wasn't curious about what they were hiding, but it wasn't that important to her. The only thing she was keen to learn about was her father. If it wasn't Nigel Whitlock, who was it?

The answers would have to wait until she was back home, as she didn't trust Daniel and Rose to tell her the truth.

But Jimmy might, she realised. He had slipped up earlier, revealing information that he wasn't supposed to.

She expected to find Daniel in the living room, but Jimmy was there alone as she entered, the dog trailing after her, and he was standing close to the fireplace, staring down at the flames, seeming mesmerised. He was still swaying a bit, the glass of what Lola assumed was whisky tilted forward and perilously close to spilling, and her breath caught when she saw him, frightened that he might topple forward.

'No Daniel?' she asked casually, relieved that her brother wasn't there.

Jimmy shook his head, glancing at her briefly as she moved to stand beside him, before returning his attention to the fire.

For a few moments, they both stood in silence and as Lola watched Monty making himself comfortable at the foot of one of the sofas, she considered whether she should just stay down here for the rest of the night. Either here or in the kitchen. The biting-cold numbness had gradually worn off and her body had stopped shivering. As she drew in a deep contented breath, she earned another sidelong glance from Jimmy.

'You don't realise quite how cold it is upstairs until you're down here again in the warm,' he commented, taking another sip from his glass. Lola noted that it was almost empty again.

'Have you and your mother lived here with Rose and

Daniel for long?' she asked, starting with what she hoped was a safe topic.

'A while,' he said, staring at the flames again.

He didn't seem suspicious of her question or guarded, but, equally, he didn't expand on his answer, instead falling silent.

'It seems very remote out here,' she tried again.

He shrugged. 'I guess it would if you're used to living in a big city. I like it. It's peaceful.'

'It's certainly that. A little too quiet for me. I'm hoping to get back to Manchester tomorrow if the weather isn't too bad.'

Jimmy paused, seeming thoughtful. 'I can give you a lift to the village tomorrow if the roads are clear enough.'

Did Jimmy ever sober up enough to drive?

Lola would rather take her chances and walk, but she would have that conversation in the morning. For now she said, 'Thanks.'

'So did you get what you came here for?' he asked after a moment.

His out-of-the-blue question caught her by surprise and briefly she wondered what he meant – if perhaps he thought she had been angling for a share of any inheritance or similar – but then he elaborated.

'Did Daniel answer all of your questions?'

Not really was the true answer, but she didn't say so. 'I know a little bit more about my parents now. And Rose gave me a couple of photos. Did you know them well, Annie and Nigel?'

'I met them at the wedding. I gave Rose away. But I didn't really know them other than that. Your mum seemed like a nice lady.'

And Nigel? He didn't say what he thought about him.

'I can see the resemblance between me and my mum. I

have the same colour hair and face shape.' Lola hesitated. 'I don't look at all like Nigel, though.'

She purposely didn't refer to him as 'dad', turning to face Jimmy, wanting to gauge his reaction. Earlier he had hastily backtracked after his slip-up, but that had been in front of Daniel and Rose. Now they were alone, would he perhaps be honest with her?

'We don't always look like both parents. I look nothing like my dad either,' he answered hastily, but guilt was written all over his face, and he refused to make eye contact with her.

Deciding to stop skirting around the issue, Lola asked him bluntly, 'Nigel wasn't my dad, though. Was he?'

Now he did look up. Blue eyes red-rimmed and glassy. And she could tell he was annoyed. 'Of course he was,' he snapped.

'You said I'm Daniel's half-sister.'

'It was a bloody joke.'

'Not a very funny one, if it was,' Lola pointed out, heat creeping into her tone.

Jimmy opened his mouth to respond, but no words came out. Instead, he frowned again at the fire, his mouth drawn in a tight line.

She was losing him. The conversation over.

Unless she tried a different approach.

'I don't want anything from Daniel and Rose,' she said quietly. 'I'm not after money or a relationship with them. I know Daniel doesn't want that. I have my life back home in Manchester and I'm happy there. I just want to know where I came from, so I can close that chapter of my life.'

Seconds ticked by as Jimmy sipped at his whisky and considered her words, a muscle working overtime in his jaw that she suspected was agitation. He was still swaying slightly, and she hoped the alcohol would loosen his tongue.

'Once I have answers, I promise none of you will ever hear from me again.'

Jimmy sighed and huffed out a breath, and Lola realised she was wasting her time. It seemed he was as determined as Rose and Daniel to stop her from finding out the truth. She didn't understand why, but she'd had enough now.

When he spoke, his tone low, it caught her off guard.

'I can't tell you anything about your dad. I never met him.'

Lola's heartbeat quickened. 'So Nigel Whitlock isn't my father?'

Jimmy glanced to the open living room door and she realised he was anxious about being overheard. 'If I tell you, you have to promise you will never breathe another word, and that you'll leave them alone.'

Lola nodded, quick to agree. 'Of course. I promise.'

'Rose told me that Annie had an affair with a man named John, who worked for them at their home in Oxford. I think he did gardening for them and manual labour, that kind of thing.'

'How did Rose know? Did Daniel tell her?'

'No, he would have been very young at the time of the affair. I don't know if he knew about John back then. He's never said. Certainly not to me. Annie was the one who told Rose. I guess Rose then talked to Daniel.'

That must have been hard, finding out his mother's huge secret from his wife.

Lola waited for Jimmy to continue, keen to know more.

'Rose said she found her one day looking at a photograph of John, and Annie admitted to the affair. She said it had ended after she had fallen pregnant and Nigel had found out.'

'And the baby was me?' Lola pushed. 'But how did Nigel know I wasn't his?'

Jimmy held up his fingers in a snipping motion. 'Vasectomy. He had his son, his heir, and didn't want another child.'

'Do you know what happened next?'

'Only that Nigel gave Annie an ultimatum. He made her choose between you and Daniel. She told Rose that he'd said he would fight for sole custody of Daniel if she didn't give you up for adoption. She couldn't take the risk that he might win, so she agreed to his terms. His name would go on your birth certificate, but you would be given up for adoption.'

Although Lola understood why Annie had done it, it was still a punch to the gut.

Her birth mother was dead and she would never get to have a conversation with her. And she had believed her father was too. Learning about John gave her fresh hope.

'Do you know his surname or if he is still alive?' she pushed. It was a stretch to think Jimmy would know any more as this would have been years before Rose started working for the Whitlocks and Jimmy had already told her he had never met John, but he knew this much, so it was worth asking.

'I'm sorry. That's all I can tell you. John stopped working for the family after the affair came to light and Annie told Rose she never heard from him after that. I think, from what Rose said, that she was just relieved to get it off her chest. Unburden her secret.'

'Okay, thank you. I really appreciate you being honest with me.'

At least Lola had a name. It was a starting point for trying to locate John.

Jimmy was quiet for a moment and she wondered if he was regretting saying anything, but then he gave her another glimmer of hope.

'I'm wondering if that photograph of John might be with

Annie's things. It was a few years ago, but she might have held on to it.'

'Are they here in this house?'

He nodded. 'It's just a couple of boxes they brought with them when they moved here. Mostly important documents they might need, but a few personal items too. I think they are stored in the cupboard next to the kitchen.'

'Are you able to look for me?'

A cough sounded in the near distance, making them both jump, and Jimmy's eyes again shot towards the door. The noise seemed to remind him he shouldn't be sharing this information with Lola because he immediately shut down again.

'I don't think that's a good idea. I'm sorry. I've told you all I know. Rose will be angry if she finds out I've said anything.'

Angry, why? What did she have to gain from keeping Lola's parentage a secret from her? This wasn't about Rose, so shouldn't be any of her concern.

Lola wanted to push him further, but the sound of approaching footsteps warned her that Rose was on her way to join them.

As she entered the room, Jimmy took a guilty step away, and Lola didn't miss the quick look of suspicion Rose gave them both as her gaze swept over them.

'I'm sorry about earlier,' she apologised to Lola, a coolly polite smile on her lips. 'We normally keep Mum locked in her room at night for her own safety. Her mind isn't really there any more. I hope she didn't give you too much of a fright.'

'It's okay. I understand,' Lola said, wanting to draw a line under the incident, even though it unsettled her that no one had mentioned Agnes even lived in the house.

'So, what have you two been talking about?' Rose asked

brightly. And perhaps it was guilt at the conversation she'd had with Jimmy, but Lola's face heated.

Rose hadn't overheard anything. Had she?

'Just the weather,' Jimmy said quickly. 'I told Lola I will give her a lift to the village tomorrow if I can get my car out.'

'I see.' Rose's face gave nothing away to suggest what she was thinking. 'Well, I suppose I should go up to bed. We're going to take a chance and leave the fire burning as it's so cold, so don't put it out,' she told her brother.

'I'm coming up too now,' he said, and Lola suspected it was because he was keen not to return to their conversation about her father.

'Is Daniel okay?' Lola asked, wondering where he had disappeared to.

'Of course. Why wouldn't he be? He's in bed.'

Lola frowned. 'Jimmy said the lift is broken. I wondered how he was managing to get upstairs.'

Rose glanced at her brother, then gave a humourless laugh. 'He's an oracle of information tonight. Yes, it is out of order. We've had a power cut, remember?'

'He said it's not worked for a while,' Lola challenged, not missing Rose shoot a glare Jimmy's way.

'Not that long, but Daniel is sleeping in the study until it can be fixed.'

Was she lying? If so, it had rolled smoothly off her tongue, and Lola realised she had no grounds to question Rose further.

Other than the fact that she's been lying to you all night.

She replayed the conversation they'd had when she had first arrived. Rose had mentioned they had looked for a house with a lift. Was it odd that she hadn't said then that it was out of order or was Lola overthinking things? Second-guessing everything was starting to give her a headache, so for now she focused on the information Jimmy had given her and the photo of her father that might be in the cupboard next to the kitchen.

If Jimmy wouldn't help her find the picture of John, she would look for it herself.

'I'm going to stay down here for a bit longer if you don't mind. It's so cold upstairs.'

If Rose had a problem with that, then she didn't say, instead nodding that it was fine and for the second time that evening, wishing her goodnight.

Lola watched them go from her position by the fireplace. She would give them fifteen minutes to get settled, then she would go and look for the box of her mother's things. It was the only way she was going to get any answers.

26

It was a mistake, letting her come here.

We knew we were taking a huge risk, that there were too many things that could go wrong, and now the snow has made things even more dangerous for us.

There is so much room for error in this game we are playing and the stakes are high. If one of us slips up now, everything we have worked towards will be wasted and this house of cards will come crashing down around us.

I keep telling myself it's just a few more hours, and that as soon as morning arrives we will be rid of her. She will be gone for good.

But will she?

I am beginning to fear that I might have overplayed my hand and that our Pandora's box of secrets has already been prised open.

If that is true, then it is too late.

I have killed once before to protect what is mine.

Could I do it again if I have to?

Already I know the answer, without hesitation, is yes.

27

No one had told Lola where the study was and as there had been no good reason for her to ask, she knew she would have to take a chance that it wasn't down the end of the house where the kitchen was.

She couldn't risk disturbing Daniel. Even though he would require help getting out of bed, he was bound to have an alarm that he could sound if he needed help, and Lola couldn't risk getting caught snooping if he heard any suspicious noises.

After waiting fifteen minutes, she decided to give it another ten just to be on the safe side. Then, reluctantly leaving the warmth of the fire and telling Monty to stay – relieved when the dog obeyed – she headed out into the hallway, keeping her footsteps light as she crept through the dark house.

Jimmy had mentioned the cupboard next to the kitchen and she located it easily, her breath catching when the door groaned as she opened it. In the silence of the night, it echoed through the house and she froze, terrified of waking the sleeping occupants. If Rose and Daniel caught her, how would she explain herself?

She gave it a few moments, then, when nothing stirred, fully eased the door open.

The beam of her phone torch swept over the interior of a large cupboard and she could see it was mostly used for storage of household items, from brooms and mops to an ironing board and vacuum cleaner. Floor-to-ceiling shelves held an array of items, including cleaning supplies, Tupperware and cumbersome casserole pots. It seemed like an odd place to store important documents and briefly Lola wondered if Jimmy had been messing with her, but then she spotted the boxes on the bottom shelf. There were three of them, all matching in a cream linen cloth with gold trim on the edges.

Were these the boxes he had been referring to?

To get to the shelves meant moving the items in front of them, and as the space was large enough, Lola stepped inside, careful this time as she pulled the door closed behind her. Although she didn't particularly relish being shut inside the cupboard with its musty odour, it was safer and cut her chance of being found.

She worked quickly, but carefully, clearing a path to the shelves and removing the first of the boxes. Setting it on the floor, then dropping down onto her knees, she lifted the lid and shone the torch inside.

This box contained Nigel's things, she soon learnt. There were important items such as his passport and birth certificate, as well as bank statements and house deeds. Things that were none of Lola's business and, feeling guilty even looking at them, she didn't delve deeper, closing the box and returning it to the shelf.

The middle box was her mother's and contained more personal items, including sketchpads and pencils, handwritten recipe books and a well-worn paperback. There were drawings that Daniel had done as a child, as well as sympathy cards sent after Annie's passing, and also a photo album.

Was this the one Rose had taken the pictures from to give to Lola?

For now, she set the album to one side, curious about the sketchpad. Had her mother liked to draw? If so, it was a hobby that they shared.

The first few pages were of nature. A vase of flowers, a chaffinch pecking at the ground and a sleeping tabby cat. While not perfect, they showed a keen eye for detail.

Leafing further through the book, the drawings changed subject to people. There was one of a young Daniel, and another that Lola assumed was of Nigel. Then there was another man, smiling eyes looking directly at her. Annie had drawn him several times at different angles.

Was this Lola's father?

She lingered over the images, looking for any sign of similarity. Perhaps it was there a little in the structure of the cheekbones and the shape of the eyes.

She finished with the sketchbook, then turned her attention to the other items, conscious that the longer she spent in the cupboard, the more risk there was that she would be found.

There were no secrets in the recipe books, the food-splattered pages suggesting cooking had been another loved pastime of her mother's, and Daniel's drawings held no interest. Lola couldn't relate to the little boy who had done these, having met the cold, mean-spirited man who was her brother.

The paperback was a spy thriller by J. T. Fagan, an author she wasn't familiar with, but it had been personally signed to Annie, suggesting it had been written by a friend. She briefly leafed through it and was about to put it down when something fell out from the dusty pages.

A photo.

She picked it up from the floor and stared at the man in the image. The same man Annie had sketched. Instinctively she knew it was John. Her father.

He had smiling earthy-green eyes. They were the same shade as her own, she realised.

Had her mother been in love with John or was it a casual encounter?

The fact she had been drawing him suggested the former and Lola clung to that, wanting their relationship to be a fairy tale, even if it was one that had ended badly.

Because it *had* ended badly. Nigel had forced Annie to choose when he had learned of the affair and Lola had been given up for adoption.

Did her father even realise she existed?

Hurt and anger choked her, hating Nigel for what he had done.

She put the photo of John to one side, already knowing she would take it home with her. It wasn't theft. He had been Lola's father, not Daniel's.

Besides, all of his parents' things were tucked away in what was effectively a laundry cupboard. He couldn't care about them that much.

Finally, she picked up the photo album, flicking through pictures of Annie and Nigel's wedding and the birth of her brother, looking at photos of Daniel as a toddler, a schoolboy and then into his early teens. Neat handwriting under each photo said what the occasion was, and it was hard not to feel the bite of envy seeing how their mother had taken care to document his life, and Lola had to remind herself that she had been loved. Kelly Henderson might not have been her biological mother, but she had made sure her daughter was given everything she needed.

One final photo showed adult Daniel holding a bottle of champagne. He was with the friend who had been in the Lamborghini with him and both had full flutes of the drink. The caption read 'Daniel and Brett celebrating getting their bachelor's degrees in culinary arts'.

Brett.

Lola remembered hearing his name at dinner. Hadn't Jimmy mentioned him visiting for Christmas a couple of years back? She assumed the man must be Daniel's best friend.

There was nothing else for her to see here and she had no desire to snoop any further. She had found the photograph of John and that was what she had come here for. Putting the album and the rest of Annie's things back in the box and sealing it, she returned it to the shelf.

She was about to move the vacuum cleaner and other items back to where she had found them when a noise came from the other side of the door.

It sounded like someone was clearing their throat.

Fuck.

Someone was out in the hallway.

Lola fumbled with her phone, turning off the torch and barely daring to breathe in case she was heard.

Now she was aware of the low sound of footsteps and the faint beam of light coming through the gap at the bottom of the door.

Did they realise she was in here?

Another thought occurred to her.

Had Jimmy set her up?

The light disappeared now, but she could still hear the faint tread of footsteps.

Had whoever it was gone into the kitchen?

Her suspicions were answered when she heard the sound of a running tap. The pipework must run through the back of the cupboard, the sudden noise of water gushing through them behind her making her jump and bash into the vacuum cleaner.

It clattered, even as she reached out to steady it.

Had she been heard?

Now there was silence and she waited with bated breath, her heart almost thumping out of her chest and her phone clutched tightly in her hand. Her whole body was trembling and it was only in part due to the cold.

As the seconds ticked by, she waited for another sound, but there was nothing.

Still, she knew she couldn't risk leaving the cupboard yet and she didn't dare look at the time on her phone for fear the light might show under the door.

Instead, she started to count slowly down from one hundred in her head, aware she needed to give it more time.

Play it safe, Lola.

When she reached one hundred, she would take a chance and open the door.

28

TWO YEARS EARLIER

Norfolk

Rose never intended to start an affair with Brett Corrigan, but she would look back later and realise that Brett's plan had been to seduce her all along.

He had once been Daniel's closest friend, and the pair of them had slipped back into a rhythm that at first left Rose feeling like an interloper. She suspected Jimmy did too. It was especially bad when Daniel and Brett reminisced about the past – something she hadn't been a part of – and how Annie and Nigel had doted on Brett almost as a second son. But running alongside that friendship, Rose noted, was an undercurrent of rivalry, and the longer that Brett stayed, the more consuming that competitiveness became.

Brett had never had the entitlement Daniel sometimes took for granted and it seemed at times he was envious. And now he was confined to a wheelchair, Daniel envied Brett's freedom. Seeing his friend still able to do all of the things he had once loved was making him bitter.

If he was aware of the furtive glances and flirty little comments Brett made to his wife, he never commented, and while Rose at first hadn't considered Brett as anything more than Daniel's friend, she gradually started to notice and to crave his attention.

She was a woman who made an effort with her appearance – not that Daniel seemed to appreciate it much these days – but now she took added care; her hair styled and her make-up perfect, an extra spritz of her favourite perfume, and she always wore matching underwear.

As winter thawed, Brett remained at Midwinter Manor, their strange little foursome bumbling along, with neither Daniel nor Rose pointing out that he had stayed far longer than he was supposed to.

It was with the birth of spring that the four learnt they were to become a five, when Rose and Jimmy's mother, Agnes, had an episode back home in Scotland that required a hospital stay and then a diagnosis of Alzheimer's.

Rose had wanted to weep when she and Jimmy had first been summoned home by her Aunt Elspeth, who lived a few doors down and had been keeping an eye on Agnes. The burden was becoming too much, she had explained over the telephone, and she had her own family dramas to contend with. It was time for Rose and Jimmy to step up and take over the responsibility for their mother.

Rose wanted to put Agnes into a care home. After the cruelty she had been subjected to throughout her childhood, why should she now be forced to care for her mum? Jimmy, though, was against the idea and he gradually wore Rose down, offering that if Agnes came to live in Norfolk, then he would do the bulk of looking after her.

His extended stay and long-term plans had never really

been discussed until this point. Rose was grateful for his help around the house, and Daniel didn't seem to mind his brother-in-law's company. Gradually Jimmy had become like part of the furniture.

It was the extortionate care home fees that finally had Rose agreeing. They could easily afford them, but she begrudged the idea of spending so much money on her mother. Daniel had already agreed to do whatever she felt was best for Agnes, so if Jimmy wanted to take on the burden of Agnes's care, let him.

The following week, he returned to Scotland alone to help clear their mother's house and terminate her rental agreement, and in the weeks that he was gone, the tension between the three who remained in the house was almost at breaking point.

Daniel and Brett seemed as if they were playing a game of chess, each fighting for dominance as they tried to outmanoeuvre the other. Daniel had a renewed desire to walk again. Where before he had loved the gardens of the manor house, now he barely ventured outside, and he was growing obsessive, spending hours with Monty, locked away in his study as he searched for new doctors who might be able to help him. He had become so tunnel-visioned, he was neglecting his marriage and it had reached the point where Rose barely recognised her husband.

Meanwhile, the slow teasing foreplay of Brett's seduction was driving her insane. He never touched her, but he often whispered in her ear, letting the caress of his warm breath heat her skin, the scent of his aftershave permeating her senses, while each sinful look he gave her burned through her clothes and suggested he was intending to fulfil an unspoken promise soon.

That day eventually happened when Rose planned a visit to the city of Norwich.

'I quite fancy heading there myself,' Brett suggested, his tone casual as he stirred his coffee. 'If you don't mind me tagging along.'

Part of the reason Rose wanted to go was to get away from him, aware she needed to shake off her shameful thoughts about cheating on her husband. The atmosphere in the house, and the undercurrent of mistrust, was so intense she could barely think straight. A day in Norwich would help her see sense as she cleared her head.

'I'm going clothes shopping,' she said lightly. 'It will be very boring for you.'

'I have my own things to do. I just thought it made sense if we rode there together.'

Rose's cheeks heated, aware Brett was watching her and looking amused as she desperately tried to think of another excuse.

'I suppose so,' she agreed, realising there wasn't one.

'You could come too if you want, Daniel,' Brett offered, his tone light, but challenging. Both of them knew Daniel had no interest in going and that he would spend the day locked away in his study.

'I have stuff to do here,' Daniel said, slipping a piece of toast crust to Monty, as he turned down the invite. 'You and Rose go, though.'

As he reached for the butter and concentrated on spreading it on his toast, Brett made a point of catching Rose's attention again. The look he gave her suggested he had just asked and been granted permission to sleep with his best friend's wife.

They never made it to Norwich that day. Brett insisted on

driving and the sexual tension as they drove away from Saham
Toney was at boiling point. When Brett changed gear, his
fingers brushing against Rose's leg, her breath hitched and she
almost whimpered.

Moments later, his fingers were inside her, teasing her
closer to the edge, neither of them speaking or acknowledging
what he was doing as he focused on the road. But later, when
he parked in a layby, pulling her from the car and into the
woods, where he roughly dragged up her skirt around her
waist and fucked her, he made his intentions very clear.

'What belongs to Daniel is mine too.'

It was as though a dam had broken, Rose's control snapping. She hadn't been wanted like this in a long time, and
Brett's all-consuming greed for her was too difficult to resist.

He pursued her whenever Daniel's back was turned, love-
bombing her with filthy messages and secretive gifts,
constantly questioning Rose as to whether he was a better
lover and making her tell him that he satisfied her more than
her husband.

And the risks he took became increasingly dangerous. It
was almost as if he wanted Daniel to catch them.

But Rose couldn't say no.

Daniel loved her, but she had never been wanted in such a
crude and primal way.

It was a shame that the arrival of her mother was going to
ruin everything.

On the eve before Jimmy returned with Agnes, Brett went
out to meet with a friend about a possible business venture,
and Rose and Daniel sat alone at the dining table with Monty
lying on the floor by Daniel's wheelchair. It was the first time it
had just been the two of them in quite a while.

'I know you're fucking him,' he said quietly as Rose speared a carrot with her fork, his tone so casual at first she thought she had misheard him.

'Sorry?'

He looked her dead in the eye. 'I know you are fucking Brett,' he repeated, each word enunciated.

Her fork wavered in the air as he smiled slowly at her, allowing her time to register his words.

He knew?

Perhaps she shouldn't be surprised. Brett hadn't exactly been discreet during their more recent encounters. Still, panic had a rush of thoughts jumbling in her head as she sought for a response, unsure whether to turn on the tears and beg for Daniel's forgiveness or to admit what had happened and go on the defensive, blaming him for his recent neglect.

In the end, she answered him with just one word. 'Okay.'

At first, she thought his eyes were going to pop out of his head. He was outraged at her reaction and she could see it had caught him off guard.

'Is that it? You're cheating on me with my best friend and all you can say about it is "okay"? I should kick you all out of the house. You and your brother. And what will you do with Agnes? She's not my responsibility now.'

Rose put her fork down, surprised at how calm she felt now this was out in the open. 'You won't do that because I know you're a good person,' she told him. 'You like Jimmy and you won't throw an old lady with Alzheimer's out in the street. And you love me. You need me too. I'm the only one who can care for you properly.'

When he didn't respond, she continued.

'I never meant for it to happen, if it's any consolation. Perhaps if you had been a little more attentive it wouldn't have done.' She watched his mouth draw a tight line, adding, 'You know I am right.'

'Do you love him?'

She thought about it and shook her head. 'No, I love you. But I have needs. This thing with Brett, it's just a fling. Or was. Obviously it's over now and I understand you will want him to leave.'

To her surprise, Daniel threw his cutlery down in temper. 'No!' he snapped. 'I don't want you to tell him I know.'

'You don't?' Rose's eyes widened. 'Okay, you've lost me. I don't understand.'

'This is classic Brett. He has always liked helping himself to what is mine, taking advantage of my hospitality, and it's time for it to stop.'

Rose bristled, not appreciating being referred to as an object. She bit down on her annoyance for now, aware she didn't have the moral high ground.

'It's all a game to him,' Daniel continued. 'Don't you under-stand? But I'm on to him, and I want to see just how far he is willing to go to get one up on me.'

'Okay.' Now she was wary, not liking the sound of being caught in the middle. 'And what is your plan?' she asked, wanting to understand where this was going, realising the implications if Daniel was to now kick her out of the house, especially with Jimmy and her mother on their way back from Scotland.

'I haven't decided yet, but you're not to say a word to him that I know. I want to test our alleged friendship and see just how disloyal he is.' Daniel picked up his knife again, running his finger casually back and forth along the dull blade as he spoke, raising his gaze to look Rose in the eye. 'If he turns out to be as much of a traitorous bastard as I suspect, then you, my darling wife, are going to help me get my own back.'

'Your own back, how?' she asked tentatively, her palms dampening as her heart thudded in her chest.

Daniel shrugged. 'If he's lucky, I'll just expose him for the liar and cheat he is.' He winked at Rose. 'Or perhaps I should make you help me kill him.'

29

PRESENT DAY

Lola had finished counting, but she was still trying to pluck up the courage to open the cupboard door.

Even though there had been no further noise from out in the hallway, she didn't trust that the coast was clear. What if whoever it had been was waiting outside to catch her out?

Problem was, she couldn't stay in there indefinitely, and she didn't want to either. Although she had now adjusted to the unpleasant odour in the cupboard, she was desperate to get back to the warmth of the fire; her toes were so cold she could barely feel them.

She was just going to have to take a chance.

Slipping the photo of John into the back pocket of her jeans, she gingerly reached out in the darkness, her cold fingers closing around the metal doorknob.

Here goes nothing.

She eased the door open slowly, relieved when it didn't make any noise this time, and stepped out into the dark hallway.

Her phone was clenched tightly in her hand, but she didn't

want to risk using the torch just yet. Once the cupboard door was shut, she would go into the kitchen for another glass of water. At least then if anyone walked in she would have a valid reason for being there.

As her eyesight gradually adjusted to the darkness, she released a breath. She was alone and whoever she had heard was gone.

Still, she took care closing the door behind her, her legs trembling as she made her way back into the warmth of the kitchen. Now she turned on the torch, sweeping the beam around the room, immediately seeing the evidence of the late-night visitor she had heard.

An empty tumbler sat on the kitchen table, along with a plate of crumbs.

One of the occupants of the house had been in here for a snack.

Daniel and Agnes were in bed and everything Lola had seen of Rose suggested she was neat and tidy. She would surely have cleared up after herself.

It must have been Jimmy.

Had he checked the living room first to see if Lola was still in there, perhaps assuming when he found it empty that she had changed her mind and gone up to bed? Or had he come downstairs and gone straight to the kitchen?

Did he suspect she would go to the cupboard?

He hadn't checked to see if she was in there, but then he might have already forgotten the conversation they'd had. He had been drinking heavily all night, so it was possible.

Picking up the tumbler that she had used earlier from the drainer, Lola poured herself a fresh glass of water, this time taking it with her as she headed back across the house to the living room, where Monty's head shot up, his tail wagging at her return.

She wouldn't go upstairs again. It was too cold and creepy. Instead she'd wait down here by the crackling fire.

The time on her phone told her it was 2.30 a.m., which meant it would be about four or five hours to dawn. Once it started to get lighter, hopefully her paranoia would ease.

Taking a seat on the sofa, the dog at her feet, she pulled the photo of John from her pocket and set it down on the coffee table in front of her.

When she was back home in Manchester, she would begin the hunt for her father. Although she only had his Christian name and this picture, it was a start.

He had worked for Nigel and Annie back at their home near Oxford. Perhaps if Lola went there and asked around locally, someone might recognise him.

It had been a blow learning that both of her birth parents were dead, but now she felt she had been handed another chance. If John was alive, she was determined to find him.

Again she wondered why Daniel and Rose had lied to her, pretending that Nigel had been her father. What could they possibly have to gain from having her believe that?

Daniel had seemed to think that Lola might be after a share of his inheritance, but if they had different fathers, surely it helped prove his case that she was due nothing.

None of it made any sense.

Unless it was Jimmy who was trying to trick her. Maybe even making a joke at her expense. After all, the adoption people had Nigel Whitlock listed as her father.

Lola didn't believe it, though. She knew in her gut that Jimmy had told her the truth. His slip-up at dinner had seemed genuine, not contrived, and he had seemed nervous telling her about John when she pushed. Almost as if he feared he would be in trouble with Rose and Daniel.

And then there was the photo amongst Annie's belongings, and the sketches too.

No. She was convinced John was her father.

And was his identity the only secret the Whitlocks were hiding from her?

They had been behaving oddly ever since she had arrived.

The sooner she was out of this house, the better.

She wondered what Quinn would make of it all when she told him, wishing she had been able to message him to let him know she was stranded here for the night.

Would he be worrying about her? She had promised she would WhatsApp him to let him know she had arrived safely.

He was the only person she had told where she was going.

As soon as she was somewhere where she could get a phone signal, she would message him so he knew she was okay.

He remained on her mind as she stayed in front of the fire, and although the room was large, the house dark and mostly silent, the crackling of the flames burning through wood comforted her, a little of the tension easing out of her shoulders.

It was going to be okay.

She had started to drift off when a noise pulled her to.

The sound, she realised, eyes open wide and sitting bolt upright, was that of a toilet flushing.

At first, she assumed it must have come from upstairs, but it felt much closer, definitely like it was on this level.

A downstairs cloakroom, perhaps.

Again she wondered who it was.

Daniel was sleeping in his study, but Lola assumed he

needed assistance to get in and out of bed. That left Jimmy or Rose, but why would they come downstairs to use the toilet when there was a perfectly good bathroom on the first floor?

Whatever the reason, whoever it was would likely put in an appearance any moment now and come to join her by the fire.

She waited, her money on Jimmy, but he didn't appear and neither did Rose.

As the seconds ticked by, Lola grew more curious.

Although she was comfortable beside the fire and reluctant to move, it was going to bother her if she didn't find out. Switching on her phone torch again, she got up from the sofa – not objecting this time when Monty started to follow.

As she headed out of the living room and down the corridor into the main hallway, she was reminded how intimidating the darkness was.

The faint sound of the cistern still flowing came from the direction of the kitchen and remembering the noises she had heard when she was in the cupboard, and the discarded plate and glass she had found in the kitchen, she suspected Jimmy was the more likely of the two to want a middle-of-the-night snack.

She found the toilet. The hallway where the cupboard was led down to a T-junction, the cloakroom to the left and the door still ajar.

There were other rooms too, but Lola wasn't interested in exploring.

As there was no one about and she wasn't able to locate who had used the cloakroom, she resigned herself to the fact it would remain a mystery, starting to retrace her steps.

As she did so, she passed another room, one she had missed as it had been behind her. But now it drew her attention, a warm glow visible through the crack in the door.

Pushing it open, she realised there was a fire lit in this room too.

The room looked like some kind of library. The walls were lined with floor-to-ceiling shelves and filled with books. But those weren't what drew Lola's attention.

Instead she was focused on the figure standing in front of the fireplace.

Tall and imposing, a heavy beard visible in the dancing shadows of the flames.

Daniel.

His legs worked.

She didn't speak his name aloud, didn't make any sound at all, but then Monty whined, and becoming aware of their presence, Daniel turned abruptly, staring right at her.

Shock had her brain trying to process what her eyes were seeing, while her feet rooted her to the spot.

'You can walk,' she gasped, her voice so low that he might not have heard her if the silence in the room hadn't been so deathly. In that long drawn-out moment, it was as though even the fire was holding its breath.

Daniel's expression mirrored hers, making her realise just how badly she had caught him out, but it quickly morphed into anger as he took a step towards her.

'I need you to come here, please,' he commanded, and although he didn't raise his voice, there was a menace to his words.

While Lola had no idea of the significance of what she had just learnt, she understood in that moment it had placed her in grave danger.

Run.

The instruction finally reached her legs.

Without a word, she turned and fled from the room.

30

'Tell me again exactly what you said to her.'

Jimmy could tell from Rose's dismayed expression that she was disappointed, but as he had hoped, she hadn't lost her temper with him, instead questioning him calmly. It was the reason he had confessed to her first.

After he had gone to bed for the second time, he had fallen asleep straight away, no doubt thanks to the topping up of booze he had pumped into his bloodstream.

Unfortunately, as the alcohol levels in his body decreased, his sleep became restless and he found himself tossing and turning. It was the usual pattern for him, but this time the bitter cold of the house didn't help and as Lola had crept into his consciousness and fragments of their conversation came back to him, he'd worried himself fully awake.

He had confessed that Nigel Whitlock wasn't her father.

Fuck.

Why, Jimmy? Why did you have to open your big mouth?

A rhetorical question. He knew exactly why. The alcohol made him act recklessly, thinking he was protecting them all.

Booze was his worst enemy, but he also couldn't cope without it, needing to numb his fuck-up of a life. He already knew that he would manage a few hours sober, but by late morning he would start repeating the cycle.

For now he was alert. Suffering, but alert; his mouth furry and dry, and his head thumping.

Unable to sleep without unburdening his sins, he had gone to wake up his sister.

He had known she was in bed alone as they had decided it wasn't worth the risk of Lola seeing her brother upstairs. Not after she had learnt the lift was out of order and they had no way of explaining how he had climbed a flight of stairs.

Another screw-up of Jimmy's. Though, at least it wasn't as big as this one.

Rose hadn't been impressed when he had woken her to confess, but at least she was listening.

He repeated the conversation he'd had with Lola, skimming over the part where he had mentioned where Rose kept the boxes of Annie's and Nigel's things. 'She was like a dog with a bone,' he said, trying to make her believe that he hadn't had a choice. 'She knew we were lying to her and she wasn't going to let it drop.'

That was good, lay it on thick. This was all Lola's doing.

'She is going to ask questions and wonder why we kept it from her,' Rose muttered, shaking her head.

'She only knows his first name. John is hardly enough to go on. We're safe. Perhaps we can tell her it was just a joke.'

Jimmy had hoped to reassure her, but instead Rose sank her fingers into her hair, pulling it tight against her skull, her expression panicked as the edges of her temper frayed.

'We purposely let her believe Nigel was her father so she

didn't go looking for John. If the truth comes out about what we did…'

'Okay, sis. You're overreacting a bit, don't you think?'

Telling an angry woman she was overreacting or to calm down was never the smartest idea and it was a mistake Jimmy had made on more than one occasion.

'You think I'm overreacting? Honestly, Jimmy, I wonder what goes on in your head sometimes. We've been so careful to keep our secret hidden!'

'Okay, okay.' He held his hands up to try to pacify. 'We'll find a way to fix it.'

'*We*?' Rose shook her head. 'Oh yes, of course *we*. Because you always need help to fix the messes you create.'

'I meant *I* will,' Jimmy quickly backtracked. 'I will fix it.'

She glared at him. 'And how exactly are you going to do that?'

Honestly, Jimmy had no idea. He had to say something to appease his sister, though. She was getting upset. He searched his groggy brain, hoping the answer would come to him, as she arched an eyebrow, the weight of her stare – the blue eyes that had once seemed to mirror his, but now seemed much colder – piercing into him.

'Well, I'm waiting, Jimmy. How are you going to undo your mess?'

As he opened and closed his mouth, searching for the right words to reason with her, a commotion came from outside the room. A woman's scream.

What the hell?

Rose and Jimmy stared at each other for a moment, eyes wide, then, without saying anything, Rose grabbed her torch and both of them ran for the open door. As they crossed the landing, something – someone – came charging up the stairs.

Lola, Jimmy realised, as the beam of the torch fell on her. She looked terrified.

'What's going on?' Rose demanded, a hand reaching out to catch Lola's arm and pull her to a halt.

Before Lola could answer, the dog barked below, then there were further footsteps heading up the stairs and she tried to jerk herself free.

Jimmy's jaw dropped as he realised who it was.

'Daniel?' Rose snapped, her tone warning, though she seemed as shocked as Jimmy. 'What are you doing?'

'It's over. She knows I can walk.'

'What's going on here?' Lola demanded, and although she was trying to sound angry, Jimmy could hear the fear in her tone.

For what felt like a long moment, no one spoke, but there was enough hint of menace in the exchanged looks for them all to realise this spelt trouble.

Lola seemed to understand this too, because the freeze frame abruptly restarted, descending into chaos, as letting out a sob of both shock and fear she ripped her arm away from Rose's grip, charging across the landing towards the second-floor staircase.

'She's getting away.'

'Quick, stop her!'

As the three of them gave chase, Jimmy understood it no longer mattered that he had told Lola about her real father.

What she had just uncovered was so much worse.

31

As Lola ran across the landing and up the narrow second-floor staircase, she was glad her eyes had adjusted enough to see in the shadowy darkness.

In hindsight, she realised she had done all of this wrong. In the heat of the moment, she had simply reacted and now she wished she had tried to get out of the house, instead of running upstairs, where she was now effectively trapped.

Though going outside into the snow could have been equally perilous and she would have frozen, as there was no time to grab her coat and her boots were upstairs.

She had been left with no choice.

Into the bedroom, she slammed shut the door, aware that Daniel and Rose were close behind her, their footsteps already on the stairs.

She needed something to put against it. The dresser was nearest and it looked heavy. There was no time to think and she had to act now. Pushing all of her weight behind the solid piece of furniture, she managed to scrape it across the floor, pushing it into place just as the knob turned and the door wedged open a crack.

Another hard shove and it clicked shut again.

'Lola, we need to talk. Can you come out please?'

It was Daniel's voice and he sounded calm. Reasonable even.

But she had seen the rage on his face when she had realised he didn't need the wheelchair. In that moment, knowing that he had fucked up, he had looked like he wanted to kill her.

'I don't think that's a good idea,' she told him, surprised at the steeliness in her tone. She might have sounded like she was holding it together and perhaps that was a good thing, but inside she was a shaking, terrified mess.

'Look, I know we have some explaining to do about Daniel and the wheelchair,' Rose said. 'But if you come downstairs, we will talk.'

When Lola didn't respond, not believing a word she was saying, Rose tried again.

'I promise you that you're overreacting. Once we have explained it, you'll understand why we tried to keep it a secret.'

'Please, just open the door and let's go downstairs,' Daniel added. 'I don't like knowing that we've frightened you.'

That was rich, Lola thought, given the way he had so far treated her.

'Tell me here,' she demanded. 'What did you have to gain by pretending you needed a wheelchair?'

It made absolutely no sense why he would lie.

'Lola, please,' Rose simpered. 'It's freezing cold up here. Let's talk about it downstairs where there is a nice warm fire.'

They were both making far too much of an effort to sound pleasant and she didn't trust them one bit. But while she didn't want to go downstairs with them, she was also fearful of staying in this room. Up here on the second floor, how was she supposed to get help? She was trapped.

Perhaps she should play along, let them think that she believed them.

If she did that, would they let her go?

No. She had seen their exchanged look before she ran. Whatever they were up to, it was important to them they kept it hidden, and she didn't even dare think about what would happen to her if she left this room.

Crap, Lola. What the hell are you going to do?

As the silence stretched, she replayed moments from the last few hours.

She had asked Daniel about the wheelchair earlier and he had blatantly lied to her, telling her he would never walk again.

Why did he feel the need to pretend?

And they had lied about her father, pretending she was Nigel's daughter.

This could end very badly.

If she finds out, she'll wish she had never come here.

Daniel had never wanted to meet her and although he had eventually invited her to the house, it had been with reluctance.

Because they were scared she might learn the truth.

Still, she felt there was a piece of the puzzle missing and she had no idea what it was.

It had suddenly gone very quiet outside the door. Were they both still outside?

The sudden creak of the doorknob turning caught her off guard. As it opened slightly, the dresser slid towards her, and alarmed, Lola threw her weight against it again, trying to push it back into place.

For the next few moments, they gave up on trying to persuade her to come out with gentle words, instead resorting to force, and there was a tussle as she fought to keep herself barricaded in the room.

Somehow she managed to hold the door shut and when they finally gave up, she heard them talking urgently in hushed whispers. Then came the sound of footsteps and she strained her ears trying to figure out if it was both of them leaving.

Lola waited, the silence stretching.

Was this a trick? Were they trying to lull her into a false sense of security?

She was too scared to open the door, fearful they would be waiting on the other side.

Fuck! What the hell was she supposed to do now?

She needed to somehow get out of this house and find help. Was it possible there was a way down out of the window?

The room was up on the second floor, so it seemed unlikely, but she needed to at least explore all options. She didn't have a coat, which would be a problem, but at least her boots were up here.

She was about to take a chance and move away from the door, when she heard movement again out in the corridor.

Drawing in a shaky breath, she resumed her position in front of the dresser.

What the hell were they up to?

The scraping against the latch answered her question, though it still took her a moment to fully register what was happening.

Hearing a twisting click, to her horror she realised they had locked her in the room.

32

Quinn was up and out of the house early on Christmas Eve, borrowing Chloe's Dacia Duster for the drive to Ely. If the family decided to make the trip to see Darren's parents, they would be going in his car, so there was no urgency to return it.

Everywhere outside was still white, though the snow had mostly stopped, with just a few odd flurries, and gritters had been out on the roads in anticipation for heavy traffic as people made the last-minute rush home for the holidays.

Still, he took it easy, aware that the driving conditions were not good, arriving at Lola's hotel just after 8 a.m.

Before leaving the car, he checked his phone. No reply from Lola and there were no blue ticks against the WhatsApp message he had left her that morning. She hadn't even read it.

His hope was that she had switched her phone off for whatever reason, or it had broken, or run out of charge. That she had either made it to Norfolk and back again safely, or changed her mind when she saw how bad the weather was, instead turning back, and she was still asleep.

He didn't care if she had forgotten to update him, or decided she didn't want to update him, changing her mind about being in contact – well, okay, that was a lie, he did care. But he would figure a way to be okay with it, so long as Lola was safe.

That was why he pulled out his police badge when approaching the reception desk. Something he knew he shouldn't do but was willing to take a risk with on this occasion, as he didn't have time to argue over privacy laws, just needing to locate Lola.

Five minutes later, he was being let into her hotel room and he could see straight away that the bed hadn't been slept in.

The unease in his gut knotted a little bit tighter.

Where was she?

He had no intention of snooping through the travel bag that was sitting under the desk, certain it wouldn't help establish her whereabouts, so, after leaving his number, asking the hotel staff to contact him urgently if she returned, he left the hotel.

Back inside the Dacia, he ran the engine, letting the heating – cranked to full blast – do its thing, while he googled the address for Safe Hands. He was grateful that Lola had told him about the client she was in Ely to meet and that the company name had stuck in his mind.

By the time he arrived at the office, it was almost 8.30 a.m. and he was relieved to see lights on in reception. He pulled into the small car park, noting two vehicles occupying spots: one an Aston Martin, the other a VW Beetle. Neither car was going to be a rental, which suggested Lola wasn't here. Unless she had already returned the hire car.

A chiming alarm announced his arrival as the door opened

to the office and Quinn immediately heard footsteps approaching.

'Glad you finally decided to join us,' an irritated male voice said.

The owner of it appeared in the reception moments later, his eyes widening when he realised Quinn wasn't Lola.

'Who are you?'

To the point and a little bit rude, but a fair question.

'Quinn Mallory. I'm looking for Lola Henderson.'

'Aren't we all.'

Well, this guy was a delight.

Quinn ignored his sarcasm. 'You must be Rich Bradford,' he guessed, recalling the name of the arsehole who had pulled Lola in for meetings right before Christmas. She hadn't been exaggerating in her description of him. 'She's supposed to have a meeting here with you this morning, right?'

'*Was* supposed to,' Rich grumbled. 'We were meant to begin at eight. She's over half an hour late.'

Okay, this wasn't good. 'And you haven't heard from her at all? She didn't call to say she was running behind?'

Rich shook his head. 'If I had, I wouldn't be wasting my time standing here talking to you.' He looked curiously at Quinn now. 'How did you say you know Lola?'

'I didn't,' Quinn said bluntly, before softening his tone. Just because Rich was an arsehole didn't mean he had to act in kind. 'She's a friend and was supposed to get in touch. She didn't and I'm worried about her.'

'She told me she was seeing family last night. I'm guessing the party carried on a little too late and she's overslept.'

That might be Rich's assumption, but Quinn suspected otherwise. He wasn't going to get into the finer details about Lola driving to Norfolk or that the family she was going to see she had never met before. It was none of Rich's business and it would only waste more time. Besides, he didn't think anything he said would change Rich's view that this was all just a great inconvenience to him. Instead, he left his number, asking for a call if Lola showed up, then went back to the car.

Everything was suggesting that Lola had definitely left to drive to Norfolk last night. Had something happened to her en route?

Quinn spent a few minutes making calls to the local police station and nearest hospitals to see if there had been any accidents, but while driving conditions had been hazardous, nothing serious had been reported.

So was she still at her brother's?

Perhaps things had gone so well she had decided to stay for longer.

But why hadn't she let Quinn know she was safe and, more worryingly, why was her phone not receiving calls and messages?

She would have contacted Rich Bradford too if she couldn't make their meeting this morning. He might be a bit of a jerk, but Lola took her business seriously. She wasn't the type of person to let down a client. At least not without any kind of warning.

He thought back over their conversation on the train, remembering what information she had told him about her brother. His name was Daniel Whitlock and he recalled her saying the man had money. She had been a little bit intimidated by his wealth, worried in case he thought her motivation for getting in touch was financially related. Hadn't she said he lived in a manor house?

A quick Google search showed him there were four properties in Saham Toney that were worth over a million pounds.

He would check them all out.

Starting the engine, he pulled out of the car park. The roads still weren't great for a trip to Saham Toney, but at least the blizzard had passed and the gritters had been out.

It was time to go find Lola's brother and figure out what the hell had happened to her.

33

There is a saying that the best-laid plans of mice and men often go awry, and the one we have tried to put in motion has failed spectacularly.

It was an ambitious plan, I have to admit, but I had faith in it. Had the circumstances not battled against us, I am convinced we would have pulled it off. Alas, the weather, the power cut, plus Lola's poor driving skills, all let us down, and I suspect there is an aspect of fate playing a role too. Perhaps punishing us.

She should have been gone by now and we should be safe, but instead she stayed and chose to snoop. We know she found the photo of John. She left it on the coffee table in the living room. Although we don't know if she has managed to piece the truth together yet, she has seen and heard too much. Despite our best efforts to try to sweet-talk her out of the room, she's not stupid. If she goes away now, she will have too many questions. And that gives us a big problem.

What are we going to do about that?

The three of us have been up all night, sitting around the

fire in the living room as darkness gave way to dawn, and then sunrise. The power is still off, but at least now we have some natural light. It is a beautiful morning, despite the snow, the sun blazing low in the winter's sky, and everyone has had breakfast – well, except for Lola. But it was her stubborn idea to barricade herself in the bedroom and not listen to reason. And because she behaved that way, instead of thinking about the upcoming festivities, we are discussing the best way to deal with her.

For now she is locked in the bedroom up on the second floor, and there are concerns about whether she can escape from there. The door is solid, and the window her only way out, but the roof will be icy and slippery, the drop will maim or possibly kill her.

I don't think she will risk it.

Though if she did, it might solve our dilemma.

We were all out early, digging her car out of the snow and pushing it towards the house and into the garage. It can't stay in there, but at least it is out of sight for now, until some decisions have been made. And we have turned off the Wi-Fi, not wanting her phone to connect to the outside world if the power suddenly comes back on.

We are confident no one will be looking for Lola. At least not over the next few days. She said she has no one at home waiting for her and she has already told us she intended to spend Christmas alone. Still, we can't keep her here indefinitely, so we need a plan.

'We'll say the doctors managed to cure you,' Jimmy suggests.

If only it was that easy.

'Don't be ridiculous,' I say, rolling my eyes. 'We all know Lola isn't gullible enough to believe that.'

'All she would have to do is go away and do her research,' I am backed up from across the room. 'Besides, she will still question why we felt the need to lie and try to trick her. Use your brain, Jimmy.'

'At least I'm coming up with suggestions,' he complains. 'Unlike you two.'

'Yes, ridiculous ones that aren't going to help us at all.'

'Well, perhaps if you idiots hadn't agreed to let her come here in the first place, we wouldn't be in this mess.' Jimmy glares. 'Why the hell didn't you just keep fobbing her off? She would've gone away eventually.'

'Don't blame me. It wasn't my stupid idea.'

'Stop!' I snap over the raised voices. 'We need to keep cool heads.'

As the hours have ticked by with no solution in sight, tensions have been rising and we have started to turn on each other. We need to stop and work together, particularly as we know the wheelchair is not our only problem. There is the truth about her father too.

How will we explain hiding that from her? Especially now she knows his name.

Plus we've kept her locked in the bedroom for hours.

What is to stop her going to the police and reporting us holding her prisoner?

Much as I don't want to suggest it, I am starting to think we can't risk letting Lola leave this house.

Not ever.

34

Lola had no idea how long she had been locked in the bedroom.

The last time she had looked at her phone, it had been just before 5 a.m., but to her alarm she realised her battery was on 9 per cent. She couldn't risk the device dying, so she had switched it off for now.

Having watched the sunlight filtering into the bedroom some time ago, she knew that it was morning. The ground outside was still covered in snow and the temperature in the house no warmer than it had been overnight. The blouse she wore offered no protection from the cold, and even with the blanket from the bed wrapped around her shoulders, she was still shivering.

Right now, she should be in a meeting room in Ely and Rich Bradford was probably choking on his coffee in rage that she hadn't shown up. There was nothing she could do about that and he was the least of her problems as she tried to figure out how the hell she was going to get out of this mess.

Just after sunrise, she had heard a commotion outside,

quickly going to the window, hopeful it might be someone coming to the house. Those hopes had plummeted when she had realised it was Rose, Daniel and Jimmy. They were moving her rental car.

At first, she had foolishly thought it was to prevent her leaving, which was unnecessary as the car wasn't driveable, but then she understood. They wanted it off the driveway. They were trying to hide all trace that she had been here.

What were they planning on doing to her?

For now all she could do was wait to find out.

She was desperately thirsty. A mint she found in the bottom of her bag had helped a little, but hours had passed and now she was beginning to worry they were going to just leave her locked in here. Unless the door was opened, she had no hope of escape.

Her bladder was aching with the need to pee and hunger pains were creeping in along with her thirst. She could take care of the first problem by using a decorative urn that stood on top of the dresser, but pride told her she wasn't that desperate. Yet.

Quinn was the only one who knew where she was. Would he care enough to be concerned and come looking for her?

She racked her brain, trying to remember what information she had given him.

Her brother's name, yes, and he knew she was going to Saham Toney.

Had she told him about the house? Mentioned that it was called Midwinter Manor? She couldn't remember. But she had said Daniel had money, sharing her concerns that he might think she was after his fortune.

They had talked about catching the train back together today, but perhaps the trains weren't running and he had decided to stay with his sister over Christmas. He might have messaged her to say that's what he was doing, the WhatsApp sitting unread on her phone.

As paranoia crept in, making her doubt every possible scenario, she realised she couldn't rely on him to be her saviour.

No, she had to figure a way out of this situation by herself.

If the damned power would come back on, she could use her phone to call for help. She was connected to the house Wi-Fi. One quick emergency call and everything would be okay.

But she couldn't wait for that to happen. And remembering Rose had mentioned sometimes they were without power for days, Lola knew that she had to come up with something else.

Already she had checked out the one potential escape route. The window.

It looked dangerous and she wasn't sure she dared risk getting out onto the roof while the weather was so bad. Besides, even if it was viable, they would be able to track her footprints in the snow.

Perhaps she should have gone back downstairs with them. Although she knew they wouldn't let her go, if they thought she had believed their lies they might have dropped their guard and she would have had the chance to escape.

It was too late now and she couldn't pretend she had suddenly changed her mind.

She was hoping they weren't going to leave her in here indefinitely and when they did eventually come back, it was going to be her one opportunity of escape.

She needed to be ready for that and it might mean fighting her way past them.

Looking over at the candlestick she had earlier considered as a weapon, she wondered if it would be enough. Especially as there were three of them and she would probably only have one shot at getting away.

Could she fool them into believing she had left through the window?

If she left it wide open then hid behind the door, would she have time to escape while they went to investigate?

The key would hopefully be in the lock and she could trap them in the room while she made a run for it.

It was a chancy plan, but perhaps one she could finesse.

Deciding that she needed to explore all options, Lola pulled open the drawers of the dresser. Perhaps there was something else she could use as a weapon.

There was nothing she found that would help. One side was packed with extra linen for the bed and she briefly wondered if she could tie everything together to make an escape rope. There weren't enough sheets, though, and she didn't trust they would be strong enough if she tore them.

She glanced at the heavy drapes around the four-poster bed. Could she use those?

A test tug of the fabric told her they would be too cumbersome to knot.

In the other side of the dresser, there was a writing pad and pen – no use in her current situation as the house was miles from anywhere. There were spare candles, though nothing to light them, and in the bottom drawer she found a storage box filled with various items.

With nothing else to do to pass the time, she went through the contents, establishing quickly that this box belonged to Rose. The scent of her floral perfume was over everything. There were a few scarves and hats, a smaller box containing costume jewellery, and a folder that held her nursing certificate of completion, birth certificate and passport, as well as other documentation. Much of it was older and from before she would have met Daniel. Lola flicked through it all, though there was nothing much of interest.

Underneath everything were a handful of loose photographs. A couple of them showed Rose when she was younger, maybe in her late teens, hanging out with friends, then there was one of her, pretty and glamorous in her wedding dress. In another picture there was a man alongside Rose. They were sat at a table and he was looking at her, while Rose smiled coyly at the camera. Immediately he looked familiar.

It took Lola a second to realise where she knew him from. It was the man from the Lamborghini. Daniel's friend, Brett.

He was older in this picture, his hair longer and curling around his ears and the nape of his neck, and from the way he was looking at Rose it was clear he was besotted with her.

Did Daniel know?

More importantly, did Rose realise?

She had the photo in a box of her personal things. It would suggest she did and that perhaps she had encouraged his attention.

There was one more item underneath the photos.

A gift bag, Lola saw, taking it out. Inside was a slim jewellery box. She opened it up to find it was empty. The shape of it, though, suggested it had contained a bracelet. As she went to put it back, she realised there was a card inside the bag.

The heart on the front left no doubt as to the nature of the gift. It had been intimate. Inside, written in an elaborate scrawl it said, *To Rose. All my love, Brett xxx.*

Lola recalled them saying that Brett had spent Christmas

with them a couple of years ago. Did Daniel have any idea that his best friend and wife had been having an affair?

And where was Brett now?

Had things ended between them, or were he and Rose still secretly seeing each other?

More importantly, was this something she could use against them if it became necessary?

If she could somehow create a divide between them and make them turn on each other, it might allow for an opportunity.

Lola was certain Daniel didn't know about the affair. He didn't strike her as a very forgiving man.

Keeping the card and the photo of Rose and Brett to one side, she replaced everything else back in the box and returned it to the drawer.

Just as she was getting to her feet, a rumbling noise from deep within the house had her head jerking towards the bedroom door.

What the hell was that?

It took a few moments to work it out, but then the hiss of water in the pipes had her glancing at the radiator.

Was the heating back on?

And the electricity?

Hope surged as she flicked the light switch, her moment of relief when the overhead chandelier lit up overwhelmed by a burst of panic that her phone was switched off. She needed to turn it back on and call the police quickly in case the power went off again.

Fumbling with the buttons, she held it in her trembling hand, staring at the screen and willing it to hurry up and load, fearful that she was going to lose this one precious chance.

When the phone was finally ready for her use, she almost wept.

Thank God.

Call the police. Message Quinn. Get the hell out of here.

Hopefully a simple to-do list.

She waited for it to connect to the Wi-Fi, eager to call 999 and alert the police to her situation, aware she needed to get help fast. But nothing was happening.

Clicking into her Wi-Fi settings, she realised the network wasn't even showing as available.

What was going on? They should be back online by now.

Unless they had turned the Wi-Fi off.

Of course they had. They had locked her in this room, so they would want to be sure she couldn't contact anyone.

Lola wanted to sob in despair.

The odds might be stacked against her, but something had to give, she reminded herself, determined not to break down. Becoming hysterical about her situation wouldn't help in the slightest. She needed to keep a cool head.

Her chance to escape would come. She just had to be ready to take it.

35

'Anything for me?'

Rose was in the hallway, having opened the morning mail and cursing at the contents, and she flinched when she heard Daniel's voice behind her.

His wheelchair was too quiet when moving on the hard floor.

'No, afraid not,' she told him, crumpling up the one letter that had arrived in her hand, glad the dress she wore had pockets as she hid it out of sight.

Not quite quick enough, she realised, seeing him narrow his eyes.

'Just a catalogue trying to tempt me to resubscribe,' she added lightly, grateful when he didn't ask which one, instead turning his attention to the daffodils she had picked from the garden and arranged in a vase on the console table.

'Fresh flowers,' he commented.

'I thought they'd brighten the hallway up.'

'They're pretty. As are you, my love.'

After he had learnt about her affair, he had stopped paying

her compliments, but in recent days he had made more of an effort and it was appreciated.

'Do you fancy any breakfast?' she asked. 'I'm going to make some poached eggs.'

'That would be nice.'

He wheeled himself up to the table, while Rose fished out the saucepan she wanted from one of the lower cupboards, then made casual conversation while she boiled the water for the eggs, and she tried to push the letter from her mind.

It was just the two of them. Brett had left the house early, muttering something about an appointment, while Jimmy was still in bed and Agnes in her room. Rose had taken her mother up a plate of toast and some juice in a plastic cup, locking the door after her. A habit she had started doing recently. When Daniel had suggested it was cruel, she had pointed out that the house had too many hazards. It was safer this way, she insisted, even though she knew deep down he was right.

Nothing more had been said about her affair following their conversation a couple of weeks ago and although everything he had said that day was still very clear in her mind – especially the threat that he might want her to help him kill Brett – she was now hoping it had all been a sick joke, one to punish her and make her cool the affair. Even if Daniel had said he didn't want that.

Rose had been on tenterhooks waiting to hear more about these challenges he had spoken about setting, but it was almost as if he had forgotten about them, and she certainly wasn't going to bring the subject up.

She had already made efforts to back away from Brett, terrified that she might end up the loser in this scenario. While she had enjoyed their time together, her marriage was too precious to her. He had satisfied her needs, but she had no intention of ever leaving her husband for him. Continuing their affair came at too great a risk.

Since Daniel had confronted her, she had consciously tried to avoid being alone with Brett, though it wasn't easy when they were living together, and she could tell that Brett, who had at first been confused, was now getting frustrated as he tried to get her to one side.

She hadn't made doing so easy for him, disappearing out early most mornings. She was spending a lot of time at the gym, making use of their pool and spa facilities, or taking herself off to different towns on shopping jaunts.

Daniel was almost always at home, so when she was in the house she had taken to spending more time with him, and perhaps it was now that her secret was out in the open between them, but it felt like he was making more of an effort with her.

If he was aware she had backed away from Brett, then he didn't say and Rose hoped that it was something they could now put behind them, though it bothered her that Brett continued to stay at the house and Daniel made no move to ask him to leave.

She couldn't say anything about it. Not without bringing the awkward situation up.

'Do you fancy doing anything today?' she asked brightly, clearing the plates away from the table after they had eaten.

'What did you have in mind?'

Truthfully, Daniel did very little these days.

When Rose had first met him, he had led quite an active social life and he often wanted to be out and about, but since his mother's death he had wanted to stay close to home, where he spent much of his time locked away in his study talking in online forums with people he had never met.

'It's a nice morning. I thought perhaps we could go out and get some fresh air.'

She was always careful not to say 'for a walk'. When she had first started working for the Whitlocks, she had slipped up a couple of times, grateful when Daniel, amused, had laughed it off. But in the months after Annie's death, he had snapped at her when she said walk.

'How the fuck do you propose I do that?'

Although it was four years ago, that moment had stuck with her.

'Is it warm out?' he asked now.

'It's a pleasant temperature and the sun's out. I went into the woods yesterday and the bluebells have already started to sprout. It's pretty in there.'

The woods surrounding the house had often been her solitude, but yesterday she had gone there to escape Brett. Although they wouldn't be able to go off the main path, as she liked to do, delighting herself with the myriad trails that snaked between the trees, at least it was level enough for Daniel's chair. It would do him good to get outside.

For a moment, she thought he was going to say no, but then he surprised her.

'Okay then.'

They spent over two hours out wandering through the woods, some of it in conversation, but mostly in companionable silence, with only birdsong and the crunch of twigs on the dirt floor beneath them offering any noise.

Again, nothing was said about Brett, but as his car overtook them as they headed back up the drive, Rose's stomach tightened and she noticed Daniel, who had been telling her about an occasion he had gone hiking, suddenly fell silent.

Brett was already out of the car and watching their

approach by the time they neared the house, and Rose didn't miss the look he gave her. It was almost accusatory, as if she had done something wrong. How dare she go out with her husband?

'Where have you two been?'

'For a walk,' Daniel told him.

There was a challenge in the words and he held eye contact with Brett, who glanced at the wheelchair but chose – perhaps wisely – to say nothing.

Instead, he unlocked the front door, stepping back for Rose and Daniel to enter.

As Rose passed him, his fingers brushed against hers and she flinched away.

'I'm going to put the kettle on. Let's go and have a cup of tea, Daniel.'

'Do you mind bringing mine through to my study? I have something I need to check on.'

Shit.

'I fancy a cup too,' Brett told her.

Rose pretended not to hear him, aware that he was following after her as she headed into the kitchen. Ignoring him, she filled the kettle at the sink, stiffening when his warm body pushed up against her back, pinning her to the counter.

'I've missed you,' he whispered close to her ear, his breath hot against her skin.

She managed to slide out from beneath him. 'Careful,' she hissed. 'Daniel might come in.'

'He said he was going through to his study. We're fine.'

'We still need to be vigilant,' she pointed out, switching on the kettle to boil.

'You didn't say that the last time I fucked you on the table in here,' Brett reminded her, yanking up her dress.

Heat spread to Rose's cheeks remembering the encounter and the huge risk they had taken. No wonder Daniel had caught them out. Their affair hadn't been discreet.

'Is that why you've been avoiding me?' Brett asked when she said nothing. He sounded sulky now, a mean edge to his voice. 'You're having second thoughts.'

'I'm not avoiding you,' she told him, purposely keeping her own tone light. There was no way she was going to admit the truth, that Daniel had found out about them, frightened of what fireworks she might set off.

It would be easier if this thing with Brett just fizzled out and he moved on to pastures new.

'So what is this then?' he demanded. 'You think you can just have your fun and then drop me?'

'*This* is nothing.' To pacify him, she turned and smoothed the palm of her hand over his cheek, mustering up a smile. 'Like I said, I just think we should be more careful. That means no more fucking on the table.'

He caught her hand roughly, tugging her close against him when she tried to pull away. 'Looked like you and Danny boy were having a nice romantic time in the woods this morning.'

Rose glared at him. 'He wanted to go out for some fresh air. I'm his carer as well as his wife. Do you really have a problem with that?'

Instead of answering her, Brett twisted her hand, sending pain shooting up her wrist.

She winced. 'Ouch, that hurts. Let me go. I mean it, Brett.'

'You'd better not be fucking with me. I don't like to play games, Rose. If I find out that you're messing me around, you're going to regret it.'

'I'm not. I swear,' she promised him, her heart thumping,

and a little unnerved by his threat. 'But we do need to be careful.'

'I'm not sure I believe you.'

For a moment, they were at a stalemate, staring at each other, neither willing to back down. Then a cough from the hallway startled them both, eyes widening as Jimmy entered the room.

Brett was lightning quick, dropping Rose's hand and stepping away.

'All right, mate?' he asked smoothly, turning his attention to Jimmy, who looked too hungover to have spotted a thing.

As the two of them spoke, Rose rubbed at her sore wrist, a little shaken by Brett's reaction. Was he really so jealous of Daniel that he didn't want her spending time with him?

She had assumed this was a passionate fling for Brett too, but now she was worrying she had judged him wrong, and she was fearful that unless she could persuade him to back off, then this whole mess could implode around her.

No matter the fallout, she could not allow that to happen.

36

PRESENT DAY

Now the power was back on, the house was really starting to warm up, while the flickering lights of the two huge pine trees Rose had decorated – one in the hall, the other in the living room – and the background music of the television, which was tuned to a festive music channel, was making it feel Christmassy again.

Beneath the tree in the living room was a pile of wrapped gifts, and Monty lay beside them, keeping a close eye. Jimmy knew the dog was hopeful there would be something for him. Knowing Rose, she had probably wrapped a couple of bones up and maybe a squeaky toy. Most of the time she saw Monty as an inconvenience, but even he was spoilt at this time of year.

His sister had always loved Christmas, though they had endured a few lousy ones after their dad had left, their mum refusing to celebrate. Perhaps it was because of those miserable years that Rose now pulled out all the stops, especially since moving into Midwinter Manor. She made sure the house was impeccably decorated, and went overboard buying festive food and presents.

Of course, this year the only gift they all wanted was a solution to their problem upstairs. Until they had figured out what to do about Lola Henderson, no one could relax and enjoy Christmas.

It didn't help that Jimmy's head was raging with the mother of all hangovers and although the alcohol would still be in his bloodstream, he was starting to sober. If it had been his choice, he would have carried on drinking throughout the night, but Rose had put her foot down after Lola had been locked in the bedroom, telling him she needed him fully aware. He had tried to point out that he needed a drink to help him think straight, but she was having none of it.

'We can't keep her locked up there indefinitely,' Rose reminded them both, earning herself a scowl from across the room.

'But if we let her go she will tell everyone what she saw and what we did to her!' Jimmy pointed out, panicked.

'Look, first things first, we should look at her phone,' Rose suggested. 'We need to see who she's been speaking with and find out who knows she was coming here.'

It was a good idea, but they would need to get it from her first.

As they discussed the logistics of that, a noise rumbled outside. It was an engine, Jimmy realised, as the three of them looked at each other.

Shit.

Rose's eyes widened in realisation. 'Crap. It's the Ocado delivery!'

They were all on their feet now, Monty included, as he wondered what they were all so excitable about.

Glancing out of the window, Jimmy saw the familiar van

heading towards the house. He looked at the others, panicked, as they all reached the same conclusion.

They needed to get to Lola before she could alert the driver she was here.

37

When the chance came, Lola grabbed at it with both hands.

She had been pacing the room restlessly, finally giving in to the urge to empty her bladder and using the urn she had earlier spotted for the task. It was humiliating, but what choice did she have?

Daniel and Rose had locked her up here for hours and she was desperately thirsty and hungry too. The one blessing was at least she had started to warm up, the radiator now hot to the touch.

Just how long did they plan to leave her up here? They couldn't keep her locked away indefinitely.

Lost in thought, she almost missed the delivery vehicle.

Up here on the second floor with the window shut, she was too far away to hear the engine, and it was by chance she happened to glance out towards the driveway, seeing it heading towards the house.

An Ocado van. She had to alert the driver.

With sudden urgency, she tried to open the window, frustrated to find the lock sticking. She likely wouldn't get another chance; she couldn't let him leave.

He was already out of the van and unloading groceries, and Lola pounded frantically on the pane of glass, hoping to attract his attention.

When he didn't look up, she tried the lock again, her finger and thumb hurting as she attempted to force it aside. It was with sheer determination that the catch finally gave.

Ignoring the pain, she forced the window open, screaming as loud as she could.

'Help me, please! They're keeping me a prisoner! Call the police!'

He wasn't looking up and frantic, Lola tried again.

She was so focused on trying to get his attention, she didn't hear the sound of footsteps on the stairs or the key unlocking in the door, but she heard the loud scrape as the dresser slid across the floor; the door opening wide. Her head snapped around.

Daniel stood in the doorway, a menacing sight, Jimmy hovering behind him.

And in the moment before hell broke loose, Lola had to decide whether to keep yelling to the delivery driver, or to try to make a run for it.

As Daniel took a sudden step forward, she panicked, acting on instinct, brushing past him as he grabbed for her and barrelling into Jimmy, hoping the momentum would knock him off his feet.

Instead, he managed to hook an arm around her chest, the reek of stale alcohol almost choking her as she fought to free herself. Kicking and screaming at him to let go, she punched out with her elbows, hearing a satisfying grunt as she hit soft flesh, pleased when she made him yelp.

He loosened his grip, but it wasn't enough. And then Daniel had hold of her ankles and despite her frantically bucking and squirming, aware that her one chance was slipping away from her, they managed with ease to carry her back into the bedroom.

'Why are you doing this?' she demanded.

Neither of them answered as she was unceremoniously dumped face down on the floor. A heavy weight pinned her down as she tried to get up.

Daniel, she realised, begging him to stop. Her words were silenced as he clamped his hand over her mouth.

'Close the window, then find something to tie her up with,' he barked at Jimmy, as Lola frantically tried to break free. 'Keep still,' he growled, as the window slammed shut, then drawers opened and closed behind them.

She ignored the instruction. Whatever they were about to do to her, she wouldn't make it easy for them.

Were they going to kill her?

Although she shuddered at the thought, she wasn't stupid. They all knew that if she left here, she would go to the police and report them.

'Here you go.'

Whatever Jimmy had found, he threw to Daniel, who roughly yanked her arms behind her. Briefly freeing her mouth, he wrapped something around her wrists, binding them tightly together, and Lola used the opportunity to scream for all she was worth.

It was short-lived, though, his hand returning the moment he was done.

Knowing her opportunity to get help was over, she had no choice but to wait as the seconds ticked by.

'He's getting back in his van,' Jimmy announced, on watch duty by the window.

Daniel gave it another few seconds, before releasing her.

Lola managed to roll over, her hands touching the floor at the small of her back, as she stared up at them.

Her heart was racing and fear spiking through her, but she tried not to show them how scared she was.

'You won't get away with this,' she snarled, trying, without success, to pull her hands free.

Neither man was taking notice of her as they spoke quietly between themselves and a few moments later there were more footsteps on the landing, as Rose joined them.

She glanced briefly at Lola, before looking away.

Did she feel guilt at what they had done?

'We need her phone,' Daniel said. 'Find out if anyone is looking for her.'

The others muttered their agreement and started looking for it. When they didn't find it, Daniel turned back to Lola.

'Where is it?' he demanded. He had a mean expression on his face that suggested he wanted to hurt her, and in that moment she wondered what kind of monster her brother was.

'Why are you doing this to me? I won't tell anyone about this, I promise. Just let me go and I'll leave here and never try to contact you again.'

'Where's your phone?' he snapped again, completely ignoring her words.

Rose and Jimmy had searched the room for it and Lola knew any time now they would check her pockets. They were going to get it and there was nothing she could do to stop them, but it was her lifeline. She couldn't just hand it over.

As though reading her mind, Rose looked at her. 'It's not in here. She must have it on her.'

With zero respect for her boundaries, Daniel pushed Lola to the floor again, looming over her as he patted her down, despite her protests.

He pulled the phone from the back pocket of her jeans, handing it to Rose.

'I'll go turn on the Wi-Fi,' Jimmy offered.

Rose nodded, turning to her husband as Jimmy disappeared downstairs. 'Hold her still so I can unlock the screen.'

Daniel nodded and twisted his hand tight in Lola's hair and she winced in pain as he tugged hard, keeping her still as Rose held the handset over her face.

As Rose scrolled through her phone, Daniel barked questions at her.

'Who knows you're here?'

'Where have you been staying in Ely?'

'Who is expecting to see you over the next few days?'

Lola refused to answer him, instead pleading again for them to let her go.

'She has several missed calls and voicemails from someone called Rich and also from a Quinn,' Rose said, glancing up from her scrolling now the phone was back on Wi-Fi. 'We can listen to those and figure out if they're going to be a problem.'

'Who are these men?' Daniel demanded.

Lola searched her scrambled mind, thinking back to the WhatsApp messages she had exchanged with Quinn. They had mostly spoken on the phone about her coming to Norfolk, but he had sent her messages telling her to drive safely and let him know when she arrived. Would those put him in danger?

And Rich. He was a bit of a wanker, but she would never do him harm. He didn't know who she had been going to see. They had no reason to hurt him.

A hard, stinging slap across her cheek knocked her head

back and she cried out, both in shock and pain, refocusing on Daniel, as he loomed in close.

'Who are Rich and Quinn?' he asked again, his tone nasty.

Had he split her lip? She could taste blood.

'I'm asking nicely, Lola. If you're going to be difficult, then we can try this another way.'

What? Her fear spiked. What the hell did he mean by that?

She pulled uselessly at her hands, wishing she could touch her throbbing cheek.

'I was supposed to have a meeting with Rich this morning. He won't be happy I haven't shown up.' She glared at Daniel. 'Knowing what he's like, he's probably already called the police.'

It was a poor bluff. Rich would do nothing of the sort. He had probably left her a dozen fuming voicemails, though.

'And what about Quinn?'

Unfortunately, Rose answered for her, having opened her WhatsApp.

'She was messaging with him last night.'

'Saying what?' Daniel asked, looking up.

'*Have a safe journey.* She then replied: *Thanks. I'll let you know once I get there.* He sent another one last night. *Are you okay?* And then again this morning. *Lola, can you please just let me know you're safe?* That's it. She never replied to the last two messages.'

'He knows about us.' Daniel sounded really pissed, and Lola's heart sank. 'Who is he? What is your relationship with him?'

'He's just an old friend I bumped into on the train to Ely.'

'Not a boyfriend, then?'

'No.' Lola hesitated, not wanting him to know about her history with Quinn. If they believed him to be a casual acquaintance, then hopefully they would drop it. 'I told you earlier, I'm single.'

Daniel glared at her, trying to work out if she was telling the truth. 'How much does he know about us?'

'He doesn't know anything about you. I told him I had to drive to Norfolk, but he has no idea where I was going or who I was coming to see.'

'Why tell him you would check in with him then when you arrived? That doesn't seem like something you would need to do with an old friend you haven't seen in a while.'

'He was worried about the weather.'

'Don't lie.'

'I'm not lying. I promise.'

This time, Lola saw his hand when he went to hit her and she managed to duck away, but she wasn't quick enough to stop him grabbing a clump of her hair again.

Her heart thumped as she tried to reason with him, his face pressed close to hers. 'He doesn't know anything, I swear. Don't you think he would have already come looking for me if he knew where I was?'

'There's no message history between them,' Rose confirmed, backing her up. 'Just those three messages.'

For the first time, Lola was grateful she had lost all of her WhatsApp messages when she upgraded her phone, after the app had failed to back them up. At the time, she had been devastated. Although she never opened her message trail with Quinn, it was a memento of their history together and she had liked knowing it was there. She had hoped that maybe one day she would be strong enough to read about their excitement in the lead-up to Milo's birth and look at the photos of the decorated nursery and the toys they had bought him.

Everything happened for a reason and if losing those

memories meant keeping Quinn safe, then it was a worthy trade. It seemed to appease Daniel, who finally stopped grilling her.

Instead, he and Rose waited in impatient silence and Lola knew they were desperate to listen to her messages.

'The Wi-Fi has connected,' Rose announced after a short while, putting Lola's phone on loudspeaker as she dialled her voicemail.

Lola's breath caught as she heard Quinn's voice asking if she was okay and urging her to call or message him, just to put his mind at rest, and she silently begged him not to reveal that he knew where she was. She could hear the concern in his voice and hoped Daniel and Rose would continue to believe her that he was simply worried about the driving conditions.

This was her mess, her stupid idea to come here, and the consequences were hers alone to deal with. She hadn't given up hope of escaping yet, even if the odds were currently stacked against her, but if the worst was to happen – because she assumed from the way they were talking that they planned to kill her – the thought of Quinn unintentionally being dragged into this and possibly being at risk was almost too much to bear.

She had worried he might have forgotten about her after she hadn't made contact, but he hadn't, and knowing that he was still looking out for her gave her the strength she needed. The train ride to Ely had offered her a second chance she hadn't been expecting and Daniel and Rose would not take that away from her without a fight.

As the message ended with nothing revealed, she let out a relieved breath. At least something was going her way.

Rich's voice boomed out next, loud, sarcastic and sounding

incredibly put out as he demanded to know where the fuck she was.

He'd left four follow-up voicemails telling her he was going to withhold her pay and then escalating to terminating her contract if she didn't get her arse into his office right now, and Lola wished his threats were the worst of her problems.

As the last message finished, Rose commented, 'He sounds like a delight.'

Right now, Lola would have given anything to be sitting in a meeting with Rich.

'Are you telling us the truth that this Quinn isn't your boyfriend?' Daniel asked, the voicemail he had listened to seeming to unsettle him again.

'I am. I promise.'

His fist twisted in her hair again, his face close to hers, and she winced. 'If you're lying to me—'

'I'm not. He's just a friend. He has nothing to do with any of this.'

He stared at her and the lack of emotion in his eyes scared her.

How was she going to get out of this?

'Shall we move her downstairs or leave her up here?' he asked Rose, as if Lola wasn't even in the room.

'People are going to miss me,' Lola hissed. She was not just a thing they could destroy because they found her inconvenient. 'You're worrying so much about Quinn and Rich, but there are plenty of other people who are going to notice if I disappear.'

Daniel's jaw clenched and his expression darkened.

'Let's all go downstairs,' Rose suggested. 'It's cosier down there with the tree lights on.' She smiled at Lola and the gesture seemed odd given the circumstances. 'I bet you'd love a cup of tea.'

A glass of water would do fine, Lola thought, though she said nothing.

She was no longer a guest in this house. She was their prisoner. And Rose's comments were unsettling. Lola was hardly going to enjoy watching the fairy lights twinkle.

Daniel dragged her to her feet. 'Come on,' he said, voice void of emotion, and as he ushered her out of the bedroom, her fear spiked.

There was no reasoning with either of them, and while she had earlier believed that Jimmy was the weak link, she now realised he would be absolutely no help to her either. She was trapped with three people who she suspected wanted her dead.

If there was a way out of this situation, she needed to think of it fast.

38

Quinn took the most logical route to Saham Toney, passing through Lakenheath and Brandon, hoping it was the one Lola had travelled the previous night. He drove slowly. Although no accidents had been reported, he still kept his eyes peeled. This wasn't a motorway. She had been travelling on B roads, some of which may not have been gritted, and it was likely that for parts of her journey they had been empty.

For the first stretch, the countryside was open and flat, with only a few pockets of trees and nothing but snow-covered fields for miles, but there were also ditches on either side of the road and he kept a close watch for any sign of a car having come off the road.

Closer to Norfolk, the landscape changed to forest roads; the frost-covered branches of the trees, thick in places, looked like a winter wonderland scene.

If Lola had skidded and lost control of the car, it was possible no one would have been around to help her.

He really hoped that she hadn't crashed, but his mind couldn't help going there. It made no sense that she would be at her brother's and not touch base. Lola wasn't the type of person to keep someone worrying. She was thoughtful and kind. Always had been. If she had hit it off with Daniel and his wife, she would have messaged Quinn even without him nudging her. That was why – try as he might to stay positive – he was instead suspecting the worst.

When she had called to say she was cancelling their dinner date, he should have insisted on going with her to Norfolk. At the time, he had held back, not wanting to be pushy, but now he regretted it. Still, difficult as it may be, he needed to set emotion to one side and treat this as if it was a job. Lola deserved nothing less.

By the time he eventually arrived in the small village where Daniel lived, he was feeling more confident that she hadn't come off the road. But while he had hoped the unease in his gut might have dissipated, instead it tightened. Though perhaps that was in part due to tiredness. He hadn't slept well and his tired brain needed a pick-me-up.

On the road up ahead was a pub, The Black Horse, and taking a chance they would be open, as it was just after 11 a.m., he pulled into the car park. Although he was keen to find Lola, he would function better after a quick cup of coffee.

Outside of the car, the bitter cold hit him, and he trudged through the snow and slush to the pub door. Pushing it open, he stepped inside, grateful to be back in the warmth, breathing in the mingling scents of alcohol and polish, as Wizzard sang in the background, wishing it could be Christmas every day.

Hearing the tinkle of the bell, a man appeared from a door at the back of the bar. He was small and wiry with very little hair left on his head.

'What can I get you?' he asked as Quinn approached.

'Just a black coffee, please.'

He was the only customer, he noted, glancing around the room at the empty tables. In the far corner, the lights of a fake tree that had been decorated to within an inch of its life twinkled through the layers of tinsel smothering it. It wasn't really a surprise that no one else was here given the weather, but as it was Christmas Eve the place would probably be much busier later on in the day.

'Not seen snow like this in a long time,' the man commented, as the coffee machine chugged and spurted.

'Yeah, it's pretty nasty out there.'

'The blizzard knocked all the power out in the village last night. I didn't think we'd be seeing anyone just yet. My missus wondered if it was even worth opening at the usual time.'

'Well, I'm glad you did,' Quinn told him as the coffee was placed in front of him. 'I need something to keep me awake.' As he took his first sip, the hot, bitter liquid a pleasing jolt to his senses, he wondered if the power cut had anything to do with why Lola hadn't made contact. Possibly, though it was back on now and she still hadn't been in touch.

'You're not from around here.'

'Is it that obvious?'

As he laughed, the bar owner smiled wryly. 'In a place like this, you get to know who everyone is.' He held out the card reader so Quinn could pay. 'So are you just passing through or do you have family around here?' he asked as Quinn tapped his phone against the screen.

'Actually, I'm looking for someone.'

'Oh right.'

As the man seemed more intrigued than suspicious, Quinn pulled up a photo of Lola he had on his phone. It was an older one from early on in their relationship, but she essentially looked the same. Her ash-brown hair falling around her shoulders and the spark evident in her earthy green eyes as she smiled at the camera.

'A friend of mine is missing. She headed over this way last night to meet her brother, but no one has heard from her since.' He held up the phone so the bar owner could see the screen. 'Her name's Lola. I don't suppose her face is familiar.'

'I'm sorry, but I wasn't working last night. My son was covering the bar. He ended up having a lock-in with some of the locals, so he was late to bed.' The man hesitated. 'I guess I could go wake him as it's important.'

Quinn shook his head. 'No, don't do that. But could I leave you my number and WhatsApp her picture? Maybe you can check with him when he's up.'

'Sure thing. You said she was meeting her brother? Does he live here in Saham Toney?'

'Yes. Daniel Whitlock. He's my next stop. Lives at a place called Midwinter Manor.'

'I know it.'

As the bar owner seemed happy to chat, making no attempt to leave Quinn with his coffee, he decided to push further. 'Do you know him?'

'I've met him once or twice. The Whitlocks, they like to keep to themselves. The brother, Jimmy, he's been in a handful of times.'

'Daniel has a brother?'

This was news to Quinn. Surely Lola would be related to this Jimmy too. Unless he was a stepbrother perhaps.

'No, the wife, Rose, is his sister. Daniel is Jimmy's brother-in-law.'

'And he lives with them?'

'Yes.' The bar owner hesitated and Quinn could see he was

starting to question whether he should be saying so much. 'I'm guessing you don't know your friend's family at all?'

'No, and neither does Lola,' Quinn told him, deciding to be honest. 'She was adopted at birth and has never met him before. They recently connected and he invited her over last night.' Pulling one of his police contact cards out of his wallet, he handed it over. 'My mobile number is on there. If you could ask your son to either call or message when he wakes, I'd appreciate it,' he asked, downing the rest of his coffee.

This wasn't a police matter, and hopefully wouldn't become one, and under normal circumstances he would have given out his personal mobile number. He understood, though, why the bar owner might question his motives for finding Lola and he needed to show him he was trustworthy. His police-issue phone was in the car, so it was no biggie if the man's kid contacted him on that.

As Quinn suspected, seeing his occupation had the desired effect.

'Do you think this friend of yours is in some kind of trouble then?' the bar owner asked, once again eager to talk.

'Hopefully not,' Quinn assured him. 'The driving conditions weren't good, but there's no sign of an accident. With any luck, Daniel will have some answers as to where she is.'

'They're a strange lot up there.'

Quinn frowned. 'How so?'

'Well, Jimmy once mentioned that his and Rose's mother lives with them too, though no one has ever seen her. Our niece's friend, Sophie, cleaned for them for a while and said the place was like a museum. There were locked doors and rooms she wasn't allowed in. The mother was never there and she asked Rose about her one day. Rose came up with some story that she went out whenever Sophie came into clean, then promptly told her they wouldn't be needing her services any more.'

Was it simply village gossip from someone with an axe to grind? Quinn wasn't sure. He made a mental note anyway.

'And then there was Brett. He was there for a while. An old friend of Daniel's, apparently. Not sure if he's still there.'

'You seem to know a lot about them given they keep to themselves?' Quinn joked.

The bar owner waggled grey eyebrows and smiled. 'Like I said, in a place like this you get to know everyone. Whether they want you to or not. I think Jimmy mentioned Brett the last time he was in here. It's been a while since I saw him, though.'

Quinn looked at his phone again, pulling up the screen-shot he had taken from Daniel's Facebook profile. The picture of him in a yellow Lamborghini. After Lola had failed to make contact, he had been keen to know who this brother was who she had gone to see. 'This is Daniel, right?'

'Yes, that's him,' the bar owner confirmed, pointing on the screen. 'Must be an old photo, though. He's aged a fair bit since then.'

'Is the manor easy to find from here?' Quinn asked, sliding off his bar stool. He was keen to get on his way now, aware that as friendly as this guy was, he wasn't going to help him locate Lola.

'Yes, turn left out of the car park and then the first right. It's about a mile down the road.'

'Okay, thanks.'

Back in the Duster, Quinn started the engine to let the heating warm up, then opened up WhatsApp on his phone, double-blinking when he saw there were now blue ticks against the WhatsApp message he had sent Lola this morning.

Like the one last night, she had read it, but yet again she hadn't replied.

For a moment, he doubted himself, an unfamiliar lack of confidence threading into his nerves and clouding his judgement. He had been so hell-bent on finding Lola, had he read all of the signs wrong? Perhaps she hadn't ever really wanted to reconnect with him but was too polite to say so, and this was her way of letting him down gently.

Was he going to look a fool showing up at Midwinter Manor looking for her?

His hesitancy was fleeting, as he considered what type of person Lola was. She didn't string people along and she often spoke her mind. There was too much history between them and a familiar intimacy that he knew both of them had immediately felt when they saw each other on the train. After everything they had been through together, she wouldn't hurt him like that. If she had been in a mindset where she wasn't comfortable around him, she would have said so.

No, his intuition told him something was wrong.

If Lola was able to, she would message him to put his mind at rest.

Certain he was right, the ball of unease in his gut twisted a little tighter.

He needed to go speak to Daniel Whitlock and see if he could find some answers.

39

After dragging Lola downstairs, Daniel had taken her through to the living room, sitting her down on one of the sofas, while Rose had continued to play the genial host, offering her drinks.

Still desperately thirsty, Lola just wanted water, and she had faced the humiliation of having to drink from the glass being held to her mouth, water slopping down her chin, unable to wipe it away with her hands tied behind her back.

Jimmy was left to keep guard, and Monty too, although the Labrador had merely slunk into the room and settled by Lola's feet. He, at least, was a comforting presence, as he watched her with soulful brown eyes. Could he pick up on her nerves?

Daniel and Rose, meanwhile, moved to the corner of the large room, where they whispered and connived. Lola was watching them closely and at times the tension between the pair of them was palpable. She couldn't figure out what it was they were saying, but she saw some of their exchanged heated glances and knew they were disagreeing, Daniel looking frustrated and angry as he loomed over Rose.

Lola knew they had to be discussing what they were going

to do with her. Something she really shouldn't think about, fresh fear rattling through her body.

Not that she intended to go quietly. Life had taken too much from her already. She deserved a happy ending and would fight for her chance to have one with everything she had left.

She stole a glance at Jimmy, relieved to see he wasn't paying her too much attention, far more focused on his phone. Taking advantage while he was distracted, she worked at the knot binding her wrists. Her fingers could just about reach it, but the silk of the scarf was slippery and the knot tight. From the position of her hands, she wasn't sure she had enough manoeuvrability. Still, for a while she continued to give it her attention. At least until she realised it wasn't going to come loose unless she found something to cut through it.

As there was nothing at her disposal and she was very much aware that the seconds were ticking down towards her fate, she decided to switch tack, challenging Daniel and Rose.

'Why did you pretend you couldn't walk?' she demanded of Daniel, her voice raised as she glared at him and Rose across the room.

They could hold her prisoner, but she decided she wouldn't make it easy for them.

To her frustration, neither of them reacted.

Only Jimmy glanced up, his eyes widening, but he wasn't relevant. It was Daniel whose attention she was seeking, though she was sure that Rose could give her answers too.

She left the silence to stretch before resigning herself to the fact that neither one of them was going to respond. Determined not to give up, she tried again.

'How did you regain the use of your legs?' she asked, this

time her voice even louder. 'I read up about you before I came here. You were paralysed from the waist down.'

While she was conscious of provoking them too much, fearful they might decide to resolve their situation faster if she was causing them trouble, they had her trapped, and she figured out she had nothing to lose at this point. She refused to cower like a mouse. She wanted – no, she deserved – answers. If they were going to kill her, then first they owed her the truth and she would keep asking questions until they gave it to her.

'Was it some kind of miracle?' she asked, unable to keep the sarcasm from her voice. 'Because you can walk perfectly well now. Or did you lie to everyone about the extent of your injury?'

This time, Daniel paused, his shoulders tightening, and Rose threw her a brief look of irritation.

Had she hit a nerve?

Lola had thrown the accusation out in the heat of the moment, but now, as she considered it, was she on the right track? Though, what would he have to gain by pretending to be confined to the wheelchair?

And how deep did the deceit go?

Rose and Jimmy knew, but had his parents?

She asked the question now, earning a scowl from Daniel.

'Does this have to do with why you lied about Nigel being my father? I don't understand what you had to gain.'

'For fuck's sake,' Daniel snapped. 'Can we please shut her the hell up?'

'It costs you nothing to give me the truth,' Lola said, trying to keep her tone reasonable, even though she was seething inside. She tried to hold on to that anger, knowing it was more productive than the heavy weight of fear coiling in the pit of her stomach. 'I came here because I wanted to connect with you, Daniel. I wanted to meet my brother. I never asked for any of this. At least let me know why you lied to me. You owe me that.'

He glowered at her. 'I owe you nothing, you stupid bitch. You should never have pushed to meet me. You should have stayed the hell away.'

'Trust me. If I'd known what I was walking into, I would have.'

'Leave it...' Rose put a warning hand on Daniel's arm when he took a menacing step towards Lola. 'Please.'

On the floor beside Lola, Monty growled.

Daniel glanced at his dog hesitantly. 'Okay, if she wants the truth so bad, let's just tell her,' he growled. 'I'm getting fed up with this whole charade anyway, and with the sound of her whiny voice.'

His words caused Rose to react in alarm. 'We agreed we wouldn't say.'

'It's over, for God's sake. She's not going anywhere. She already knows too much.'

'Please, just think for a minute. It's too dangerous.'

'I'm not letting her leave this house, Rose.'

Daniel's words had Lola's heart hammering, horror choking her throat as she realised her fate was sealed, and, instinctively, she struggled to free herself. Whatever he wanted to confess to, it had to be bad.

What was it they had done that was so terrible it had to stay a secret?

Was it something to do with her real dad?

Daniel and Rose had pretended that Nigel was her father. Was it to try to throw her off track, so she didn't ask questions about John?

Why didn't they want her to find him? Was it because they had done something to him?

Were they about to confess to his murder?

Oh God, now her mind was jumping ahead. She was being ridiculous.

Except, the reality wasn't that stupid. Daniel might be her brother and Rose her sister-in-law, but they were strangers she knew nothing about. And the fact she was currently tied up in their house as they discussed her fate was warning enough that they were dangerous people.

It made sense that they wouldn't want her to know about John if they had killed him, because of course she would want to try to find him. But why would they kill him in the first place, and how was this connected to Daniel being able to walk?

Was it because of Annie's affair? Had Daniel wanted revenge, coercing Rose and Jimmy into helping him?

And if he hated John so much, then Daniel was going to hate her too.

Enough to kill her? From the way he was talking, it seemed so.

Beneath the fear, she was aware of the simmering heat of anger and she tried to hold on to that, aware that if there was any way of surviving her predicament, she needed to fight with everything she had. Fear would break her. She needed to be strong, be fierce, and try to keep her wits about her.

If the opportunity arose, she could not afford to hesitate.

For now, she had nothing to lose and she decided to throw the accusation out there.

'This is about my real father, isn't it?' she demanded, certain she was on the right track when Rose's eyes widened. 'Is he dead? Did you kill him?'

Daniel's expression was unreadable, but she could see she now had his attention. Leaving Rose's side, he strode over to where Lola was sitting.

'Take a break, Jimmy,' he snapped. 'Now.'

Jimmy stared up, his eyes bulging, and Lola wondered if he was going to challenge him, but then he jerked his head in a nod and left the room.

'Now it all makes sense why you didn't want me to come here,' Lola pushed, as soon as he was gone and Daniel had taken his vacant seat. 'You must think I'm stupid.' She glared at Rose, who had wandered over to join them, and then at Daniel. 'You did kill him, didn't you?'

Rose's gaze flickered her husband's way, but her expression was unreadable.

'Your father was becoming a pain,' she admitted.

'That's why you lied about Nigel. You knew if I found out the truth that I would go looking for John and your secret would be exposed?'

Lola could see she had both Rose's and Daniel's full attention now and was determined to keep it.

'You know, if I can figure it out, other people will too eventually. You might silence me, but you won't get away with what you've done. Why did you do it?' she demanded, shaking her head in disgust as she addressed Daniel. 'Was it because of our mother's affair? Did you really hate John that much?'

'You don't know anything,' he seethed. 'Bastard child, jumping to conclusions.'

'Tell me what happened and why. He was my dad and I deserve to know the truth.' She looked at Rose, who seemed to be wavering. 'Please?'

'Enough,' Daniel demanded. 'This has dragged on for too long. We can't let her leave, and that means we only have one option, so let's just get it the fuck over with. There's some plastic sheeting in the garage. Go get it for me. Now.'

Lola's eyes widened as she gasped, horror choking her throat as she fought again to free her hands.

'No. I won't have you doing it in here,' Rose hissed. 'You'll ruin my sofas.'

She was worried about the furniture?

Lola stared at her incredulously, noticing for the first time that Rose's face was perfectly made up, her hair neatly pinned back. They had all been awake for much of the night. When had Rose found the time or the inclination to make such an effort with her appearance?

She was less aggressive than Daniel, who seemed to rule the house, and Lola had thought her to be the softer of the two, but now she saw the shallowness of the woman. Rose was all about materialism. How she looked and the way her house was styled – currently dressed for Christmas with the flair of an interior designer, no expense spared – was more important to her than anything else. She didn't like to be inconvenienced and was happy to turn a blind eye to things, like letting her husband lock someone in the attic bedroom or end their life, as long as it didn't interrupt her plans or destroy her things.

In her own way, she was as much of a psychopath as Daniel.

'Then I'll take her outside,' he said now, rolling his eyes. 'I want this over with, Rose, now. The bloody woman is getting on my nerves.'

As Daniel got up, Lola tried to scoot back across the sofa, her heart thudding as she realised her time was up.

Unless she could find a way to keep him talking or to escape, he was going to kill her.

40

MARCH 2023

Oxford

Rose chose an outside table at the cafe where she had agreed to meet John. It was too crowded inside and she didn't like the idea of anyone listening in to their conversation. Out here, beneath the canopy of the front window, the other tables were empty and she had the perfect vantage point to see John when he arrived.

The cool March day would also hopefully keep their meeting brief. Neither of them wanting to linger longer than necessary.

As she replayed their conversation from the previous day, she lit a cigarette, not liking that her fingers were trembling. It wasn't from the cold. The fur-trimmed coat she wore took care of that. She was nervous, she realised, about meeting with John behind Daniel's back.

It was the contents of that letter that had brought him to their house, and it was fortuitous that Rose had been the one to open the door. Her husband had no idea about their visitor.

He had been in the shower at the time, using the specially adapted wet room at the back of the house, and wouldn't have heard the knock at the door as Rose did.

She had been packing up the house, deciding what they were going to take with them to Norfolk, and which pieces to sell, and John's visit had caught her off guard.

Dressed in jeans, her face free of make-up, and her dark hair tied back, she had not been prepared for a visitor. She prided herself on her impeccable attention to detail. How she presented herself to the world was important. Her image was her shield and she was naked without it. Seeing the stranger on her doorstep had immediately thrown her.

He was older, but attractive. He had fine lines on his face and threads of silver in his tawny brown hair. And there was a spark in his intelligent olive-green eyes that unnerved her. It made her feel exposed and uncomfortable. Then he had introduced himself in a calm and kind manner, telling her who he was and why he was there.

It was because of the letter that Annie had written to him shortly before she passed away. Rose remembered posting it for her mother-in-law, but that had been three years ago. Why was John only reaching out now?

But then he had explained. The letter had gone to his mother's home address. It was where he had been living at the time of his affair with Annie, but, shortly afterwards, after their affair had come to light, he had moved abroad.

His mother, who had the early stages of dementia, had tucked it away in one of her safe places. Although he had come back to the UK when her illness worsened, it wasn't until recently, as her house was being cleared out for sale, that he had found it in a box full of cleaning supplies.

He seemed to know about the family situation, that Nigel

had passed and that Daniel still lived here, that it was his house now, and he didn't seem surprised when Rose introduced herself as his wife.

'Is he home?' he had wanted to know. 'It's about the contents of his mother's letter. I really need to speak with him.'

The word yes was on Rose's lips and she was about to explain that he was in the shower, but something had her hesitating. A gut feeling that whatever Annie had written to John, it wasn't good.

Had she confessed about the child she had given up?

She was fairly certain that Daniel knew nothing about his sister, and she wanted it to stay that way. So she had plastered a fake smile on to her face, telling John that her husband wasn't there. If he knew about Daniel's condition, he didn't say.

It was a lie that could have easily blown up in her face if Daniel had called out or if John had insisted on coming back.

As it was, he had been persistent that he needed to speak with Daniel, but eventually Rose had managed to persuade him to leave by offering that they would meet him at a cafe in Oxford city centre the following day.

Of course, John had believed he would be meeting Daniel, which was why he had agreed, and as Rose watched him now as he crossed the street, latching eyes on her, she saw his face drop with disappointment.

'Where is Daniel?' he asked by way of greeting.

'I'm sorry. He wasn't happy about you showing up at the house,' Rose apologised, doing her best to frame her expression into one of regret. 'He knows about your affair with his mother and... well, I'm afraid he's still very bitter about it.'

As she hoped, John reacted with guilt, his cheeks staining red and a tic working in his jaw. 'I'm sorry. I should have known this might be difficult for him. I promise I wouldn't have just shown up like that if it wasn't important.'

'I understand.' Rose nodded sympathetically. 'Perhaps it's something I can help with.'

She watched him hesitate. Was he wary of trusting her?

'Can I buy you another coffee?' he offered after a brief silence. 'And then we can talk.'

'Thank you.' She smiled then, not letting on how desperate she was to know about the contents of Annie's letter to him. She could be patient. Waiting a few more minutes wouldn't hurt.

As she suspected, John knew about his daughter. Annie had revealed in her letter about the child they shared, confessing how she had kept her existence a secret from him, giving her up for adoption.

Of course, that was why he had shown up at Rose and Daniel's house. He wanted to track his daughter down and hoped that Daniel might know where she was.

Rose listened to him talk, hearing about his frustration that because his name hadn't been on the birth certificate, it was almost impossible for him to get any answers, and she made all of the right noises, even as panic built inside of her.

John had moved on from being a handyman. He was now a successful author, she learned, writing spy thrillers under the name of J. T. Fagan. She had heard of him, Rose realised, remembering the signed paperback of Annie's that she had packed away in a box just days ago, in preparation for the move. It stood out because it was a spy novel and Annie had preferred sagas and romance. Rose had been tempted to sling it, but then she had realised it was signed, so she had put it in the box of keepsakes.

She asked John about it now, curious as Annie had told her they had never met up again following their affair.

'I sent it to her,' John confessed sheepishly. 'She used to read my stories and encouraged me to try to find a publisher. Although we were no longer in contact, I wanted her to know that I had finally followed her advice.'

Was this why Annie had eventually decided to come clean with him? The paperback was old and worn, so she must have held on to it for years, still carrying a torch for John.

Whatever her reason, Rose now cursed her late mother-in-law to hell. Why had the stupid woman decided to write those letters?

It had been when she had first taken to her sickbed, before any of them realised how serious the virus would be, but perhaps it was a premonition, Annie somehow knowing that she wouldn't get another chance to make her peace with those she had either wronged or needed to clear the air with.

Rose should have slung them in the bin instead of posting them. Because now she had a problem. If the daughter found out about Daniel's fortune, was she going to expect a share?

Annie had confided her secret with Rose, admitting that she had no idea how much her son knew or remembered about her pregnancy. He had been young at the time and Nigel had been so ashamed, it was a taboo subject. Annie had worn clothes that had disguised her bump, not wanting to anger her husband, and she had struggled through a difficult birth, then was alone in hospital as she recovered. After she had returned home without her daughter, it was as if the whole experience had never happened. The matter was never spoken of again and, growing up, Daniel hadn't asked any questions.

He had never mentioned his sister to Rose either, and

before the conversation with Annie, where she had admitted her secret, Rose had assumed him to be an only child.

She had decided to keep what her mother-in-law told her to herself, even after Annie died, working on the basis that Daniel didn't know about his sister. Rose now took it as her own responsibility to protect his inheritance, and in turn safeguard her own future. This sister, whoever she was, wasn't entitled to a penny. As far as Rose knew, she had never tried to make contact either, and it was better it stayed that way.

But now John was here and the secret was at risk of being exposed.

Rose needed to make her problem go away, but how?

'Daniel isn't in contact with her. I don't think he even knows of her existence,' she said, playing dumb. 'He's certainly never mentioned anything to me about a sister.'

'I know he's angry with me,' John said. 'But surely he would want to know. She's his flesh and blood too and he will be able to get the answers I can't.'

The poor, pathetic man looked so hopeful, for a moment Rose actually felt sorry for him. She quickly quashed that feeling.

They were moving next week. All she had to do was keep John and Daniel apart until then. John didn't know they were leaving and even if he did find out where they had gone, surely he wouldn't follow them all the way to Norfolk.

'I will speak to him again and tell him everything you've told me, but I'm certain I know what the answer is. He won't want anything to do with his sister if he realises you're her father.'

Rose knew her words were harsh. She intended them to be, pleased at John's crestfallen expression.

She took his phone number and left it with him that she would speak to Daniel.

Of course, she did no such thing, instead fobbing John off on the two occasions he messaged her to see if she had managed to talk her husband round.

On the day the removal lorries showed up, Rose sent John one final message.

> I'm very sorry, John, but Daniel is insistent that he wants nothing to do with his sister. He is also very clear that he would like you to leave us alone. Please respect his wishes. Regards, Rose.

She had deleted and blocked his number before they left Oxfordshire and as they settled into their new home in Norfolk, she gradually forgot all about him.

At least she did until the following spring.

The letter from John arrived on 1 April 2024, with a forwarding sticker that told her it had been delivered to their Oxford address. Had she not known better, she would have thought it to be an April Fool's prank.

Thank fuck it was addressed to both her and Daniel, and she had seen it first.

As she opened the envelope and read the letter inside, rage coiled inside of her.

John was hoping that they might have changed their minds and he was pleading with Daniel to help him find his daughter.

Had he not listened to a word she had said?

More than a whole year had passed without any word from him and as the days had rolled into months, here safe and secure in their new home, Rose had honestly believed he had given up. By the time spring came around again, she had pretty much forgotten about John Fagan and the secret love child.

But it was just a letter, she reminded herself. He had no idea that they had moved and it wasn't as if he had shown up on their doorstep. That could have been disastrous.

Was it too much to hope that he would give up when he didn't get a reply?

He had written it nearly four months ago, she noted, seeing the typed date at the top of the page was a couple of weeks before Christmas. That suggested it must have been lost within the postal system. Maybe the time of year had him feeling nostalgic. All she could hope was that within those four months without a response, he had decided to move on.

Or perhaps he had spent that time trying to track them down? If he went to the Oxfordshire house, he would soon learn they no longer lived there. Had he figured out that her and Daniel were now living in Norfolk? What if he showed up here unannounced?

Midwinter Manor was isolated and not clearly signposted, but it wouldn't be impossible for him to find them.

'Anything for me?'

Daniel's voice startled her and she swung around, crumpling the letter in her hand, as he came up behind her.

'No, afraid not.' She knew how guilty she must look as she shoved the letter in her pocket. Quickly adding, 'Just a catalogue trying to tempt me to resubscribe.'

Luckily he didn't ask any questions and she tried to push the letter to the back of her mind, hopeful that John wouldn't try to make further contact.

With hindsight, she should have got rid of it that same day.

Either burnt it or ripped it into pieces and buried it in the bottom of the bin. Instead, she had foolishly held on to the stupid piece of paper, not realising that John's letter was about to change everything.

41

PRESENT DAY

'Stay here with her. I'll go get the plastic,' Daniel ordered, and instead of grabbing Lola, as she had anticipated, she watched him leave the room.

For now, it was just her and Rose, along with Monty, and an awkward silence descended.

Lola was the first to break it, knowing it was her last chance to try to reason her way out of this situation. Rose seemed to value material possessions over life, but was there a way to get through to her?

'Please tell me what happened?' she asked, making an effort to keep her tone soft as she started working again at the knot binding her wrists. 'You're going to kill me anyway. At least give me the truth.'

Rose's gaze flickered towards her, but her expression was stoic. 'It's better that you don't know what we did. If it's any consolation, I'm sorry it's come to this. If there was another way...' She trailed off, choosing to look instead at the beautifully decorated Christmas tree with its baubles in reds and golds.

She was sorry? Lola wanted to scream at her, to demand her attention back, but it would be a waste of her strength. She knew she would require all of that when Daniel returned.

Would Quinn search for her when she didn't show up? And what about her friends back home in Manchester? How long before they realised she was missing?

She thought of her kittens, Casper and Tilly. They lived indoors and her neighbour, Jamie, had been going in to put down food, but only up until this morning. Lola knew Jamie was heading down to Somerset to spend Christmas with her family and they had agreed she would post the key through Lola's letterbox on her last visit.

That meant the kittens would be trapped all alone inside her flat and without any food or water once it ran out. They were going to wonder why she had left them.

The thought was unbearable. They were her babies.

Knowing what she would be leaving behind had tears pricking at the back of her eyes and she blinked them away furiously.

Focus, Lola.

She had to take her mind off her cats and Quinn, and use what little time she had left productively. Getting her hands free was most important. She had to escape before Daniel came back. It was her only chance.

'Why did you invite me to the house?' she asked, determined to try to get Rose talking again while she worked at the knot.

At first, the woman didn't seem to hear her. She seemed zoned out and preoccupied, and Lola actually considered if she could try to make a dash for the door.

But then Rose looked up. 'We didn't think you would let it drop. And we couldn't risk you showing up unannounced. You should never have pushed for a meeting, Lola. I'm very sorry, but what happens next is all your own fault.'

'Stop saying that,' Lola snapped, her temper fraying. Both Rose and Monty stared at her. 'Stop saying you're sorry. I know you killed my father and now you're going to kill me. You're not sorry at all.'

Although her outburst seemed to shock Rose, she had the nerve to look offended.

'I was trying to make this easy on you,' she bit back, her tone hardening. 'You ungrateful bitch.'

Daniel chose that moment to return to the room, glancing between them both, and Lola realised her time was up. There would be no reasoning with Daniel. As fresh fear quaked through her, she managed to hook a fingernail into the knot. At first, as she tugged there seemed to be no give, but she kept patiently at it, certain after a few attempts that it was gradually coming looser.

She needed a distraction, just a brief one. Something to buy her a little more time to get free.

'What's all the yelling for?' Daniel asked.

Shaking her head, Rose got up and went to him. 'It's not important. But you're right. We need this over with. Can I leave you to take care of it while I go and fix us some lunch?'

She ran an affectionate hand over his cheek, as if she had just asked him to go fetch her bags in from out of the car, not commit murder, leaning into him as he kissed her on the mouth.

'Of course, my love,' he assured her. 'Consider it done.'

This marriage was really fucked up. But was it as strong as they tried to portray?

Lola remembered the gift bag she had found upstairs with

the empty jewellery box. The gift card reading *To Rose. All my love, Brett xxx*

Did Daniel know all of Rose's secrets?

'Rose is very lucky to have such a devoted husband,' she said sarcastically. 'Forgiving too, given how many secrets she has kept from you over the years. Did you also forgive her for her affair with your best friend, Brett?'

She expected a reaction of either shock or anger. The short burst of laughter Daniel gave completely threw her off balance.

He and Rose looked at one another and there was something in their silent exchange that unnerved Lola. This was another secret they shared, she realised.

He already knew.

So what had happened with Brett and how did he figure into this?

Had Daniel found out and made him leave?

How come he had forgiven Rose so easily?

Then another thought occurred to her.

Had Rose helped her husband murder her lover?

Lola was about to ask the question when Jimmy came running back into the room, a look of panic on his face. 'Someone's here.'

'What?'

Rose and Daniel spoke in unison and Lola could see they were immediately panicked.

'There's a car coming up the driveway.'

'Who?' Rose's voice was almost a squeak, as she lost all of her composure.

'Wait here,' Daniel ordered, striding from the room.

Lola's mouth was dry, her heart thumping in her chest. Was this her chance? She had managed to loosen the knot enough to give her wrists more movement, but there wasn't quite enough slack to pull her hands free. Anxiously, she kept working.

She didn't know who was approaching the house, but suddenly she had hope. If she could find a way to alert the visitor, let them know she was here and in danger.

Her hopes sank with Rose's next words. An order to Jimmy.

'Get her back upstairs. Wait with her and keep her quiet.'

Jimmy didn't need to be asked twice. Lola could see he was shaken too and he roughly caught hold of her arm as she tried to get away from him, yanking her to her feet.

'Please, you don't have to do this,' she begged. She couldn't lose this one precious opportunity.

Her plea fell on deaf ears, and the man she had assumed was the weak link, whom she had last night persuaded to reveal the truth about her father, was now only interested in saving his own skin.

His allegiance was clear. He was part of this fucked-up family and he would no longer be any use to Lola.

Still, as he dragged her from the sofa, she fought him with everything she had, desperately trying to free her hands as Monty started barking, on his feet and following after them.

She hadn't missed that Jimmy was the clumsy one, and that he was a little overweight and less reactive than Daniel. That was probably down to the alcohol, and while he had mostly sobered up over the last few hours, Lola could now smell the whisky on his breath as he manhandled her.

He had been sent on a break and it seemed he had used that time to top himself up.

Unfortunately, he was still stronger than her and despite her best efforts, he easily managed to half carry, half drag her down the narrow corridor and into the main hallway, where

Daniel was peering out of one of the narrow windows at their approaching visitor.

Hearing Jimmy, he swung around.

'Get her the fuck out of here,' he barked.

'But Rose told me—'

'To get her upstairs,' Rose finished for Jimmy, as she appeared behind them. She glared at her brother. 'Go on. What are you waiting for? And Monty, in the kitchen. Now!'

When the dog ignored her, still barking at Jimmy and Lola, Rose caught hold of him by the collar, marching him away.

Lola was unable to use her hands, but she still had two working feet and she used them now, kicking out at Jimmy as she struggled against him, screaming at the top of her lungs, *'Help me! Please, call the police!'*

For a moment, it felt like she was making progress, Jimmy struggling to maintain his grasp, let alone to shut her up, but Daniel reacted faster than his brother-in-law. He was upon them both in seconds and pulling Lola from Jimmy's grasp, clamping one arm across her chest, and his free hand over her mouth.

'Get hold of her legs,' he demanded, swearing when Jimmy tried and failed to do as asked, as Lola kicked out at him. 'For fuck's sake, you idiot.'

The second time, he was successful, but Lola bucked and thrashed against them both as they carried her upstairs, aware she was losing her chance to raise the alarm.

As they carried her across the landing, the doorbell rang below, and she fought with everything she had, biting down on Daniel's hand and managing to kick Jimmy in the chest.

Still, they both held on.

At the foot of the narrow second-floor staircase Daniel

handed her back to Jimmy with a warning. 'Get her upstairs, keep her quiet. Do not fuck this up.'

Then Jimmy's clammy hand was replacing Daniel's, covering her mouth.

Despite his allegiance to Rose, he *was* still the weakest link. He might be on his sister's side, but she had more chance against him than she did against Rose and Daniel.

As he pulled her up the stairs and into the bedroom where they had first held her prisoner, she ordered herself to breathe and to focus.

There would be a way to trip Jimmy up. She was certain of it.

But she needed to wait for the right moment and take her chance.

42

The woman who eventually answered the door to Quinn greeted him with a smile, though he noticed immediately that it didn't touch her eyes. Those were wary and she seemed a little jittery.

Yes, it could simply be because he was a stranger on her doorstep, but it didn't do anything to help the knot tightening in his stomach.

He quickly took in her appearance, committing it to memory, something he had learnt to do early on in his police role. Arctic blue gaze, immaculately presented, with her wavy, dark hair pinned back from her face. This was Daniel's wife, he guessed. Rose Whitlock.

He had done his research.

'May I help you?'

The hesitancy as she spoke those four words revealed she was cautious too. His arrival had definitely unsettled her.

Quinn reminded himself that he shouldn't jump to conclusions. He had already reached far too many of those. The snow out here had been deep and he had driven slowly and with care, allowing him to take in extra details, and as he had passed through the main gate that led up to the house, he hadn't failed to notice that part of the driveway had been freshly cleared and that there were tyre tracks leading to the garage.

Someone had been out this morning, though there had been no tracks in the woods, so they hadn't left the property.

It probably meant nothing, but the detective part of his brain had worked overtime anyway, storing the detail away.

The only thing that mattered was finding out that Lola was safe. Once he knew that, then he could rest easy. If she didn't want to see him, then yes it would hurt, but he would figure out a way to deal with it.

'Hi, yes. I'm looking for someone, actually.' He offered his most friendly smile, hoping to win Rose over. 'Her name's Lola Henderson. Her brother is Daniel Whitlock. She was coming here to meet him last night?'

There was the slightest pause, but then Rose shook her head. 'I'm sorry. She's not here.'

Was she lying?

'Not here as in she never showed up, or she was here, but has already left?' he pushed.

'She never showed up.'

This time, there was no hesitation, but Quinn's guard was still up. He prided himself on his ability at making correct first impressions, rarely judging people wrong. Something in Rose's demeanour was setting off his spider sense. Was it because she was covering for Lola, or something else?

For the moment, he played along. 'Okay? Well, did she contact you to say she wasn't coming or give a reason why?'

'No. She was supposed to show up at seven, but didn't, and we haven't heard from her since.'

'I see.'

Rose's eyes suddenly narrowed, her expression hardening, as if she was only just getting the memo that Quinn was a stranger and hadn't introduced himself, so she shouldn't be giving so much information away. 'I'm sorry. Who are you exactly?'

'My name's Quinn Mallory. I'm Lola's...' He stopped himself from saying ex-boyfriend, instead saying, 'I'm her friend.'

Keep it simple.

Rose nodded and although she was keeping her expression neutral, Quinn couldn't decide if he imagined a flicker of recognition at his name.

There was no way she would know who he was, though, unless Lola had told her. Which wouldn't be possible unless Lola had been here.

'Is Daniel home, please? I'd like to speak with him if possible.'

'He's resting at the moment.'

Rose was regarding him through hostile eyes now, a subtle shift in the way she was watching him, and he knew she wanted him gone.

'I'm sorry, I can't help you,' she added, starting to close the door.

'Wait.'

'What?' she asked, sounding harassed.

'I do need to speak with him, so perhaps you could ask him to call me when he's awake.'

'Look, it's Christmas Eve and not convenient,' Rose protested. 'We're busy.'

'I'm sorry Lola's disappearance is disrupting your celebra-tions, but this is important,' Quinn said smoothly, pleased when she flinched at his dig. 'I promise I won't take up much of his time.'

She glared at him and the fake smile that tugged at her lips told him she was getting irritated.

He reached for his wallet, then changed his mind. He wouldn't give her his police contact card. For now, he decided he didn't want her knowing his occupation, fearful she might shut down on him completely.

Right now, he had no idea if Lola was inside the house or if Rose was telling the truth and she had never arrived. Until he had a clearer idea, he would keep his cards close.

'Do you have a pen and paper?' he asked. 'I'll give you my number.'

For a moment, he thought she was going to refuse, but then, with a brief shake of her head, she ordered, 'Wait here,' before shutting the door on him.

She was gone for a while and, although the sun was out, low in the sky and casting the Christmas card scene surrounding him with a warm glow, it did little to alleviate the harshness of the chilly air. The tips of his ears and nose burned with the cold, and Quinn was grateful for his scarf and thick jacket. As he pulled his hands from his pockets and huffed out a few breaths to try to warm them, it crossed his mind that she might not come back at all.

Perhaps she was hoping he might leave if she ignored him, which would be a very stupid assumption for her to make, as he had no intention of going anywhere.

Still, he was fearing the worst, his mind already working overtime as he considered a plan B, when he saw her appear through the glass.

No paper or pen, he noted, but someone was with her. A man in a wheelchair.

So Daniel was awake after all.

The door opened again and this time the smile Rose greeted him with wasn't forced. It seemed smug.

'It seems I was wrong. My husband is awake.'

She stepped to one side and Daniel wheeled his chair forward.

The full beard he wore distracted Quinn momentarily, but then he focused on the man's features. His hooded eyes, wide forehead and long nose.

There was no mistaking him. He was instantly recognisable from the Lamborghini photo, and Quinn had to stop himself from staring.

'My wife tells me you have some questions about the woman claiming to be my sister. This is all very inconsiderate given that it's Christmas Eve,' he grumbled.

'I do. I'm sorry to disturb you, but I promise I will keep it quick.' Quinn fought hard to keep his expression neutral. Until he figured out what the hell was going on here, he would be genial and give nothing away.

'You'd better.'

'Mr Whitlock? Daniel?' He made an effort to smile at the glaring man.

'Yes! Now what do you want? You're wasting our time, just like the Henderson woman did yesterday.'

'Her name's Lola. So you didn't meet her last night?'

'I already told you the answer to that,' Rose interjected, her tone snappy. 'She never showed up.'

Quinn ignored her. 'When was the last time you heard from her?'

He watched as the two of them exchanged a glance, both of them answering.

'Yesterday lunchtime,' Rose got in first. 'She said she would be here at 7 p.m., but we heard nothing from her after that.'

'We wasted our evening waiting around for her.'

Neither of them seemed concerned about Lola's whereabouts. Only how inconvenienced they were.

'So you didn't think to check on her, to make sure she was okay?' he asked.

'No.' Rose shook her head. 'We assumed she had changed her mind.'

Quinn was getting irritated with her constant butting in. 'I was asking your husband, Mrs Whitlock,' he said, keeping his tone polite. 'Mr Whitlock, she's your sister. Did you not want to make sure she was okay?'

Scowling eyes stared up at him from the chair. 'I don't know her. So of course not. We might be blood related, but she's a stranger to me. If I had known she was going to waste my time, I would never have agreed to meet with her in the first place.'

'She's been missing since last night when she left Ely to come here,' Quinn pointed out, his patience slipping. 'It sounds like something has happened to her rather than her wasting your time for the fun of it.'

'The weather's terrible. Perhaps she changed her mind and stopped somewhere to wait out the storm,' Rose suggested.

Quinn made a point of looking around him at the snowy, but calm landscape. 'The storm's passed. Besides, she's not answering her phone or responding to messages.'

'Well, I'm sorry,' Rose shrugged, refusing to make eye contact. 'But I don't know what else to tell you. We never saw her.'

She was lying. They both were. He had interviewed enough suspects over the years to recognise the signs. And he now had so many questions, he had no idea where to even begin.

Most importantly, he had to find Lola.

Was she in the house, or had they done something to her? Because this situation seemed so fucked up, he couldn't help but assume the worst.

He couldn't force his way in, but he would get to the truth somehow. He was wasting his time talking to the pair of them, though. That much he knew.

'Okay,' he nodded, aware he now needed to convince them he was going to leave and continue his search for Lola elsewhere. 'I can see I'm wasting my time here. I'm going to retrace her route again, in case she came off the road.'

'That does sound the most likely scenario,' Rose agreed.

'I'm sorry to disturb your Christmas Eve. I'll leave you alone to enjoy it now.'

Quinn nodded at both of them, not missing the look of relief they shared before the door was closed in his face.

What the fuck was going on inside that house?

He knew they would be watching him leave, so he made a show of turning and walking back up the driveway, resisting the urge to look back.

Once he was in the shelter of the woods, he would find a way to angle back without being seen.

Lola was here. He was certain of it.

He just had to figure out where.

43

'You don't have to do this, Jimmy. You can let me go.'

Jimmy had only released his hand from Lola's mouth for the briefest second, while he tried to adjust his grip. The damn woman was as slippery as an eel as she struggled against him, fighting with everything she had to free herself. Although he was bigger, he wasn't in great physical condition and his morning top up of whisky wasn't helping. It was taking all of his strength to control her.

He went to clamp his hand back, to shut her up again, squealing when she bit down on his fingers. Before he could recover from the shock, she trod down hard on his foot, and the double-barrelled assault had him loosening his grip momentarily.

It was all Lola needed, managing to break free, and as the doorbell sounded below, echoing through the house, Jimmy realised he was in deep trouble.

As she ran for the door, she started to scream, and panicking, knowing he had to stop her, he launched himself at her, somehow managing to knock her to the ground with his bulky frame. She landed inelegantly and he threw all of his weight on top of her back, pinning her down as she wriggled beneath him, gasping and out of breath as she cried out.

He soon put paid to that, covering her mouth again, then, for what felt like an hour, he clung on to her as if his life depended on it. Which, he supposed, it did. He couldn't risk letting his sister down. There was too much riding on it.

'Sit still,' he hissed, as she continued to fight him. 'I don't want to hurt you.'

Trying to keep her still was exhausting, even with her hands tied behind her back, and he had no idea how long he was supposed to wait up here like this. Was the man he had seen approaching the house still on the doorstep or had Rose managed to get rid of him yet?

Jimmy didn't dare move until he was given the all-clear.

It would help if he had something to gag her with, so he could at least use both hands to hold her down, but a frantic look around the room showed him there was nothing in reach.

Unless he used part of his clothing.

His jumper was too bulky and would be difficult to remove while holding her down, but could he use a sock? If he balled it up and forced it in her mouth, it would certainly keep her quiet.

Not daring to remove his hand from her mouth, he tried to adjust his position atop her, so his legs were holding her in place. Knowing he would have to be quick, he released the hand that was holding her, stretching it behind him as he reached for his left foot.

Beneath him, Lola bucked like a rodeo bull and he wobbled, almost losing his grip. His heart thudded as he tried again, straining as his fingers found his foot. He tugged hard at the toe of the sock, falling forward as it came free, his bare foot slapping back against the ground, and clinging on to his prize for dear life.

Scrunching up the sock, he pushed it in front of Lola's face, removing the hand covering her mouth as he tried to force the gag past her lips.

Realising what he was doing, she renewed her attempts to get free, taking advantage of the fact both of his hands were in front of her face, with only his weight and his legs holding her in place. The next thing Jimmy knew, he was losing his balance, all of his weight falling forward, and as he toppled over his own head, Lola was wriggling out from behind him.

He landed inelegantly on his back, sprawled across the carpet, the shock of what had just happened momentarily slowing him down.

As he registered the fact Lola was on her feet, he scrambled to get up. He was barely on his knees when he realised she had managed to get her hands untied, and she was holding something. He double-blinked, realising it was a large candlestick, just moments before she charged towards him.

The first blow was so sudden, he had no time to react, the crack of metal against flesh knocking his head sideways, blistering pain erupting in his jaw.

As he tried to put up his hands to shield the second blow, the candlestick caught the tips of fingers, before smashing into his nose. He yowled in agony, hands now fully covering his face, certain she had broken it.

He didn't even see the third blow come, smashing into his skull and sending him sprawling back to the ground.

By the time his head hit the carpet, his world had turned black.

44

Lola stared at the candlestick in her hand and then at Jimmy, face down on the floor, and her heart was beating out of her chest as she spotted a small puddle of blood oozing from beneath him.

Was he dead?

She had wanted to incapacitate, not to kill, but even in that moment of shock, she knew she had been fighting for survival.

That was why there was no time to check for a pulse. She owed Jimmy nothing and knew she had to get out of this house now while she had the chance.

As he had pinned her to the ground, she had almost given up hope of escaping. His weight was heavy as he had sat himself on top of her, crushing her hands so she couldn't try to pull them free of the scarf, but then he had adjusted his position, leaning forward as he tried to gag her.

With his sock, she realised, staring now at his bare foot.

Gross.

As his weight had shifted, she had managed to pull her

right hand free from the scarf, then tip him forward, crawling out from beneath him and grabbing her weapon.

Now she was free, but she still had to escape from this house, and quickly, before Daniel and Rose realised what she had done to Jimmy.

The candlestick was heavy in her hand, and she was about to let it drop to the ground, but then she checked herself. She had yelled at the characters in horror movies far too many times for leaving their weapons with unconscious killers. Even if Jimmy was dead, she still needed to get past Daniel and Rose. She would keep it close in case she had to defend herself again.

Was the visitor still at the front door?

While part of her was tempted to scream for help, she also didn't want to alert the others that she was out of the room. Instead, she fled along the second-floor corridor and down the narrow staircase, checking that the coast was clear before making her way across the landing to the main staircase, freezing when she heard voices in the hallway below.

Rose and Daniel.

'He knows about us.'

Although Rose was making an effort to talk quieter, Lola could hear her angry hiss.

'How does he know?'

'She lied to us. He knew exactly why she was coming here.'

'So what have you told him?' Daniel demanded.

'I said she never showed up. He wants to leave his number. You need to go out there and persuade him to go away.'

Lola strained to listen, and although her mouth was uncomfortably dry, her shoulder muscles aching from where her arms had been pulled behind her back, and she was still jumpy with nerves, a tiny spark of hope ignited in the pit of her stomach.

Were they talking about Quinn? Had he come to find her?

They had to be, because no one else knew that she was coming here.

In the distance came the faint sounds of Monty barking – had he been locked in the kitchen? – then Rose yelling at him to shut up.

If Quinn was still outside, should Lola start screaming and hope to get his attention?

It was too risky with both Rose and Daniel at the foot of the stairs, blocking her escape. If they managed to intercept her, or if she had it all wrong and Quinn wasn't there, she could place herself back in danger.

Remembering the window at the other end of the first-floor landing, the one that looked over the front of the property, Lola ran towards it. If he was outside, then she could try to alert him and make him realise she was trapped inside?

As she passed the narrow staircase, she glanced warily at it, fear almost stopping her heart when she spotted movement at the top.

Shit. Jimmy was awake and coming down the steps.

Had he seen her?

She didn't think so, but now she was trapped. She couldn't go back towards the main staircase and Jimmy would soon tell Daniel and Rose what she had done.

Biting down on her urge to scream, she fled towards the window and the room she suspected belonged to Rose and Jimmy's mother, Agnes.

Just as she reached the turn on the landing, a loud thud sounded behind her and she turned just in time to see Jimmy collapse at the foot of the stairs.

Had he fallen down them?

As she stood frozen to the spot, he slowly raised his head, locking eyes with her. Silently, he started to drag himself across the floor towards her, leaving a trail of blood behind him.

Lola's eyes widened in horror. He wasn't moving fast and she could probably go bash him over the head again, but in that moment, fear took hold and she wanted to be as far away from him as possible.

She turned her attention back to the window, seriously considering clambering out onto the roof, reasoning that she had a better chance at making it to ground level safely than when she had been locked in the second-floor bedroom.

Lifting the latch, she understood that wasn't going to be an option. The window was locked. It wouldn't budge.

Lola drew in a deep, shaky breath, trying her best to stay calm as tears pricked at the back of her eyes. She could not afford to give in to emotion, not while she was still trapped here, but right now she didn't know what the hell to do.

Frantically, she looked around for something to try to break the glass.

The click of a door latch made her jump and her head shot up.

Agnes stood in the open door of her bedroom. Still in the white nightdress and barefoot. She stared directly at Lola, and for a moment, Lola was convinced she was going to cry out, alerting everyone where she was. But then the woman stepped back into the bedroom and held out her hand, beckoning.

'Come on.'

45

It is starting to unravel.

This is all Lola's fault. She should never have come here.

More importantly, she lied to us, insistent that Quinn Mallory only knew she was going to Norfolk, not who she was planning to see.

Not only does he know where we live, he is also aware of the family connection.

I have met his type before. He asked too many questions and I suspect he will be like a dog with a bone, looking for a scent of Lola.

We can't let him find her.

'You know he's going to come back here when he doesn't find her. And if he starts telling people she's missing and we were the last to see her, it's going to bring scrutiny to our doorstep.' I am aware of the rising note of panic in my voice, but I can't help it. I'm worried. 'And it's not like we can let her go now. She knows too much; plus, she will tell people what we did to her.'

'We're not going to let her go. Relax. He knows nothing.'

'What if he comes back before we've dealt with everything? He might bring the police.'

'Don't worry, my love. It's all going to be okay.'

I want to believe the words, but I am scared.

Everything is starting to unravel and there is nothing I can do to stop it.

46

Agnes's room was stark and depressing, and although it was generous in size, it reminded Lola more of a prison cell than a bedroom, containing little in the way of furniture or personal effects. Plain white sheets covered the single bed with its cheap plastic frame, and they were greying in colour and fraying at the edges, while a threadbare yellow blanket was spread haphazardly across the end of the mattress and a pine bedside table with one drawer missing stood beside it.

The rest of the items were mismatched and in a state of disrepair: a cherrywood freestanding wardrobe with one door falling off its hinges; a white dressing table with a dusty mirror and one of its thin, spindly legs taped in place; and a leather armchair by the window that looked as if it had seen better days.

There were no pictures on the walls nor a lampshade covering the bare bulb hanging from the ceiling rose, no television, and the curtains hanging at the two windows were torn and tatty. On the floor was a tray containing an empty plastic plate and knocked-over beaker, orange juice spilling out of it.

They were the kind of things you would give to a small child. But this was Rose and Jimmy's mother and she was ill. Both mentally and physically, judging by her waif-like appearance. Lola could see how stick-thin her legs were through the thin nightdress and her arms were like twigs. She seemed malnourished, and she was dirty too – her bare feet filthy and her hair a greasy mess – and there was a soiled, rancid odour about her, suggesting she was in desperate need of a wash.

Why did they leave her in this state? Did they not care?

Agnes was staring at Lola with the curiosity of a child, and Lola's sudden surge of compassion was almost as compelling as her need to escape this hellhole of a house.

Someone had to help this poor woman.

'Do you remember me?' she asked, setting the candlestick down on the dressing table, so as not to frighten her, and keeping her voice low, scared that Jimmy might hear them.

There was no key in the lock and the furniture that was in the room would not be strong enough to use as a barricade for the door.

She needed to check the windows, to see if there was a way out, but the way Agnes was looking at her, she felt she owed her something. Especially after the woman had just offered her a lifeline.

If that's what it was.

The woman's poor mind seemed so far gone, she perhaps had no idea what she had even done.

But then she surprised Lola with a seeming moment of clarity, her gaze locking on hers.

'They want to hurt you,' she warned. 'My ungrateful daughter and the bad man. If they find you, they will hurt you.'

Lola nodded, forcing a smile, even though the words chilled her. 'I know.'

So Daniel was unkind to his mother-in-law too? Perhaps that shouldn't surprise her, given how he had acted towards her since her arrival last night.

Although she needed to go, she found herself hesitating. 'Do they hurt you, Agnes?' she asked softly.

The woman stared at her and for a moment Lola didn't think she was going to respond to the question, but then she raised her bony arms, revealing bruises on her delicate, pale skin.

Was that from where they manhandled her?

It surprised Lola that Jimmy willingly went along with this, though. Agnes was his mother too. Was he really that weak-willed that he bowed down to his younger sister?

'They keep me in here. They lock the door,' Agnes told her. 'But Jimmy, he sometimes forgets.'

Purposely? Lola wondered, curious about the relationship between mother and son. Did he leave the door unlocked to give Agnes some freedom?

There had been no key in the lock. Had the woman taken it? Was it in this room?

She asked the question, but Agnes's face had gone blank and Lola realised she had lost her. She was now staring at Lola as if seeing her for the first time, and seemed a little fright-ened, her eyes widening as she took a step back towards the bed.

'What are you doing in my room?'

Shit, this wasn't good. If she cried out for help, Lola was screwed.

'Hello, Agnes,' she introduced herself again, smiling. 'My name is Lola.'

Agnes was studying her warily, but she didn't respond, retreating further, though to Lola's relief she seemed content to sit down on her bed, drawing her legs up like a child as she watched her.

Lola would get help for her. But first she had to help herself.

Keeping her movements calm and steady, not wanting to do anything that might trigger Agnes, she moved over to the windows. There were two in the room and she went to the larger one first, which was on the wall facing the bed. It overlooked the side of the house and the scene was a countryside winter wonderland with bare branches coated in silver frost and the morning sun already low in a cool blue sky, glinting through the trees, above a carpet of untouched crisp snow. If she wasn't trapped in this awful situation, the view would be perfect, and she imagined it would only get better as spring blossomed.

It struck her as particularly cruel that Agnes was forced to live in this soulless room, day after day, while taunted with a beautiful world outside her window. One that she could never go outside and explore.

That thought was on her mind as she tried the latch, finding that, like the window on the landing, this one too was locked, and even through her despair she realised she had been a fool expecting it to open. Of course they were going to lock Agnes's windows. She was their prisoner too.

It didn't stop Lola trying the other smaller window, frustrated when it wouldn't budge. This one had a view of the front of the property, but there was no sign of Quinn or of a car. Had he already left?

The only tyre tracks were those made by her rental car, along the path they had earlier cleared, when they had hidden it away in the garage.

Panic clawed its way up her throat. It was a reminder that

unless she found a way out of this house, they were going to destroy every trace of her existence. But, right now, she had no idea how she was going to do that.

She could smash one of the windows, she supposed, looking around the room for something she could use, but the noise would alert Rose, Daniel and Jimmy to her hiding place.

Getting out onto the roof and down to the ground wouldn't be an easy task, not with all the snow and the ice, but taking it slowly wouldn't be an option.

She couldn't risk breaking a bone. If she did, her fight would be over.

The other option was to leave this room, but would Jimmy be waiting outside?

She had hurt him badly and had thought for a few minutes that he was dead. She had no idea what kind of state he would be in. But even if she managed to get past him, there was still Daniel and Rose to contend with.

Could she get down the staircase without them seeing her or without Jimmy raising the alarm? If she could find somewhere on the ground floor to hide, then perhaps she would be able to slip out when they weren't looking.

Unfortunately, time wasn't on her side and they would surely be heading upstairs at any moment to find her and Jimmy.

She had to do something.

'Rose! Get away from the window.'

The voice came from behind her and Lola's head shot around, expecting to see Rose in the room.

It was still just her and Agnes, and it took a second to register that it was Agnes who had spoken and that she was addressing Lola by her daughter's name. Her voice had completely changed and whereas before she had been shy and almost childlike, now she sounded fierce, a scowl on her face as she got up from the bed.

Unnerved, Lola took a step back as the woman approached.

'I'm not Rose. My name is Lola.'

'Don't tell lies, you little bitch.'

Agnes's hand flew out from nowhere and given how frail she looked, she had no trouble delivering a stinging slap to Lola's cheek.

She took another step back, shocked. 'Agnes, I'm not Rose.'

Lola could see she wasn't getting through. The woman's eyes were wild and angry.

'It's all your fault.' Agnes's voice was raised now. 'You're the reason your father left. He hated having you for a daughter, you ungrateful spoilt little brat, with your conniving and your lies.'

Was this just crazy talk? Or did Rose really have this kind of relationship with her mother?

Realising she wasn't going to convince Agnes she wasn't her daughter, and knowing she needed to calm the woman down, Lola decided to play along.

'I'm sorry I lied, Mum. Please forgive me.'

'No dinner for you. You'll spend the night in the cupboard, where you belong.'

What? Had Agnes really treated her daughter that way?

'I should have sent you away, instead of wasting my time trying to discipline you. You're a good-for-nothing waste of space.'

'I promise I'll be good,' Lola told her. 'I won't do it again.'

Was she getting through?

She was scared that the whole house had been alerted to

the commotion and she eyed the door cautiously, half expecting it to open.

Agnes was quietly sobbing now and while that wasn't any better, at least she was making less noise. Lola watched awkwardly as she backed away, sitting herself down on the edge of the bed. She seemed caught up in her own world, opening the top drawer of the bedside table and taking out a photo that she clutched to her chest as she continued to cry.

Was she even aware that Lola was still in the room?

'My James,' she said, staring at the wall as she rocked the picture back and forth, all trace of anger gone from her voice.

Was she talking about Jimmy? Was it a picture of her son?

'He loved me. He promised we would be together forever.'

Not her son. Her husband.

'I was a beautiful bride.'

Taking a chance that Agnes no longer believed she was Rose, Lola took a tentative step towards the bed.

'Is that a photo from your wedding day?' she asked.

When Agnes nodded, she tried again.

'May I see?'

Agnes glanced up, her eyes red-rimmed and back to being shy and almost childlike.

She handed over the picture. 'He was so handsome.'

Lola stared at the couple in the photo, for a moment taken aback.

This wasn't Agnes in the photograph. It was Rose.

The woman was getting muddled. This was Rose and Daniel's wedding day.

Except, the man in the picture wasn't Daniel.

She recognised who he was instantly, remembering him from the photos she had seen. The two men in the Lamborghini and then with the champagne when they had graduated, posing with Daniel's parents. It was his best friend, Brett.

But why was Brett married to Rose? It made no sense. She was Daniel's wife.

Lola thought of the jewellery box and the loving note from Brett. Then the photo of the other man sitting at the table with Rose in the box she had found upstairs. She had thought he was Brett, but no, here he was in the wedding picture. The groom.

Lola's mind was trying to catch up as she registered what she was seeing, but it wasn't until she turned over the photograph, reading the caption on the back – *Daniel and Rose's wedding day. 2018* – confirming his identity, that it clicked into place and she finally understood.

The man downstairs who had been in a wheelchair when she arrived, but was now miraculously walking, wasn't Daniel at all.

He was Brett. Rose's lover and Daniel's supposed best friend.

The other man in the pictures was the real Daniel.

So in that case, where the hell was he?

47

Quinn waited until he had reached the woods before pulling off the driveway and between the trees.

The snow both aided and hampered his efforts. While it helped him see where he was going, he was also conscious that the white carpet would make it easier to spot him from the house, and also that his footsteps would be visible, so he kept to the edge while returning to the property, glad that his clothing was all dark greys and black, helping to keep him inconspicuous.

This was not the way he had planned on spending Christmas Eve, but his encounter with the Whitlocks had left him even more certain now that Lola was in danger.

The man he had met, who had come to the door in a wheelchair, was not Daniel Whitlock. The bar owner had identified Lola's brother in the photograph.

Quinn did recognise him, though. He was the other man in the Lamborghini.

So why was he pretending to be Daniel?

Quinn was determined to find out.

The cleared path on the driveway and the tyre tracks had piqued his interest when he had first arrived and he was even keener to see what was inside.

Rose had insisted they were busy, with it being Christmas Eve, so why had they been up early that morning putting their car away in the garage? Surely they would just leave it.

Quinn had reasoned that perhaps they had cleared the car and the driveway because they were planning to go out somewhere, but if that were the case, it made no sense sticking the vehicle in the garage, as the storm had already passed.

Perhaps it was nothing sinister, though it was difficult to suspect otherwise at this point, especially given what he had just seen.

He was conscious that he needed to be careful. If he was caught breaking and entering, then he would lose his badge. It was a risk he was willing to take, though, after they had lied to him. He couldn't walk away. Lola had disappeared without a trace after leaving to come here. And yes, Quinn couldn't prove that she had ever arrived, but his gut told him she was inside the house.

There was no mobile signal out here. He knew because he had checked his phone.

There was no way to call for assistance, and heading back to the village would eat into precious time. No, he was on his own, so he wouldn't do anything stupid.

He didn't know what bizarre kind of game was being played out inside Midwinter Manor, but he was determined to find out.

First he would satisfy his curiosity with the garage. What he did or didn't find inside would determine his next move.

He followed the woods round to the side of the property,

where there were fewer windows and taller shrubs to hide behind as he approached the house.

Unfortunately, there was no way of getting close without disturbing the snow, but he reasoned that his footprints were less likely to be noticed here. Hopefully the snow would soon melt away any evidence.

The main garage door was at the front of the building, albeit set a little further back from the main house, but Quinn hoped to avoid that if possible, knowing it carried a greater risk of detection. Luckily, he discovered another door to the side of the garage, and after a quick glance around him to check the coast was clear, he pushed down on the handle, unsurprised to find it locked.

Taking a credit card from his wallet, he slid it into the gap between the door and the frame, finding the lock mechanism and wiggling it back and forth until the door sprang open.

Quickly, he stepped inside the dark garage, closing the door behind him.

After replacing the card in his wallet, he took out his phone and activated the torch. The faint beam showed him four vehicles: a Ford Transit van was parked towards the back of the large room, next to a Volvo XC60, while to the front of the garage was a 25-plate Range Rover and beside it a Peugeot 208.

Disability stickers on the van told Quinn that this was Daniel's mode of transport.

He moved past the Ford and peered in the front window of the Volvo and then the Range Rover, but there was nothing suspicious with either vehicle.

Finally he moved on to the Peugeot. Once more, nothing odd about the interior of the vehicle, but it had snow on it, telling him it had recently been moved from outside, and as he circled around the back, he spotted a rental agency sticker on the rear passenger window, the knot in his stomach coiling a little tighter.

Was this the car that Lola had hired?

It made absolutely no sense why there would be a rental car in here otherwise.

So in that case, where the fuck was she?

Quinn knew he needed to get inside the house and fast. Something was wrong here.

He thought about Daniel Whitlock, and of his initial reluctance to meet his sister. For the first time, his mind went to a darker place as he tried to piece everything together.

If he was correct and on the right track about what was being covered up here, then Lola could be in big trouble.

Had she figured out the truth about her brother and who he really was?

She had dropped off the face of the planet since coming here to meet Daniel.

What if they had hurt her? Or worse.

No. Quinn couldn't think like that. She had to be okay.

He would not lose her a second time.

Desperate to find her, no longer caring if he broke a dozen laws in doing so, he let himself back out of the garage, closing the door behind him.

As he started to turn, a shadow fell upon him and he caught a brief glance of a figure in his periphery.

Then came the smash of something cracking against his skull.

He was out cold before he hit the ground.

48

Quinn's visit to the house had left me unsettled.

I just didn't buy that he would travel all the way to Saham Toney looking for Lola, then be persuaded to leave so easily.

Had we really been that convincing?

Given the tension of our situation, I didn't think so.

That was why I had kept a lookout, fearful for his return, every one of my nerves on edge. Especially when that stupid dog of Daniel's kept barking, wanting to be let out of the kitchen.

'Shut up, Monty!' I yelled again.

When I caught sight of Quinn moving between the trees as he circled back towards the property, I realised I was right to trust my gut. He hadn't believed us and the cheeky bastard was now trespassing on our land.

It didn't take long to figure out that he was trying to break into the garage.

Was he looking for Lola's car?

Perhaps we should have moved it round to the house and

hidden it in one of the long-abandoned stables, but we honestly hadn't anticipated any visitors.

Not that it mattered now. The damage was done.

At least he was making things easier for us, as we would have the element of surprise when he stepped out.

We had watched him open the back door and disappear inside. Then it was only a matter of waiting.

Now he is lying unconscious in the garage, an added problem we have to deal with, thanks to Lola.

We might be related, this sister-in-law and me, but she has caused too much trouble, and I hate her with every bone in my body.

To make matters a whole lot worse, we've just discovered Quinn has been holding out on us too. Inside his pockets is a warrant card.

He's a bloody police detective.

The discovery has me hyperventilating and I need a few moments to calm down.

How are we going to fix this?

I look to the man beside me, hoping he has the answers, but instead he berates me.

'This was all your stupid idea, just remember that. If you had just told that irritating Henderson woman to fuck off, we wouldn't be in this mess.'

Tears fall, even though I know he is right. It is my fault. I was the one who persuaded him to pretend to be Daniel, despite him pointing out a dozen reasons why it wouldn't work.

Truthfully, Brett Corrigan is nothing like my husband. He doesn't suffer fools and he has a fiery temper. I love him, though, with every bone in my body.

He is angry with me now for messing up and I don't blame him. I have jeopardised everything we have worked so hard for.

'I'm sorry. I thought if we met with her once she would leave us alone.'

'Instead it's blown up in our faces. I can't believe I let you talk me into this, Rose. You're a damn fool. And so am I for agreeing. You've gambled with our future.'

I swipe my hand across my wet cheeks. 'How are we going to fix this?' I plead. 'We can't let him go.'

Brett falls silent for a moment and I can tell he is seething.

'He was trespassing. We were just defending our property.'

'But the police will want to make a report. We can't have them come here.' My voice is shrill with panic.

It's one thing pretending to Lola, but convincing the police of our situation will never work.

Brett scowls at me, but he knows I am right.

'Okay. We drive them down to Thetford, put them both in his car in the middle of the forest. Make it look like they were fighting. He strangles her, then is overcome with guilt. Murder-suicide.'

I am listening. Is it possible this could work?

'No one is going to connect them to us,' Brett pushes on.

Could this be our answer?

Honestly, I don't see that we have a choice.

For now, we tie Quinn up and leave him in the garage.

Brett has his key fob and sets out to get Quinn's car and he orders me upstairs to fetch Lola, handing me an axe.

'It's just for precaution,' he says, seeing my look of alarm. 'It's good to have a weapon. It will help keep her subdued.'

I hope he is right, but deep down I know I will use it if I

have to. I will not allow Lola Henderson to spoil everything I have here.

If all goes to plan, this whole horrible mess will be cleared up in a couple of hours.

49

Realising that she had met with an imposter and not her actual brother had left Lola reeling.

What the hell was going on in this house and why was Daniel's friend, Brett, pretending to be him? And why the hell was Rose going along with it all, acting as if Brett was her husband?

Just what had Lola walked into?

Now she understood why they hadn't wanted her to leave and she was cursing herself that she hadn't joined the dots earlier when she first saw Brett up and out of the wheelchair.

But even as she again questioned where her real brother was, her mind crept towards a dark truth.

Was Daniel their big secret?

Was he dead?

She had to get out of this house and fast. And short of smashing the windows, she knew she had no choice but to go back out onto the landing.

As she started to cross the room, the door suddenly swung open and Jimmy came crashing into the room. He didn't look well, his face deathly pale and blood streaking all over the side of his neck and the top of his T-shirt, and he seemed a little out of it, his eyes wild and as he came to an abrupt stop, he was swaying from side to side. But then he zoned in on Lola, his gaze sharpening and turning mean, and her heart rate accelerated.

Oh shit.

Growling loudly, he launched himself at her, catching her off guard, and although she managed to sidestep out of his way, he was still able to grab hold of her arm.

As she frantically tried to pull herself free, another voice came from the landing and Rose appeared in the doorway. To her horror, Lola realised she was holding an axe.

'Jimmy?' Rose's eyes widened at the state of him. 'What the hell have you done to my brother?' she snapped at Lola.

Managing to get her free elbow under Jimmy's chin, then a well-placed knee slamming into his crotch, had him yowling out in pain and loosening his grip, and she managed to wrench her arm away, turning her attention to Rose.

'That's a question I should be asking you!' she threw back, furious. 'What have you done to *my* brother?'

That was good. Hold on to the anger. It kept her fear at bay.

Rose's mouth dropped open, but then she closed it again, and her expression became guarded. Lola could tell she was trying to decide how much she knew.

'Where is he? Why was Brett pretending to be Daniel? Did you kill him?'

'So you have worked it out.' Rose nodded. 'Well done.'

'You were his wife,' Lola snapped, glaring at her. 'And Brett was his friend.'

'And you knew nothing of our situation.'

'Tell me what he did then that was so bad he deserved to die?'

Things were getting heated, but instead of shouting back, Rose paused, her face breaking out into a wide grin. It was the most animated Lola had seen her, and she seemed genuinely amused.

'It's not what I did, Lola,' she said after a moment, shaking her head. 'It's your fault your brother is dead.'

50

EIGHTEEN MONTHS EARLIER

It was the letter from John Fagan that had unravelled everything.

By the summer of 2024, I really believed my relationship with Daniel was back on track. He had seemed to forgive me for my affair and I had put his threats to kill Brett down to nothing more than an idle attempt to scare me.

It had worked. In doing so, he had reminded me of everything I would be giving up if we were no longer married, and I was greedy enough to bite the hook he dangled.

The friendship I had formed with Daniel Whitlock when I'd first met him had been genuine. He was easy to get along with and he was kind. The lure of his fortune had always made him seem more attractive to me than he actually was, but that was okay. So when he had flirted with me, I reciprocated, flattered by the lavish gifts and treats he bought me, and when he said he loved me and wanted to marry me, I was happy to go along with it, caught up in everything he could offer.

I could compromise. He was an attractive man and a good one too. So what if it wasn't true love? That didn't matter. I would fulfil my duties looking after his needs and in return he would give me the riches I had always dreamt of.

It was a marriage of convenience, even if Daniel didn't realise it.

At first, everything had been easy enough. Nigel was a tough nut to crack, but Annie offered a steady maternal friendship that I came to treasure. When my mother-in-law passed away, I had been distraught.

That was when Daniel's and my relationship started to disintegrate.

There was no great underlying knot of love to hold us together.

Well, perhaps there was on Daniel's part, but certainly not on mine, and the wealth that I had once coveted now became the trap keeping me in this marriage.

I had signed a prenup, assuming I would be able to go along with this marriage forever, but Daniel, who had been so laid-back in those early years, became more difficult to live with. I couldn't leave him, though. If I walked away now, I would have nothing. The idea of that was simply unbearable.

So I stayed, and I tolerated both his and Nigel's behaviour, even as my resentment for them grew.

Nigel and I had never seen eye to eye, and I suspected it was because he saw me for who I really was. He knew I had never truly loved his son. That, for me, it had always been about the money.

A late-night conversation in his office, where he offered me £500,000 to walk away, had ended badly.

I had been a fool and greed had been my downfall. What I should have done was insist I loved his son. Not let the mask slip and refuse to be swayed. Instead, I had seen a way to escape my marriage and set myself up with a nice, fat bank balance.

It wasn't enough money, I had told him, certain this was a negotiation. I wanted more if I was to go, boldly telling him to double his offer.

What I hadn't realised was our conversation was being recorded on a stupid little camera Nigel had hidden on the bookcase behind his desk.

He had gleefully played it back to me, revealing that he didn't intend to give me a penny. Once Daniel knew the truth about his beloved wife, it would devastate him and he would end the marriage.

I had been beside myself as I realised I'd walked right into Nigel's trap. My dream was over and the lifestyle I had become accustomed to was about to be snatched away from me.

I had followed Nigel out of his study and up the stairs, begging and pleading with him to stop, as he went to wake Daniel, determined to share the recording.

As we reached the landing, Nigel turned, giving me a withering look.

'I always knew you were trash,' he growled. 'My son deserves so much better.'

When I later thought back to that moment, I wasn't sure if it was that last scathing remark or the fact I was about to lose everything that had tipped me over the edge. All I remembered was grabbing hold of Nigel's collar and pulling him close, glaring at him as I hissed, 'I'll see you in hell.'

I barely registered letting go of his shirt or giving him a hard shove, sending him flying down the stairs. But I never forgot the look in his eyes in that moment before he fell. The horror of realising he had overplayed his hand.

I had stood and looked down at him, lying crumpled at the

foot of the stairs. He had gasped in the moment that he lost his footing, but other than that he hadn't made a sound, the only noise coming from his body bumping against each step.

If Daniel had heard, he didn't call out, and once I trusted my legs to hold me, I had gone downstairs to check for Nigel's pulse.

There was still a faint one, but the blood oozing from a wound in his head suggested he wouldn't survive much longer without help.

Calmly, I took the camera from him, going back into his study and leaving him to bleed out on the floor, as I deleted the footage of our conversation. Afterwards, barely sparing him a glance, I had gone back upstairs, climbing into bed beside my husband, and sleeping surprisingly well given what I had done.

The following morning, I had 'discovered' Nigel's body at the foot of the stairs, putting on the performance of my life as I cried out in shock to Daniel and then called the police.

I had never killed before and I thought I was going to be a complete mess. Somehow, though, I managed to hold myself together enough to convince everyone it had been a terrible accident. The one thing that pulled me through, that I kept my focus on, was the prize: the inheritance Daniel would gain as an only son. I would not give that up, and it influenced every lie I told and every fake tear I shed at the terrible tragedy.

Still, my demons haunted me. Each time I climbed the stairs, I saw Nigel's face as I pushed him, and I remembered my panic that he was going to expose me. Did he now walk the hallways in the afterlife, looking for revenge? In my calmer moments, I reminded myself I wasn't a believer of such rubbish, but sometimes, late at night, my skin would chill and dread would choke me. Deep down, I knew it was guilt at what I had done.

Not long after the police investigation into Nigel's death was wound down, I persuaded Daniel to put the house in Oxfordshire on the market. Things hadn't been great between us for some time, but I was determined to make our marriage work. I refused to give up everything I had fought for. Away from his family home, isolated and living in the sticks in rural Norfolk, Daniel would be completely reliant on me and easier for me to control.

I didn't consider myself to be a wicked person, despite what I had done. Nigel had backed me into a corner and I had a right to defend myself. His death wasn't premeditated. What had happened, he had brought upon himself.

I intended to still care for my husband and make sure he had a good quality of life, but it would be under my supervision. When we had first met, he still had a large circle of friends, but gradually I had driven them all away, wanting him entirely reliant on me. In some cases, I had managed to talk him into cutting people off, putting the idea into his head that they were either a bad influence or that they hadn't been there for him after his accident. It helped that he trusted me and my judgement implicitly.

Then there were those who needed a firmer hand. A few cancelled catch-ups or forgetting to show up to planned meet-ups had deterred many of them, who started to see him as unreliable and flaky.

And for the last few who didn't get the hint, I had taken control of Daniel's phone, deleting messages, and in some cases pretending to be him, doing whatever necessary to make sure they stayed away from my husband.

By the time we moved into Midwinter Manor, I was his

world. And I intended to keep it that way. I kept Daniel satisfied and made sure he had a happy enough life, and in turn I got to play lady of the manor, with no expense spared. There were spa days and lunch dates, and an endless budget for my ever-growing wardrobe. I even persuaded my loving husband to allow me to bring in a temporary carer so I could enjoy a sun-soaked holiday abroad.

Then Jimmy had come to stay, followed by Brett. The one friend I hadn't really known about, so hadn't been able to drive away.

When he had first shown up, I knew I had my work cut out for me. He had a strong will and was unpredictable. Completely different from all of Daniel's other friends, and he had an allure about him, awakening something inside of me that I had forgotten existed.

At first, I believed I could have everything: still be a wife to Daniel, yet enjoy my lover, but my husband had put paid to that when he cornered me, telling me he knew of the affair.

I did my best to fix things, to be the good wife that he wanted. I swear I did. I tried to distance myself from Brett and focused solely on my husband. I couldn't allow my marriage to crumble. That had to come first.

But Brett was a difficult man to say no to and eventually I stopped trying. This time, though, I insisted we were more discreet. And I made sure he knew the reason why.

Brett had laughed off Daniel's threat to kill him, agreeing with me that Daniel had lashed out wanting to scare me, and it was no more than an attempt to keep us apart. Still, he seemed in no hurry to leave Midwinter Manor, and both of us were more careful with our time together.

If Daniel had any inkling that the affair had restarted, he

never said. I tried my best to keep him satisfied too, and his competitive friendship with Brett continued.

In the end, it wasn't Brett who messed things up. It was John Fagan.

With hindsight, I should have destroyed the letter as soon as it arrived, but I didn't. And when Daniel went snooping, finding it in the pocket of my dress, I knew I was in big trouble.

'You kept my sister a secret from me.' Daniel had been furious with me when he learned of Lola's existence, realising that I had met with John and that the interfering man had been trying to contact him. 'Why the hell would you do this?'

'Because I was trying to protect you. Protect what we have.'

'Protect what we have?' he repeated, his tone incredulous. 'You mean *my* inheritance? You did this for money?'

'We don't know anything about her,' I tried to reason, although in truth he had it spot on. 'We don't know what kind of person she is. I know you share a mother, Daniel, but she could be trouble.'

'She's my sister. My own flesh and blood. How dare you?'

He had been so angry with me and I had waited for the storm to pass.

Except it didn't.

After he had festered for a while, he came to find me.

'I don't know if I can forgive you for this,' he had said quietly. He sounded resigned and panic fluttered in my chest.

'We can fix things. Have you spoken to John?'

He shook his head. 'Not yet. I need a little time to let everything sink in.'

'That's wise. You shouldn't rush into anything.'

I was trying to be supportive, hopeful that I would win him round, but his next words crushed me.

'I'm not. That's why you can stay until you've found somewhere else and I have arranged a new carer. I know it will take a little time for you to find a place to move into, especially as you have your mother to consider.'

He might as well have kicked me in the stomach; deep dread and sickness clogged my throat so I could barely breathe. 'I don't understand.'

'Our marriage is over, Rose. I want a divorce. You've already betrayed me once by sleeping with Brett. Now I realise I shouldn't have clung on and tried to make things work. I'm not forgiving you this time.'

'I made a mistake. I promise I was only trying to protect you.'

'Protect yourself, you mean.'

I tried to talk him round, tearfully begging for his forgiveness, but his mind was made up.

What the hell was I going to do? The prenup I had signed meant I wasn't entitled to a penny of the estate. I couldn't lose this life I had built for myself and go back to nothing.

Later that night, I sought solace in Brett's arms.

He was quiet and thoughtful, seeming unsure what this would mean for him too. Daniel had allowed him to stay while there was a full house, but if he now kicked me, Jimmy and Agnes out, would he give Brett his marching orders as well?

'I don't have anywhere to go,' he admitted, revealing a rare moment of vulnerability.

'We can get somewhere together,' I suggested, even though I still secretly hoped Daniel would calm down and realise he was overreacting.

'You'll need to hire a solicitor. See how much you're entitled to,' he mused, as he ran his fingers up and down my arm.

His words were a harsh reminder of my dire situation.

'I won't get anything,' I whispered, telling him about the prenup.

Brett's body tensed beside me, his hand stilling, and for several minutes we lay in silence.

'What if we could stay here?' he said eventually, his breath warm against my ear. 'What if there was a way that you and I could keep this house... but without Daniel.'

I hesitated, a small, dark part of me already knowing what he was going to suggest. I knew, because I had been thinking about it too. Still I feigned ignorance.

'And how exactly would we do that?'

51

PRESENT DAY

Quinn awoke in blackness, his head pounding, and for a few moments he had no recollection of where he was.

He had been at his sister's, he remembered that much. And Lola. He had reconnected with Lola. Gradually, the morning's events came back to him. It was Christmas Eve and Lola was missing. He had gone to her brother's to look for her, meeting Rose Whitlock and then her husband... Except the man in the wheelchair who had come to the door wasn't Daniel.

Quinn had recognised him. He was in the Lamborghini picture he had on his phone, but the bar owner had told him the other man was Daniel. Okay, it was possible he had pointed out the wrong man, but that seemed unlikely. Especially given how hostile the couple had been and their complete lack of interest in whether Lola was safe, plus the rental car in the garage.

He remembered snooping now, and some fucker – fake Daniel – had smacked him in the head with something heavy.

Was that where he was, still in the garage? There was a faint odour of petrol that suggested he was, plus the floor he was lying on was hard – concrete? – and it was bloody cold, which suggested he was in some kind of outdoor building.

And his wrists were bound, he realised now. Pulled tightly behind his back, which would account for his uncomfortable position, curled on his side.

He started to sit up, realising the task would require more than one attempt, as a woozy sense of heaviness throbbed in his head and sudden sickness curdled in his gut.

Sucking in a breath, he tried again, this time prepared for the nausea and managing to get himself upright.

He picked at the knot – rope, he guessed from the texture – and knew from how tight it was that he needed something to cut through it. As his eyes gradually adjusted to the darkness, shapes coming more into focus, he looked around for any tools he could use.

There would be something.

He suspected the ambush had been in haste, and fake Daniel had figured he was out for the count. The rope had probably just been a precaution.

Managing to get up onto his knees and then to his feet, Quinn allowed himself a few moments to steady his head, then began to search around the garage.

He knew he should take things slowly, but unfortunately time wasn't on his side.

While before he had suspected Lola was inside the house, now he was certain.

She was smart and a fighter, but up against both Rose and Brett would she stand a chance?

He needed to focus, get himself free, then break his way into the house and find her.

52

EIGHTEEN MONTHS EARLIER

Daniel died on a warm Friday evening in June, two days after he had told me he wanted a divorce.

After Brett had suggested we kill him – an ironic turn of events given Daniel's own pathetic threat of murder, which had planted the seed in both of our heads – I hadn't wasted much time getting on board with the idea.

Of course, I had pretended to be surprised, shocked even, when Brett first spoke the words, but I quickly allowed myself to be talked round.

Yes, I had access to his accounts. Yes, I knew the code to the safe. I wasn't stupid. I had made sure over the years that I could get my hands on everything my husband owned.

Perhaps we should have taken what cash was available and fled. It wasn't enough, though. I wanted this house.

And it wasn't as if he was in contact with anyone in the real world. He rarely saw anyone. Any interactions he had were online or by phone. I could cover those, I was sure.

Daniel had backed me into a corner. If he hadn't mentioned divorce, then I would have stayed in my marriage, hopefully carrying on my affair, but that was no longer an option and I knew if we were going to do this, then it had to be before he made contact with John Fagan.

The beauty of living in such remote countryside is how cut off you are. Midwinter Manor is isolated, meaning Daniel was unable to go anywhere without one of us driving him. We also relied on the Wi-Fi for communication. There was no phone signal and no landline.

After we agreed that Daniel needed to die, our plan moved forward quickly. Brett disabled the internet, telling my husband the following morning that it seemed to be down.

I could tell he was frustrated. Had he been planning to start making calls?

Thank goodness we had acted when we did.

After breakfast, I took Jimmy to one side. Back then, my brother didn't start drinking until later in the afternoon. I wanted him sober for the conversation we were about to have.

I knew he was fond of Daniel, so, I'll be honest, I wasn't sure how he was going to react. But we needed him on board with our plan if it was going to work, and I was hoping self-preservation would weigh heavier than loyalty to his brother-in-law.

He had listened in sympathy as I told him my marriage was over, and fear when I explained we would all have to leave Midwinter Manor, but what I then proposed had his eyes bulging in horror.

'You want to do what?' he had squeaked.

It took a good hour of talking him round and making him understand there was no other choice, and I had to repeatedly promise him that Brett and I would take care of everything. All Jimmy had to do was keep his mouth shut.

'What about Mam?' he had asked, worried that she would give up our secret.

I waved my hand dismissively, already certain she wasn't going to be a problem. She barely knew her own name these days. Besides, with Daniel gone, it would be easier to keep her locked away and out of my sight.

It wasn't cruel. I fed her and let her live here. She should be grateful.

'And at least we won't have the burden of trying to pay for her care,' I pointed out to Jimmy, to add to his fear.

I knew it was something he would struggle with.

It took a while, but, as I had hoped, self-preservation eventually outweighed Jimmy's fondness for his brother-in-law, and he reluctantly agreed we had no other choice.

On the night of Daniel's death, anticipation and nerves thrummed through me and I was anxious to get it over with. I had proposed the four of us eat in the conservatory as it was such a pleasant evening, figuring the large room with its tiled floor would be easier to clean up any mess. Although we didn't expect any blood, I knew from being a nurse what happens when a body's muscles relax in the moments after death.

I had cooked Daniel his favourite pasta bake dish, followed by tiramisu. A little summer treat, I told him when he looked surprised, as we didn't often have dessert.

It was a last meal for the condemned man, though I could see he thought I was trying to win his forgiveness.

No, darling, I had smiled to myself. It's a little too late for that now.

Brett had been given the role of executioner. He was bigger and stronger than me, and Jimmy had agreed to go along with our plan as long as he wasn't involved in killing Daniel. Besides, this whole thing had been Brett's idea, I reasoned. He used an old belt of Daniel's, silently moving behind him, then slipping the leather noose around his neck, and he had pulled so hard, I actually thought Daniel might come out of his chair.

In hindsight, I wished I hadn't sat facing my husband. The look of shock and then terror on Daniel's face as he realised what was happening still haunts me and it was the most bizarre spectacle to watch, his hands going to his throat as he tugged futilely at the belt, while those poor useless legs of his sat perfectly still. Had he still had the use of them, I would have expected to see him desperately kicking out.

I had always believed strangulation to be quick, but I guess that is a lie the movies tell us. Poor defenceless Daniel was thrashing and gurgling, his eyes bulging for what felt like an eternity as Brett twisted the belt tighter.

When it was finally over, a huge surge of emotion hit. Disbelief at what we had just done, sorrow that it had come to this, but also a rush of giddiness. We were free of Daniel's threats and Midwinter Manor was now ours.

Later, when Daniel's body was buried in the spot we had picked out in the garden, the three of us sat down in the kitchen and drank whisky. It was already 3 a.m., but we didn't go to bed until we had worked our way through two bottles.

We were careful around each other over the following weeks, and I think all three of us were scared that the uneasy alliance we had formed might break, but then with the dying embers of summer as we headed into a spectacular autumn which showered golden and rust-red leaves over Daniel's resting place, we settled into a routine, adjusting to our new roles.

Brett and I could now be openly affectionate with one another and the crime we had committed had brought us closer together. My new man had a stubborn streak and at times a mean temper and I couldn't manipulate him as I had Daniel, but somehow we made it work.

As long as we convinced the outside world that my husband was still alive, I would get to stay here in my dream home.

Meanwhile, Jimmy struggled with his demons. He had never been as strong as me and it was like living with Jekyll and Hyde. Part of him determined that no one could ever learn our secret, while another side of him was wracked with remorse and drinking himself silly.

We kept him close, both aware that he was our weakest link.

At one point, Brett had talked about silencing him in case any secrets came out, but he was my brother. Buffoon as he was, I couldn't kill him.

I already had enough blood on my hands. No more death, I insisted.

Then Lola Henderson reached out.

There had been no more correspondence from John Fagan, and foolishly, I had assumed that trouble had passed, so when I first heard from the adoption agency, dread had sat heavily in my stomach. Daniel was dead and couldn't respond.

I had access to my husband's phone and in turn his email account and all of his socials. In the time since we'd killed him, I replied to the messages I needed to, and even posted a few times on Facebook, but responding to the adoption agency seemed too dangerous, so instead I ignored it.

Damn Lola for tracking us down.

She has brought this on herself.

My plan was for Brett to convince her he was Daniel. She had no idea what her brother looked like, as there were very few pictures of Daniel online.

Brett would make it clear that 'Daniel' had no interest in a relationship with her, but hopefully satisfy her curiosity, and then she would be on her way.

Although it was risky, I was sure we could pull it off. Brett was less convinced, but I managed to talk him round, telling him we needed to give her the answers she craved without letting slip that Daniel was dead.

And it was easier for us if we let her believe that Nigel Whitlock was her father.

If she learnt about John Fagan and went looking for him, there was a chance it would bring him back into our lives. Unlike Lola, he would know immediately that Brett wasn't Daniel.

For a short while, I thought our plan had worked. But that was before the bad weather, Lola crashing her rental car, and then the power cut.

Everything worked against us.

We never meant to kill again, but things have spiralled out of control and Lola and Quinn now know too much.

We cannot risk letting them leave.

53

PRESENT DAY

As Rose spoke, her tone cool and detached, admitting to what she and Brett had done to Daniel, she edged further into the room, the axe swinging ominously by her side.

Lola had taken a couple of steps back herself, but she had reached the wall and there was nowhere else to go.

She eyed the axe warily. The crazy woman was giving off *Friday the 13th* vibes, and Lola was growing increasingly fearful she might use it.

Although her hands were now free, the candlestick she had bludgeoned Jimmy with was sat on the dressing table on the other side of the room. Plus there was Jimmy himself, who perhaps posed less of a threat because of his injury, but he was still gamely trying to get back up onto his feet.

Meanwhile, Agnes, who had watched everything unfold with the wonderment of a child, would be no help at all. Lola suspected she had no concept of what was going on, as she just seemed delighted to have everyone in her room.

'Jimmy, find something to tie her up with again,' Rose

demanded. 'See if there is anything in Mam's wardrobe that you can use.'

'Okay,' he managed, speaking for the first time since Lola had knocked him out.

She watched him stagger towards the wardrobe, losing his balance at one point and stumbling forward, though, by some miracle, managing to stay upright.

'Hurry up,' Rose urged, seeming oblivious to his struggles, but that was perhaps because she was watching Lola like a hawk, making sure she stayed cornered.

Although she was desperate to make a break for it and try to flee the room, Lola didn't dare.

'I'm trying.' Jimmy was propping himself up against the wardrobe now, a sheen of sweat covering his face. 'Rose, I don't feel too good.'

'Just find something and throw it to me. Quick.'

Lola's mind was frantically racing, aware she needed to do something. She couldn't allow them to tie her up again.

'It was Quinn at the door a little while ago, wasn't it?' she questioned, trying to get Rose talking. 'He was looking for me.'

Rose glowered. 'You lied to us. You said he didn't know where you were going.'

Yes, Lola had lied, because she didn't want to put him at risk. But he had come here and apparently left again, so whatever they had told him had obviously been convincing enough. With Quinn now gone and safe, could she use him to her advantage.

'Yes, I did lie,' she admitted. 'He knew. He knows all about Daniel being my brother and how he asked me to meet him here. You might have fooled him with your lies for now, but he will keep looking for me and he won't give up.'

She had hoped to scare Rose, but instead all she did was make her laugh.

What was so funny?

'He is very persistent, I agree.' Rose's expression was pure smugness. No trace of the woman who had apologised for Lola's predicament earlier, telling her she was sorry. 'A good thing he never left and is passed out cold in the garage.'

'What?'

For a moment, Lola wasn't sure if she had heard the woman correctly, but even as the words sank in and she questioned if it was a bluff, her throat tightened with alarm, knowing deep down it was true.

'Don't worry, you'll get to be with him very soon.'

A wave of fresh despair had Lola's eyes pricking with tears. It was her fault he was in this mess. She should never have told him she was coming here.

She couldn't succumb to these psychos now, though. Even with only a slim chance, she needed to fight them with everything she had, especially now Quinn was counting on her too.

As she debated whether to take a chance of running at Rose, trying to catch her off guard before she could swing the axe, Agnes cried out.

'*You dirty little bitch!*'

Lola jumped, her attention snapping to the frail woman on the bed who was focused on her daughter. And Rose, she realised, was looking back, her eyes wide.

'Shut up, Mam. You're in my house now,' she barked back. 'My rules.'

'I'll give you something to cry about,' Agnes continued. 'Get over here.'

When Rose didn't comply, Agnes started screeching the words again and again.

'Get over here! Get over here! Get over here!'

She now had Rose's full attention and Lola glanced over at Jimmy.

He was sitting slumped on the floor by the wardrobe, his eyes glazed. Without warning, he suddenly lurched forward, vomiting all over the bedroom carpet.

Lola's heart was thumping in her ears. This was her moment.

Not allowing time to second-guess herself, she charged at Rose, making a grab for the axe as she knocked the woman off balance.

There was a brief struggle, but Lola had the momentum, and as Rose landed on her backside, Lola managed to gain control of the axe.

She swung it at Rose in warning, as she backed up to the door, wishing the key was in the lock so she could bolt it shut behind her. As soon as she was the other side, she turned and fled, the sound of Agnes's screams ringing in her ears.

Rose wasted no time coming after her, screaming at Lola to stop, the clack of her footsteps getting closer as they neared the top of the stairs.

Lola had no idea where Brett was, and if he was downstairs, she didn't want to get caught between them, so she made the split-second decision to turn on Rose. Halting at the top of the staircase, she swung the axe in the woman's direction, relieved when she came to an abrupt halt, her eyes wary.

'Put down the axe, Lola.'

'I don't think so.'

'You're not a killer. I know you don't want to do this. Look, just put it down and let's talk.'

She sounded so bloody reasonable, as if she hadn't done all of these awful things.

Was Rose debating if she had it in her to use the axe?

The honest answer was, Lola didn't know herself. She had never intentionally hurt anyone before she had attacked Jimmy with the candlestick, but this was her life she was fighting for and she had to remember that these people had murdered her brother and they wouldn't hesitate before doing the same to her and Quinn.

She found out the answer moments later when Rose, apparently deciding she was safe to do so, took another step towards her.

The swing of the axe was reflex, catching the side of Rose's arm, and she let out a pained yelp. Both hers and Lola's eyes widened in horror seeing the patch of red appear through the material of her blouse.

'You bitch,' Rose gasped. She sounded stunned.

Then she was charging at Lola, catching her off guard and trying to wrestle back control of the axe.

Lola held on tightly to the handle, even as Rose managed to push her up against the balustrade running across the landing at the top of the stairs. As she leaned in, she raised the handle up Lola's chest, wedging it closer to her neck, forcing her head back so she was trapped above the hallway far below. Beneath her back, the wooden spindles of the balustrade creaked ominously and she was certain she could feel them starting to give under the pressure.

If they snapped, she would fall.

No, she couldn't think about that. Instead, she tried her hardest to push back, even as she heard the sound of a door opening.

'I've got the car.'

Brett's voice echoed in the space below them, and Rose glanced down at him.

As fresh fear pounded through Lola, she summoned every last bit of the strength she had left, managing to slam the handle back into Rose, then push herself away from the top of the stairs. As Rose charged at her again, Lola sidestepped just in time, so it was Rose closer to the balustrade.

Before the woman could react, Lola gave her a hard shove, letting go of the handle that was tethering them together. The motion knocked both women off balance, but as Lola fell back, landing on her bum, Rose crashed into the balustrade. This time, the bearing of body weight was too much and as the spindles snapped beneath her, Rose's blue eyes went wide. Then she was flying through the air, as Brett screamed below.

The loud slap of flesh hitting the porcelain floor tiles was followed by several seconds of deathly silence. Brett had stopped screaming and Lola was in shock, initially rooted to the spot and unable to believe what had just happened. As she eventually summoned up the nerve to peer over the edge of the broken balustrade, she saw he was leaning over Rose's motionless body. The axe lay on the ground beside her.

As if sensing he was being watched, he looked up, his eyes locking on Lola's and his stricken expression twisting into one of thunder.

'You did this,' he said, quietly but with menace, and as he climbed to his feet, Lola backed away.

Where the hell was she supposed to go?

She had seen Brett's face and could already hear him climbing the stairs. She was no longer dealing with a cold, calculating man, but instead one who was incandescent with rage and wanting to avenge the death of his lover.

She had to hide.

But where? He was almost upon her. There was no time.

Blindly she ran, aware of his gaining footsteps, the roar of

his temper bellowing behind her, and she screamed as he
caught hold of a clump of her hair, jerking her backwards off
her feet.

He threw her down onto the ground, her limbs taking the
brunt as she landed and her breath wheezing out of her. As
she fought to get up, he kicked her hard in the side and she
cried out in agony. Then he was pushing her onto her back and
climbing on top of her, pinning her wrists either side of her
head.

'You killed Rose, you fucking bitch,' he snarled, his face
pressing close to hers, and she could see the blind fury in his
eyes. In that moment, she was so scared, the irony that he had
also taken her brother's life was lost on her.

Before she could manage any kind of response, he let go of
her, his hands moving to her throat and squeezing hard. Lola
tried to cry out, but she could barely manage a sound as he
crushed her windpipe, stealing her breath. Instead, she
thrashed uselessly with her legs as her hands covered his
much bigger ones, in a desperate attempt to make him stop.

Black spots were appearing in front of her eyes and she
wasn't sure she could fight for much longer, but as she slipped
closer to unconsciousness, she heard an angry yell, then the
weight of Brett's body suddenly disappeared and she was
coughing and spluttering for air.

It took several moments to realise Quinn was there, grap-
pling with Brett on the floor.

Lola watched as the momentum switched, Quinn's fist
cracking into Brett's jaw, before the other man managed to roll
them over, getting in his own punch. But then Quinn had him
pinned face down on the floor, managing to pull Brett's hands
behind his back so he could cuff him.

As he glanced over at Lola, she noticed he had a gaping cut

on his forehead, his usually tanned skin pale, and, concerned, she started to crawl over to him.

He met her halfway, catching her in a tight hug.

'I told you I should have come with you,' he gently chastised, hushing her when she tried to respond and only a croak came out. 'Don't try to speak if it hurts. We need to get a phone signal to call for help, and then we'll get you checked out.'

Of course he was right, but it was frustrating as there was so much she needed to tell him, but for now she nodded, aware that Brett was watching them from his position on the floor. He scowled at her, realising that he had her attention, rattling his cuffs menacingly, and although the action had her flinching, she steadily held his stare.

This man had stolen the chance from her to ever know her brother. She would not cower to him.

But after everything that had happened since she had arrived at Midwinter Manor, was she finally safe?

Quinn was alive and with her, she rationalised, and the monsters who had killed Daniel and held her prisoner no longer seemed to be a threat. Still, it wasn't until much later, when the sound of sirens filled the air, that she finally dared to believe that her nightmare was really over.

EPILOGUE

After making sure that Lola was okay, Quinn had gone to check on Jimmy and Agnes, finding them both in Agnes's room. Satisfied that they weren't going anywhere, he and Lola had taken Brett downstairs with them, finding the Wi-Fi router and password, so Quinn could call for help.

By mid-afternoon, the grounds of the manor were swarming with police and paramedics as the secret Rose Whitlock and Brett Corrigan had tried to hide from the world was finally exposed.

With the exception of Brett, who was driven straight to the police station, the other members of the household were taken to hospital. Rose, by some miracle, had survived her fall, though she was in a bad way, while Jimmy was in and out of consciousness. Agnes needed to be checked out too, and the paramedics were shocked at the conditions they had found her in.

Lola was given the all-clear, though warned that as her throat was bruised, eating and drinking might be a little uncomfortable for a few days.

After croakily managing to give a statement, she then rested her voice as she listened to Quinn talking with the detectives, learning that he had realised something wasn't right when Brett came to the door pretending to be Daniel, then he explained how he had been attacked in the garage after finding Lola's rental car. After regaining consciousness and managing to get free, he had seen Brett driving up to the house in Chloe's car and retrieved his handcuffs from the glovebox before heading inside to find Lola.

There were still a lot of questions to be asked, but satisfied for now, the lead detective had allowed Quinn and Lola to leave. Chloe had offered for them to go to hers, but Lola was keen to get back and check on her cats, so after agreeing with Chloe that she would pick her car up in Ely, Lola had checked out of her hotel and she and Quinn had caught a late train back to her flat in Manchester, where they had fallen into bed, then spent a quiet Christmas Day together.

The following day, they went to Quinn's and he packed up what he needed before returning home with Lola.

Both of them had spoken about the second chance they were being given and after everything that had happened, they didn't want to waste another day apart.

And in the weeks that followed, Lola appreciated having Quinn by her side.

She also had a new companion. After hearing that Daniel's dog Monty had been put into an animal shelter, she knew she wanted him to come and live with her and Quinn. He had been her only friend in Midwinter Manor and giving him love and comfort in his twilight years was the very least she could do.

Although she tried to focus on work, it was difficult not to let her mind stray to developments back in Norfolk.

Rich Bradford, who had left her several angry voicemails while she had been trapped in Midwinter Manor telling her he was going to terminate their contract, had come grovelling back with an apology once the truth came out – a first for him – and she was busy catching up on his account. But news that Daniel's body had been found, then word that Brett and Rose had both been charged with his murder as well as false imprisonment, distracted her. Especially when they both pleaded not guilty.

The police were also now looking closely at Nigel's death, wondering if Rose had played a part in this, although she claimed she was innocent.

The only one who did admit wrongdoing was Jimmy, who had revealed the location of Daniel's body, and was facing charges of assisting an offender and false imprisonment. He had already struck a deal with the prosecution for agreeing to testify against his sister and her lover, who had been deluded enough to believe they would be able to remain at Midwinter Manor after Daniel's death, with no one ever twigging what they had done.

As for Agnes, Lola was torn. She had heard that journals were found belonging to Rose that detailed her childhood living with her mother and some of the cruel things Agnes did to her. Of course, though, two wrongs didn't make a right or justify Rose's actions, and it was perhaps kinder for Agnes when she passed away in hospital a fortnight after Christmas.

Lola was Daniel's only surviving relative and eventually his body had been released so she could give him a funeral. Expecting it to be a quiet affair, she was heartened when several of his friends from his university days showed up. There was guilt from some of them, fearing they had let him down as communication dwindled, while others had actively tried to stay in his life, but had gradually been pushed out by Rose.

For her part, Lola relished spending time with them all. They had stories of her brother and new photos too, that helped to build up a picture of the man he had been, bringing him to life for her. As well as his love for sports, he had also been passionate about the planet he lived on and the creatures he shared it with. Lola knew she would have liked the real Daniel very much, and she swapped details with a few of his friends, planning on keeping in touch.

Another person who was also now in her life was her father.

She had reached out to John via his publisher in the first week of the new year and he hadn't wasted any time in responding or travelling up to Manchester, having read about Daniel's murder and the arrest of his wife.

Their first meeting had been tentative, both of them a little scared of a relationship that meant so much, but after a coffee date with just the two of them, Lola had invited John to her flat for dinner and to meet Quinn. It was still a relationship in its infancy, and they wouldn't get to see each other daily, as John, who was divorced and a bit of a workaholic, was based in London. But already they had so much in common, and through John she learnt more about her mother, Annie, and how in love the pair of them had been before Nigel had threatened their happiness.

After so much loss in her life, Lola would keep her father close and never take him for granted.

As the days became longer, the fresh buds of spring now giving way to the full bloom of summer, Rose had turned on her lover, agreeing to a plea bargain deal which would see her serving a lesser sentence. She had also confessed to pushing Nigel down the stairs, aware a case was building against her.

For Lola it was mixed blessings. She wanted Rose to pay dearly for what she had done, but at least she had pleaded her guilt, and it wasn't as if karma hadn't caught her up. The accident that had almost killed her after Lola had shoved her through the balustrade had left her as a paraplegic in a wheelchair.

Now Rose truly knew how Daniel had felt.

Brett's trial was set for October and Lola was dreading testifying, but her father and Quinn were by her side before and after, and along with Quinn's testimony, as well as the damning evidence from Jimmy and Rose, a guilty verdict was never in doubt.

Days after the judge sentenced Brett to life without parole, Lola received two lots of unexpected news.

Firstly, she learnt that she was the sole heir to her brother's estate. As soon as Rose had pleaded guilty to the murder of her husband, a forfeiture ruling had come into effect, and she was no longer entitled to a penny of Daniel's money.

Everything now belonged to Lola.

Initially, she was stunned, then a little overwhelmed. She had never been a person to live beyond her means and she had no idea what to do with her sudden fortune.

Just a few days later, she was also shocked to find out she was pregnant, something that both terrified and delighted her, and she knew Quinn felt the same.

Would the past repeat itself?

Over the following months as she adjusted to the news, her baby growing inside of her, she made some important decisions. With Quinn's blessing, she put Midwinter Manor on the market. Lola didn't want the house and was keen to sever her connection with what had happened there.

It took a while to sell and they had to reduce the price, but eventually they found a buyer.

Six weeks later, Lola gave birth to a healthy baby boy. She and Quinn named him Noah Daniel Mallory, and it was bringing Noah into the world that made her realise what she wanted to do with her brother's money.

Their first night at home as a family, as Noah slept in his cot, and Monty lay on the sofa, she talked to Quinn about her plan.

'I'd like to set aside enough for us to buy a new home,' she told him, as he cooked dinner, while she sat at the table with a cup of tea, the window ledge beside her adorned with picture frames, containing photos of her birth mother and father, Annie and John, and the mother who had raised her, Kelly. 'We'll get somewhere nice, with a decent-sized garden for Monty, and for Noah to play in as he grows, and you can have that hot tub you always wanted.'

He glanced over at her and grinned. 'I like that plan.'

'And I want to put some money into a trust for Noah too.'

Quinn nodded, approving of her decision. But would he be on board with the next bit?

'As for the rest...' Lola hesitated before telling him. 'I want to give it away.'

She held her breath, realising how much his reaction mattered.

Although the money was hers and it was her decision to make, it was important to her that she had his blessing. It was his future too.

He didn't look horrified, continuing to stir the sauce he was making as he glanced her way again. 'Okay,' he said calmly. 'So what is your plan?'

That was when the words all came tumbling out and she explained how she felt about the inheritance.

'Daniel died because of Rose's greed and I don't ever want to risk becoming materialistic like her.'

Quinn gave a wry smile. 'I think there's little chance of that happening.'

'We don't need a fortune to be happy.'

She told him then about the charities she had been researching that supported bereaved parents and people with spinal cord injuries.

'I want to donate to them, but I also want to support the causes that Daniel was passionate about as well.'

She had learnt through Daniel's friends that although he had trained as a chef, he had been considering a change of career before his accident, wanting to help endangered wildlife. He may not have had the chance to fulfil his dream, but she could help fund the causes he had cared for.

Quinn remained silent after she finished speaking as he considered everything she had just said, and Lola waited for his response, hopeful but a little anxious. He had never been a man obsessed with money. She had always liked that about him. But would he feel differently now they had it?

'So what do you think?' she pushed, impatient to know.

She watched him remove the pan from the heat, before he walked over to the table, crouching down in front of her and taking hold of both of her hands.

As his dark eyes locked on hers, he smiled. 'I think it's a good idea. An excellent idea, actually,' he told her, before pulling her forward so he could kiss the tip of her nose. 'I always knew there was a reason why I fell in love with you, Lola Henderson. Your brother would be proud.'

He squeezed her hands and she let out a relieved breath, a little annoyed with herself that she had ever doubted him.

'I still want that hot tub, though,' he warned playfully, getting up and returning to the stove.

Lola grinned. 'It will be our top priority,' she joked, genuinely happy with the decision she had made.

The things she loved most were right here in this flat. The man she wanted to one day marry and the baby boy she had been scared she would never get to hold.

And she had gained a father too.

Her heart still broke for Daniel, but donating his inheritance would hopefully help it to heal. It was the best way she could honour the brother she would never get to meet.

* * *

MORE FROM KERI BEEVIS

Another book from Keri Beevis, is available to order now here:
https://mybook.to/KerisnewBackAd

ACKNOWLEDGEMENTS

People often ask me where I get my ideas from. In this case, I was inspired after reading about Virginia McCullough, the British lady who killed her parents and lived with their bodies in the family home for four years before she was caught.

I was fascinated by how she managed to keep her secret hidden away from her siblings and other relatives, plus everyone who knew her parents, for so long, and the plot for *Dead of Winter* and the characters of Brett and Rose grew from there.

As always, this book is a group effort and huge thanks must first go to my lovely editor, Caroline, who continues to keep me on track. Thank you for everything you do for me.

And thanks too to the rest of the Boldwood team. To Wendy, Jenna, Claire, Hayley, Issy, Ben, and not forgetting our chief extraordinaire, Amanda. Thanks as well go to my copyeditor, Jade, and my proofreader, Gary.

A few of my readers also helped with this story. To the real Rich Bradford, who is much nicer in real life than he is in my book, to Willow Innes for naming Monty, to Sarah Hodgson for naming Safe Hands, and to Cindi Peterson, to whom *Dead of Winter* is dedicated. A worthy winner of my competition as she shouts loudly everywhere about how everyone should read my books.

Thank you to my lovely author friends for keeping me sane: Patricia Dixon, Val Keogh, Natasha Boydell and Amanda

Brittany in particular deserve a mention. Thank you to my family and friends. To my fab beta readers, Tina Jackson and Jo Bilton, who have to put up with me constantly tweaking what they read. To the brilliant admins in my author group: Bev Hopper, Tracy Robinson and Allison Valentine. To the amazing blogging community, and to my wonderful readers. I love you all.

Finally to my fluffy family – Ellie, Poppy and Finn. Thank you for being my morning alarm clocks, for the mouthfuls of cat hair in my coffee, and for making sure I get plenty of exercise away from my desk, as I chase you all around the house when you get something in your mouth you shouldn't. And not forgetting my precious Lola puss, who gained her angel wings last year, but is remembered every day. This one is for you, my little sweetheart. xxx

ABOUT THE AUTHOR

Keri Beevis is the internationally bestselling author of several psychological thrillers and romantic suspense mysteries, including the very successful *Dying to Tell*. She sets many of her books in the county of Norfolk, where she was born and still lives and which provides much of her inspiration.

Download your exclusive bonus content from Keri Beevis here:

Visit Keri's website: www.keribeevis.com

Follow Keri on social media here:

facebook.com/allaboutbeev

x.com/keribeevis

instagram.com/keri.beevis

bookbub.com/profile/keri-beevis

tiktok.com/@keribeevis

ALSO BY KERI BEEVIS

THE *Murder* LIST

THE MURDER LIST IS A NEWSLETTER DEDICATED TO SPINE-CHILLING FICTION AND GRIPPING PAGE-TURNERS!

SIGN UP TO MAKE SURE YOU'RE ON OUR HIT LIST FOR EXCLUSIVE DEALS, AUTHOR CONTENT, AND COMPETITIONS.

SIGN UP TO OUR NEWSLETTER

BIT.LY/THEMURDERLISTNEWS

Boldwood

Boldwood Books is an award-winning fiction publishing company seeking out the best stories from around the world.

Find out more at www.boldwoodbooks.com

Join our reader community for brilliant books, competitions and offers!

Follow us
@BoldwoodBooks
@TheBoldBookClub

Sign up to our weekly deals newsletter

https://bit.ly/BoldwoodBNewsletter

Printed in Dunstable, United Kingdom